BROUGHT TO YOU BY THE COLOR DRAB

NORMA JEAN LUTZ

Brought To You By The Color Drab

ISBN:0-9908037-8-3
ISBN:978-0-9908037-8-2

Copyright © 2017 by NUWSLink, Inc. and Norma Jean Lutz.

Except for use in any review, the reproduction or utilization of this work in whole or in part in any form by any electronic, mechanical, or other means, now known or hereafter invented is forbidden without the permission of the publisher, NUWSLink, Inc., 8703-R North Owasso Expressway, Ste. 143, Owasso, OK 74055

All of the characters in this book are fictitious. Any resemblance to actual persons living or dead is purely coincidental.

Publisher's Cataloging-In-Publication Data

Names: Lutz, Norma Jean.

Title: Brought to you by the color drab / Norma Jean Lutz.

Description: Owasso, OK : NUWSLink, Inc., [2017] | Interest age level: 012-018. | Summary: "Race Paloma's world violently turns upside-down after his older brother, Vince, is murdered in a drive-by. Without Vince's strong leadership, their once-powerful, hood-ruling pack unravels at the speed of light. The Deuce Dragons threaten takeover in their Cincinnati Over-The-Rhine hood."--Provided by publisher.

Identifiers: ISBN 9780990803782 | ISBN 0990803783 | ISBN 9780990803775 (Kindle)

Subjects: LCSH: Brothers--Death--Juvenile fiction. | Gangs--Juvenile fiction. | Juvenile delinquency--Juvenile fiction. | Single-parent families--Juvenile fiction. | Inner cities--Juvenile fiction. | CYAC: Brothers--Death--Fiction. | Gangs--Fiction. | Juvenile delinquency--Fiction. | Single-parent families--Fiction. | Inner cities--Fiction.

Classification: LCC PZ7.1.L88 Br 2017 (print) | LCC PZ7.1.L88 (ebook) | DDC [Fic]--dc23

TABLE OF CONTENTS

A NOTE FROM THE AUTHOR:

I love to hear from my readers.
You may contact me here:
NormaJean@BeANovelist.com
http://www.CleanTeenReads.net
https://www.facebook.com/CleanTeenReadsNet/

DEDICATION

To Jeremy Donovan, the only one I know personally who could relate to Race's life. Like Race, Jeremy found the freedom he so desperately sought. Victory by God's grace.

Jeremiah was a bullfrog. He was a good friend of mine...

[Today, Jeremy Donovan is a committed, dedicated youth pastor, husband to beautiful Annie, and dad to three incredible children.]

ACKNOWLEDGMENTS

My deepest gratitude to the Carmichael family, James (Jamie), and Kathy, and their two daughters, Christy Acheampong, and Melissa, who so graciously took me under their wing for my Cincinnati visit all those years ago. Who knew it would take so long for this novel to finally be completed and published?

It was totally a *God-incident* that in 2004, I called Cincinnati Christian College (now University), to find a student to escort me around the inner city for my research. What I got instead was an entire family (because it was Christy— then Carmichael—who answered the phone that day). Plus, I learned from Christy that I could procure lodging at the campus rather than go to a hotel. Only God can pull off a miracle like that. And these are only the surface details.

Thank you, James Carmichael family, for your warm hospitality, dinner at your table, rich conversation, and many drives around the city. What a blessing!

CINCINNATI, OH IN 2001

If you think that riots in the streets in this country are a recent phenomenon, you would be sadly mistaken. In my Tulsa Series novels, the setting is 1921, the year of the infamous Tulsa Race Riots. (Titles listed below.)

A quick Google search shows that riots have plagued our nation for decades.

In *Brought To You By The Color Drab*, set in 2001, a riot takes place in Cincinnati, and I use that incident as a part of the story. I've taken license to rearrange so that details fit with the plot. If you were there, and you remember it differently, I apologize in advance.

This 4-title series is available in the Kindle Store:

Tulsa Tempest
Tulsa Turning
Tulsa Trespass
Return to Tulsa

CHAPTER 1

The moment Race heard the gunshots explode, he knew it was Vince. Somehow he just knew.

Throwing the remote across the room, he leaped over the back of the ratty couch and flew down the dimly lit stairs out into the hot August night.

He screamed his brother's name as he ran through the trash-littered streets toward the playground. For three blocks his feet barely touched the ground.

Then he saw it. Beneath the streetlight, Vince's six-foot frame sprawled face-forward across the broken sidewalk, lying ghostly still, the blood pooling in bizarre patterns, trickling worm-like toward the curb. His basketball had rolled into the weeds along the chain link fence.

"Filthy scum! You filthy dirty scum!" Race screamed. The screams were drowned out by the wail of approaching sirens.

As Race lunged toward his brother's body, strong black arms from behind grasped him in a vice grip that knocked his wind out.

Race writhed and jerked to free himself. "No! No! Let me go! Oh God, please no! Answer me, Vince. Vince!"

"Hold it, Race. Just hold it."

Through the pounding in his head, Race heard Wynn's voice like a distant whisper. Race twisted violently, but the rock-hard arms held him fast. "Gotta touch him, Wynn," he pleaded. "Please. I gotta touch him. Just one time. Please."

"Can't touch him, bro. You can't. The police..." Wynn's voice cracked in a deep sob.

Suddenly Race's knees buckled and he started to fall. Wynn spun Race around and they clung to each other sobbing until the police cars splashed eerie red light into the deserted street.

No crowd gathered. No witnesses would come forward. Killings in Cincinnati's Over-the-Rhine district were too common. Police officers, with barely concealed boredom, asked a few questions and ordered Race and Wynn to report to the station. Race watched as they loaded Vince's lifeless body into an ambulance. It was over.

Race's brother and Wynn's tightest bud—the glue that had held them together—was gone.

That night was the last time Race cried.

CHAPTER 2

The warm, clammy air of the September night hung on Race like wet laundry. He and his four buddies walked along Cincinnati's Liberty Street as though they had purpose and a mission, but of course they had neither. Chains looped on their baggy pants jangled as they walked.

Wynn strode on one side of Race. Toon was on the other, jiving as he walked, his black dreadlocks bouncing. Toon always had a rap running through his head. His long, loose, skinny frame seemed to be in perpetual motion. If Vince had been there, Toon would have had to walk behind them with the younger punks, Pinky and Hawk.

"So where we headed?" Wynn threw out the question.

"How about finding a set of wheels in Clifton Heights?" Toon offered.

"Clifton," Wynn echoed Toon's idea. "Sound good to you, Race?" Wynn Jamison moved like a sleek panther–no wasted motion. Total opposite of Toon. Muscles bulged under his black t-shirt. People on the streets of Over-the-Rhine both feared and respected Wynn's power and his presence.

Race didn't answer right away. He hated Clifton Heights with its fancy houses and clean streets. Even though Clifton was a straight shot up Vine Street from Over-the-Rhine, the exclusive neighborhood was like another planet compared to their home turf. So when the suggestion came up to steal cars in Clifton, Race just shrugged his shoulders and kept his eyes ahead. "Whatever."

Race was sure Wynn expected a better answer. Like all of a sudden Race was supposed to be calling the shots now that Vince was gone. He swallowed hard around the word *gone* and kept walking.

Over his shoulder, Wynn motioned to Pinky and Hawk. "Hey punks, you be keeping up or you outta this action."

It wasn't as though Wynn's two younger cousins were falling behind. They clung to Wynn like double shadows. But at his command, Race heard them double step to close the gap.

"We gonna walk up to Clifton?" Toon wanted to know.

"Nah," Race smarted back. "Taking the ferry."

Toon laughed. He laughed at most everything. Race had never heard a hyena's laugh, but it was a cinch it was real close to Toon's.

Toon's full name was Alan Toomey but his street name was Looney Toon because he enjoyed frying his brains now and then sniffing glue, and had since grade school. There was nothing about Toon that Race liked. Why Vince and Wynn ever let him start running with their pack was a mystery.

Vince and Wynn had always agreed on most everything and that included Toon's entrance into their group. Toon just seemed to materialize out of a dark Cincinnati night. He had moved into a small rented room down the street from Vince and Race's building. His long skinny frame was perched on the stoop every time they passed by and he took to saying, "Yo bro," to them real friendly-like. And he wore no gang colors. The next thing Race knew, Toon was tagging them on one of their shoplifting sprees. That was last spring and he'd stuck like a leech ever since.

When Race had asked Vince about Toon's hanging with them, his brother was cool. "Notice we haven't had to fake IDs to get the beer since Toon came on board," he said, flashing his famous grin that the girls went ape for. Race wanted to say that he'd never remembered them having a shortage of beer—ever.

Vince, as though reading his thoughts, waved his hand to silence any protest. "He's got connections, Race. He knows choice buyers. He's been in juvie and knows tricks we never heard of."

The *tricks* Vince referred to meant getting stolen cars to the chop shops where they were quickly stripped and the ones who did the stealing got a cut of the take. Any guy who came back from juvenile detention usually knew more and better ways to beat the system.

"And," Vince had added, his dark eyes growing serious like they did when he thought hard on something, "we don't gotta hook up with no set gangs, like the Deuce Dragons, to do it."

Sets were a big deal with Vince and Wynn. Sets were all these little gang wannabes coming around, putting pressure on them to take their colors. Neither Vince nor Wynn wanted anything to do with them. Their own little pack hung tight, but they had nothing in common with gang bangers.

"Don't need you," Wynn'd tell the Dragon leaders when they came around to get them to join.

"Got our own," Vince would add.

"We watch each other's backs." That was Race's little piece to put in.

The Deuce Dragons weren't the Crips. Not the Nations. Not the Folks. They appeared to have no connection whatever to any *real* gang anywhere. They were snot-nosed little wannabes trying to act cool. While street people called them *sets,* Vince had other choice names for them. They'd rumbled the Dragons a couple times. And messed them over real good, too. But they never seemed to get the message. The three of them—Vince, Wynn and Race—were tough when it came to fighting. They'd learned young. Toon was okay, but Race could tell right away he was too loopy to hold his own.

They turned off Liberty to head up Race Street toward Clifton. As they passed by a darkened alley, Race glanced that direction and shivered. He'd had his first real fight in that alley when he was in fourth grade. The other kid was bigger. A loudmouth bully was all he was. Race remembered the stench from the overflowing garbage bins, smelling like every other alley in Over-the-Rhine. He remembered the gritty pavement scraping against his face and tearing at his bare arms as he was knocked down again and again. He remembered hard, solid punches pummeling pain into his small body, jarring his head and making his teeth slam together. But Vince was there yelling, "Punch him out, bro. You can do it. Punch him out."

Vince's voice in Race's head pumped the adrenaline that forced him to get back up again and again till he finally pinned the bully, yelling, "Don't never call me Cracker ever again. Cause if you do, I'm gonna smash your ugly face in."

Graham Kyle—what a stupid name his mother had saddled him with. It caused him no end of grief in his early grade school days when kids called him first *Graham Cracker*, then simply *Cracker*. Even his mother had dropped the Graham, preferring to call him Kyle. He'd probably been named for one of her here-today-gone-tomorrow boyfriends. There'd been dozens of them. But no one ever called him Graham Cracker after that. His rep stood solid at age ten.

After that victory, Vince started calling him Race. Perfect name. "You creamed him on Race Street," Vince crowed as he helped Race home, then nursed the scrapes, cuts, and bruises in their small kitchen. "Way to go bro. Don't ever forget," Vince said in all his fifth-grade wisdom, "you and me, we don't take nothin' off nobody. Ever!"

Race never forgot. He didn't take nothin' off nobody. Ever.

Race Street, like many in OTR, had its fair share of vacant buildings where the winos, bums, and crack addicts could get in out of the weather. Broken glass crunched under their feet as they passed where someone had smashed out a few windows. One brick wall sported fresh graffiti, obviously a work of the Deuce Dragons. The dual meaning of deuce—*devil* and *two*—was clearly portrayed by a dragon carrying a numeral two in one hand and a pitchfork in the other. Race glanced over at Wynn to see if he'd seen it as well. He had. Evidence of the Dragons' tagging activities kept popping up in the streets and alleys around Over-the-Rhine.

As he walked, Race felt the bounce of his knife in his pocket against his leg. He liked the feel of it there. He'd sunk it into a few dimwitted characters who should have known better than to tangle with him. "Just show 'em a little of their own red blood," Vince used to tell him. "That'll strengthen your rep and scare 'em off." It usually did. Race was good with a knife and he knew it. Vince and Wynn had taught him well.

Toon was probably toting a piece. But Wynn, Vince and Race had always shied away from packing guns. First of all, guns cost plenty, and the three of them were always short on cash. And like Vince always said, "It's easier to trace a gun than a knife. I'm not looking to get sent away."

Now how crazy is that? Vince never being too cool about packing and he's the one who gets shot. Made no sense at all. Race thought about those bullets that slammed into Vince's back and wondered if his brother had felt them. A new wave of bile-tasting anger bubbled up in his throat. He shivered in the heat and forced his head to shut up. *Don't think about nothing. Don't think; don't feel.*

The trek to Clifton was uphill all the way. By the time they reached Ludlow Street, they were all sweat-soaked and doing some heavy huffing and puffing. How could September be so blasted hot?

"I don't sweat this much for PE class," Pinky's voice sounded from behind. "This hill goes straight up."

"Quit bellyaching," Hawk answered him.

"See if you're big enough to make me," Pinky popped back, followed by sounds of the cousins scuffling behind them.

The cousins had been the same size for years until the past few months when Hawk had shot up a couple of inches. Now he enjoyed throwing around his new-found power.

"You whining about sweating," Wynn said over his shoulder, "we'll pick you some wheels with AC that sings, and cool, soft upholstery."

"Mmm mmm. Now you talking my language," Pinky said. Then, "Now Hawk cut it out 'fore I make pudding outta you."

"You and who else, twerp?" came Hawk's retort.

More scuffling sounds came from behind as the larger tormented the smaller. Race glanced around to see Hawk with his cousin's head in a hammerlock and Pinky's fists flailing the air whamming Hawk's back. Just like he and Vince used to do. *Used to do?* Barely three weeks ago. Before...

"Hey, Punks! Cut it out!" Wynn said. "You gonna get us in trouble before we ever get what we going after."

The rebuke stopped the scuffling for the time being. The tight little group walked on a block or two with no one talking.

Sometimes they cased a busy parking lot for a set of wheels to jack. Sometimes a quiet neighborhood. Mostly the latter. Vince, their undisputed leader, had always determined which one at which time. Some dummy might leave the keys in. Sweet times those were. They scoped those out first. If they found no keys, Vince was cool about knowing the slickest ones to open. Vince knew everything. Except how to cover his own back.

"What'll it be?" Wynn threw out, his dark face glistening with sweat beads. His ball cap was twisted slightly so the bill set cock-eyed. He always wore it that way. Sort of like his trademark.

Race quickly said, "Hoods." At the same instant Toon said, "Parking lots."

Wynn slowed his pace. Pinky and Hawk nearly slammed into him.

"Hoods are quieter. Fewer eyes," Race retorted, miffed that Toon would even dream that he had any say in the matter.

"Parking lots give better cover," Toon said. "If an alarm screams, people got no idea where it's coming from."

Race glanced over at Wynn and in a split second saw the twitch in his jaw. "Toon's got it, Race. Remember the alarm there in Fairview last month? That was a close one. Close as I wanna get."

Race bit his lip. Actually, stealing cars wasn't their big thing anyway. Shoplifting was. The three of them got darn slick at it. Oh sure, they'd grabbed a car once in a while when they wanted a thrill. But then they ditched it. Usually with only a few new scratches on it. That was before Toon. It was all because of Toon they were doing all this stuff. Did that mean Toon had become their shot-caller? It looked that way.

Race shrugged and started walking again. "Whatever." What did he care anyway?

Toon seemed to take on a new air. "Now then," he said with a twinge of authority in his voice, "they's a ritzy club a few blocks up ahead. Lotsa nifty wheels in that lot. Especially on a Friday night."

"That cool with you, Race?" Wynn asked catching up with him.

"Whatever," Race said again. "How do we split? Who goes with who?"

Before this—when Vince was still with them—Race and Vince always took Hawk, and Wynn and Toon took Pinky. Pinky was a little more jumpy and edgy than Hawk, so Wynn thought the kid needed close watching. Since the shooting, Wynn hovered over both his cousins like an old hen. So Race wasn't surprised when he said he'd take both Pinky and Hawk. That left Race with Looney Toon. His gut tightened at the thought.

Clifton Heights seemed to beam with pride, showing off all its shiny cars and stately, castle-like houses. No slummy bars or panhandlers on these clean street corners. The pack hung to the dark back streets. Wynn wasn't saying much.

Race kept waiting for Wynn to give the plan, but nothing came forth. Ever since Vince got shot, Wynn acted like he expected Race to Vince-think and Vince-act. What a crock that was. Race pressed his lips together tight and kept walking, wondering how close they'd get before Wynn said anything. But it was Toon who finally said, "Race and me'll come in from this side." He pointed to the west side of the filled parking lot.

The place was lit up brighter than day. Race looked at it and shook his head. So dumb.

"Wynn, you and your punks come in from the other side. First one to find keys give the whistle and we'll all come running."

"And if no keys?" It was Hawk, his voice all quivery with fear and excitement.

At thirteen, he was four years Race's junior. Only four years, and he seemed like such a baby. Pinky was twelve. Is that what he and Vince were like at that age? *At that age. Vince and me led the pack. We never followed. I never remember us ever following nobody. Not ever.*

"Only five full minutes of looking," Toon answered Hawk's question. "Then Wynn jacks one. We all jump in and ride."

"Any trouble," Wynn added, "you knows how to split, where to go and where to meet."

At that, Wynn and his boys headed toward the far end of the parking lot. Race and Toon entered the other end. Race squinted against the dazzling brightness. *Give me a dark neighborhood street any day.* Sweat trickled down his ribs under his thin t-shirt.

They scrunched down low, tripping car to car. They knew how to look quick and move quick. After only a few minutes, Race heard the whistle. Hawk had found the winner. Toon motioned that direction—as if Race didn't have sense enough to follow the sound of a whistle.

When they got there, Wynn had already slipped behind the wheel of a gun-metal blue Acura. Sweet. Toon took the shotgun seat and Race slid in back with Hawk who was beaming. His find—he had a right.

"Check it out, man," Hawk said to Race. "Cool, huh?"

"Cool," Race agreed. He looked out the back window and saw Pinky scurrying.

"Hurry up, kid," Toon said cursing under his breath. In his panic, Pinky slipped against another car and set off an alarm. Someone across the parking lot yelled something they couldn't understand.

Wynn revved up the car, and as Pinky dove in beside Hawk, slamming the door, they laid down a layer of rubber out of the lot.

"Better do some fancy driving, man," Toon said. Then over his shoulder, he said to Pinky, "Clumsy punk."

"Hey, I slipped. Coulda happened to anybody."

"Forget it," Wynn said, keeping his eyes on the road. Deftly, he started going down back streets with the headlights out till they could get out of the Clifton neighborhood. But they hadn't gone half a dozen blocks when sirens screamed behind them.

"Man," Wynn said, "them cops musta been having coffee right across the street or something."

"Just a siren," Hawk stated, his voice still trembly, "don't mean they's after us. Lotsa sirens late at night."

Toon laughed at the remark. "Stupid kid. Course it's us."

"Ditch?" Wynn threw the question back at Race.

"Ditch, jump, and split," Toon said. "Too hot to maintain."

Once again, Toon calling the shots. Race didn't like it.

Wynn swung into a dark alley, barely missing a tall wooden privacy fence. All four doors opened and they piled out. Toon was laughing his hyena laugh as he sped off through a nearby back yard.

Race could almost smell the fear coming off Pinky and Hawk. "Follow the plan," Wynn told them, giving the nearest one a shove as he said it.

Race was already sprinting down the alley. "See you back at OTR," he called back softly to Wynn.

"OTR," Wynn echoed.

It had become their code, long ago. When it was just the three of them—Wynn, Vince and Race. Before splitting, it was always, "Over-the-Rhine." Only now it wrenched Race's guts to say it.

CHAPTER 3

No cash tonight, Race realized as he cut through manicured lawns and zig-zagged around barking neighborhood dogs. The Acura would have brought a pretty penny. So easy. Keys and everything. Dumb Toon. They would've been better off downing a few beers, then heading downtown to locate an easy shoplifting target.

He jogged downhill south, avoiding streetlights. All of Cincinnati glowed in the basin below the hill, the city lights shimmering in the mist. All the glitter, he knew, simply glossed over the ugliness, the drabness, so familiar in his life. An unfair, one-sided joke, just like the trim houses that lined either side of the street he was on. Kids lived inside those houses who were snug in their own safe, clean little worlds. Kids who could get up in the middle of the night and find leftover roast beef in the fridge instead of a carton of spoiled milk, dried bread, and mouse droppings on the kitchen cabinet. Vince once said these people had garbage that didn't dare stink. Talking about the people who lived along the clean streets in the hills above the city.

The night Vince said that, the three of them—Vince, Wynn, and Race—had been standing on a littered Over-the-Rhine street corner passing around a bottle of beer on a hot summer night when the stench of rotting garbage hung thick in the air. Lightheaded from the beer, Wynn and Race both laughed at Vince's crack.

"Hey. No, listen," Vince said waving the bottle at them for emphasis. "It's true, I swear it. Not only can their garbage not stink, it can't even run over. They train their garbage to stay in its place and not stink. If you don't believe me, just go through one of their alleys some night late."

Vince could say things like that, poker-face expression, things that made Race and Wynn hold their stomachs from laughing so hard. Had that been only a couple months ago?

Accustomed to jumping fences on a dead run, Race bounded down an alley and leaped a fence into a manicured yard clinging to the shadows. He stopped in his tracks and did a double-take. There on the lawn lay a shiny blue and silver ten-speed. Some fool kid must've forgotten to put it away.

He looked up at the quiet two-story house with all the lights out. "Your mama's gonna kill you in the morning," he whispered to the nameless, careless kid as he walked carefully to where the bike lay.

It was just like Vince always said whenever they made a good haul shoplifting: "The fat cats got the system all sewed up, Race," he'd say. "That type don't deserve to have it in the first place."

Race picked up the bike and heaved it over the fence into the back alley. Springing back over himself, he hopped astride and rode off. No cops looking for a white guy on a slick ten-speed. This was easier than the Acura. Quieter too.

Winding through neighborhoods, he considered several places to stash the bike till the next day. Then he'd take it to

Sharkey's. Sharkey might not deal in Acuras, but he'd sure enough fork over cash for a cherry ten-speed.

Dumb Toon. Race had tried to tell him neighborhoods were better. Race turned the corner to ride nearer the University. No one pedaling a bike looked suspicious around the sprawling campus. Then it hit him where to stash the bike—the car wash where he and Vince had worked for a few weeks last spring spiffying up all the rich folks' wheels. The thickly wooded hill behind the car wash dropped off into a steep slope.

Located just a few blocks away from the west University campus, it was the perfect spot to ditch the bike. He and Wynn could come and get it after dark the next night and take it to Sharkey's Salvage Yard down by the river.

It was after two by the time Race let himself into the decrepit building where he and his mother lived on the third floor. The inner hallway reeked with the aromas of cheap cooking and soiled diapers, held thick and heavy by the dampness of the night. Vince used to say each floor told you what people had had for dinner that night. But at nearly two in the morning, the smells were mingled and dulled into nothing specific, just generally disgusting.

Race remembered the times he and Vince climbed these stairs with Vince waving his arms and spouting, "Here you have it, folks. This lovely apartment complex has been brought to you this evening by the color drab. D–r–a–b, drab." With one hand, he pretended to hold a microphone. "Can you say *drab?* Now tell me, is your drab drabbier today than it was yesterday? Never fear. We can help you to up-drab your drab. Join us today in the absolute drabbiest of drabs." Race would be laughing so hard he'd stumble up the steps.

Then there was the day they were sitting on the flat rock down the hill from the car wash sharing a smoke. Vince was in one of his quiet, melancholy moods. "My entire life," he said quietly, "every freaking part of it has been brought to you by the color drab. And I do mean the drabbiest."

Race forced himself to shake off the memory. He couldn't afford to allow himself to think. It wasn't until he neared the third floor of the apartment house that he remembered he'd not gone to his designated hideout. The bike had distracted him. Oh well, who really gives a rip? Having hideouts was one of Toon's numbskull ideas anyway.

"If you're gonna pull the big stuff," Toon had told them after he started hanging with them, "when you split after a job, the stupidest thing you can do is head back to your own place. That's the kinda stupid that'll land you in juvie real fast."

Race had been picked up by the cops only a couple times in his life. He'd always been questioned and released. Wynn, who'd seen the inside of juvenile hall dozens of time, said it was because Race was white. Maybe. But Race knew a lot of white guys who'd spent the night in detention center. Like Vince, for instance.

Race remembered how scared he'd been the first time Vince was nabbed. He was only twelve at the time; Vince, thirteen. It took the cops several hours to locate their mom, so they held Vince at the center most of the night.

Race sat home alone, petrified with fear. When Race asked Vince later about the red marks on his wrists, Vince rubbed the place and just said "Cuffs." Then he added, "But I never cried, bro. Not one tear." Race gazed at his brother in awe and disbelief to think he could be roughed up by the police and not cry. Even way back then, Race had known his brother was one tough dude.

Toon's hideout plan was for them to each have a place in which to disappear because, as he put it, "They ain't got enough cops in Cincinnati to follow us going a zillion different directions."

Vince and Wynn had agreed, so Race fell in. His designated hideout—chosen by Toon—was a dilapidated guard shack at a deserted industrial plant. He was supposed to hole up there for at least two to three hours after a heist. He hated the idea and had from the very first. Hated the spooky old plant with broken-out windows, rusted chain-link fences, and tall weeds pushing their way up through cracked concrete. Hated not being with Vince and Wynn. Before Toon came along, Vince always said, "We hang together no matter what." They might be forced to split, but not for very long. It was always, "See you back at OTR."

Toon had changed all that.

As he turned the key in his apartment door, Race realized he was secretly glad he'd forgotten about the hideout. The bike was more important. "Take that, Toon, you goon," he whispered under his breath.

He knew as he pushed through the door that his mom was still out. Who knew where. Nealia Paloma never was one for staying home much, but ever since Vince's murder, it was worse. Late at night, she'd leave the bar where she worked, walk down the street to another bar and stay till closing. Race could hardly blame her. Vince left behind an emptiness bigger than the Grand Canyon. Several times in the past few weeks, Race felt himself nearing the edge of that chasm of emptiness, clawing and scrambling not to tumble off.

Suddenly he was starved. Heading through the living room to the postage-stamp kitchen, he checked the fridge, which was nearly empty. He shook a milk carton. Felt like enough for a bowl of cornflakes. He opened it gingerly and took a sniff. Not spoiled. Enough cornflakes, enough milk. He fixed the bowl and went in and flicked on the TV.

He watched mindless stuff as he shoveled in big spoonsful. The cereal hit his stomach like a lead weight. All food did that to him these past few weeks. Nothing he could do about it.

He sat there for a minute holding the empty bowl in his hand, not daring to breathe. Waiting. Listening. Vince could sneak up on him and nail him *so fast*. Like lightning. Race trained himself to listen, listen hard. If he sat there and willed it hard enough, Vince'd come slamming in the door, leap over the back of the couch, dive in beside him and have Race's neck in a hammerlock that at one time he couldn't get out of, but later he could. More times than not, he could.

He waited. Nothing. Just nothing. Great big sickening nothing.

Suddenly he flung the plastic bowl at the wall and watched it bounce off, splattering drops of milk and bits of cornflakes everywhere. Curling into a ball, he buried his face in the ratty, smelly couch pillow.

That's where he was when Nealia came dragging in at four. He roused enough to hear her ask in her slurred I've-been-at-the-bottle-again voice, why he wasn't in bed. When he acted like he didn't hear, she went on to bed. Thank God she was alone, not dragging along one of her men friends, the majority of whom both Race and Vince always hated with a passion.

Race flopped over on his back and stared at the yellowed water stain decorating the living room ceiling, watching it turn shades of pink and green from the reflection of the neon sign outside the window and waited for morning to come. Being in their bedroom without Vince was bad in the daytime; a hundred times worse at night. Race had always suffered with nightmares, but they were scarier now—now that Vince was not there to talk to when he woke up in a cold sweat.

Nealia kept saying they'd go through Vince's stuff together, but she couldn't face it and neither could Race. Maybe he'd just start sleeping on the couch for a while. Maybe for a long while.

The next thing he knew it was light outside and Wynn was banging at the door asking to be let in. Race groaned and rolled off the lumpy couch. The floor would have been more comfortable.

"Hey dude," Wynn greeted when he opened the door. His bulked-up frame nearly filled the doorway.

"Hey back at you." Race ran his fingers through his hair and yawned.

"You still sleeping?"

"Naw. I hadda get up and answer the door."

Wynn punched his shoulder, his grin shining in his dark face, his ball cap cocked off to the side as usual. Pushing his way in, he stopped for one brief second and looked around the apartment. Race acted like he didn't notice. They all did it. Would they always be looking and waiting for Vince to appear?

"Everybody get home okay?" Race wanted to know.

Wynn nodded as he loped toward the kitchen. There was never much food at Wynn's house either. "All safe, but Pinky had a close call. He almost ran smack into a cop car."

Race felt his stomach tighten. Wynn must have seen him flinch. "Hey, man, it's cool. Anyhow Aunt Ginger woulda been downtown in a heartbeat to get him. They woulda had to let him loose. They always let the babies loose." Wynn opened cabinet doors and peered in. "The little dunce got his directions turned around. But it was cool. He'll learn."

"Sheesh. Hope he learns before he gets fried. So where are your two shadows?"

"Aunt Ginger come down hard on 'em for being out so late. They be doin' housework detail."

Race pictured Ginger, who stood not much taller than Hawk or Pinky, guarding over the boys instructing them to scrub the toilet and mop the floor. Ginger held her own as one of the hard-nosed moms in the neighborhood. "Did she know they were with us?"

Wynn smiled as he continued opening cupboard doors. "Why you think she be so mad?"

"You're outta luck, man," Race told him. "The cupboards are bare. Sure coulda used the cash from that Acura last night."

"You ain't the only one. Cool set of wheels wasn't it? Drove like a dream." He opened the fridge, then looked back over his shoulder at Race. "Leastwise it drove good the short way I drove it." He chuckled.

"Man you is right on about that word *bare*." Wynn shook his head and shut the fridge door. "Is goin' hungry on top your *to do* list for the day?"

"Heck no, man. I found me a bike."

Wynn brightened. "No way. A bike?" By now he'd found a box with a few stale crackers in the bottom. He pulled out a handful and shoved them in his mouth. He led the way back to the living room and collapsed on the couch.

"Nice one too. Ten speed. Blue and silver. I think Sharkey'll be pleased as punch to see it."

"Where'd you stash it?"

"Down behind the car wash."

Wynn gave a low whistle. "Good thinking, man. You thinking like Vince now."

The words cut deep and clean, like a well-honed shank. He *wasn't* thinking like Vince. He never could and wasn't going to start now. He'd come up with the idea all on his own. He turned toward the hallway so Wynn couldn't check out his reaction.

"Where you goin' man?"

"Hang loose. Let me wash my face and get a clean shirt on. We'll lift breakfast at the open-air market."

"Cool!" Race heard Wynn say as he ducked into the bathroom to get the grime off his face, the grit from his teeth, and run a comb through his hair. No curls on this boy's head. He combed the dark brown stuff over to the side, but it'd been getting long causing it to fall down across his face. He sort of liked it long. Nealia nagged at him to get it cut, but he sure didn't see her handing out any cash for haircuts. Paying for the cheapest of cheap funerals had strapped them bad.

Some of the funeral money his mom had borrowed from a druggie she knew who frequented Mad Malone's bar where she worked. A few dollars came from her aunt who still lived in Lower Price Hill where Nealia grew up. A few people in the apartment helped; Wynn's aunt Ginger pitched in. The rest of the cash they just scraped together by doing without. But what was new? Going without was what they did best. They'd had plenty of practice.

By some small miracle Race found a clean t-shirt in the dresser he'd shared with Vince. Nealia hadn't done up the laundry regular-like for several weeks. Most of it was heaped in the corner of her bedroom across the hall where she now slept off her binge. To her credit, she'd stayed sober for two whole weeks after Vince's funeral. Of course she'd spent most of that time screaming and crying out her grief. Since then, she'd been pretty much worthless.

On top the dresser lay the Zippo lighter Vince had found one night when they were hanging out on the Serpentine Stairs down by the river. Vince had been pretty jacked about finding it because it wasn't just any lighter. On the side was an embossed leather medallion commemorating the new year of 2000. Vince and Wynn had bantered a lot about what was being called the new millennium. Who knew it would turn out to be the last year of Vince's life? Race picked up the lighter and ran his thumb over the circle of leather, then slipped it into his left pocket—opposite from his knife.

When Race came back out to the living room, Wynn jabbed his thumb toward the wall past where the TV sat on a low, paint-chipped wooden table. "You into interior decorating? Cornflakes on the wall?"

Race shrugged and turned to open the front door. "You comin' or not?"

"You know, bro, it's gonna take a chisel to get them dried flakes off that wall."

"The roaches'll take care of 'em. They eat better than we do anyhow."

CHAPTER 4

Outside Race's apartment door, eight-year-old Marcus sat on the top step fiddling with his inhaler. Even on the sunniest days, the single bulb in the hallway struggled to ward off the darkness, and Wynn nearly stumbled over the kid before seeing him sitting there all alone.

"Whoa!" Wynn did a double step, and jumped over Marcus' head. He stopped on the lower step and turned around. "Hey there little gangsta. I nearly creamed you." Wynn extended his clenched fist and in return Marcus tapped it with his small black fist.

Marcus lived in the next apartment with his mom and baby brother. He was used to the ragging. "Naw. You couldn't. No way," he said. "Vince and Race wouldn't let you." He looked up at Race. "You wouldn't, would you, Race?"

Race leaned over and rubbed the boy's nappy head. "Not on your life, Marcus."

"See there, Wynn Jamison. Can't nobody cream me when Race and Vince be here."

If the kid said Vince's name one more time, Race was sure he'd implode on the spot. "You okay, Marcus? Your asthma okay? Been taking your meds?"

Marcus shook his head, his brow wrinkling into worry lines too old for his little face. "Can't afford no meds no more, Mama says. But I still gots this." He waved the inhaler. "I been coughing a lot in the night." He rubbed his chest. "Hurts."

Race wondered why he hadn't heard the coughing. They usually heard Marcus through their paper-thin walls. Then he remembered. First of all, he'd been gone most of the night and second, he'd not been in his bedroom.

"Catch you later, little gangsta," Wynn said bounding down the steps two at a time. Near the landing he vaulted his long legs over the railing, and landed neatly on the next flight of steps, making Marcus laugh.

"Way cool, Wynn," he called out. "I be doing that when I get bigger."

If you get bigger, Race thought. The kid spent half his life fighting for the next breath.

Fruit was always the easiest items to lift at the stalls in the open-air market. If they spotted an unsuspecting tourist, snagging a wallet was slick and quick. Cash meant they could buy a real breakfast. The best trick was to find a family with the mom herding a few kids. Vince had always been the one who could walk up and ask them the time, pointing to his wrist with no watch. Because of his dark curls and olive skin, he'd pretend he was Hispanic and couldn't understand English. That stalled for time. While he had them distracted, Wynn would bump into the dad and lift the wallet.

The first time Toon saw their action, he called it baby stuff. "Man, I'd at least turn tricks with the credit cards," he said. Because they usually just grabbed the cash and tossed the wallet—credit cards and all—into a dumpster in some alley. "Juvie's one thing," Vince had countered Toon's remark, "prison's another. And credit cards equal prison time, man."

That particular morning Race and Wynn didn't even look for hapless tourists, but just jostled in the crowd grabbing up fruit, stashing it inside their jackets and then sauntered off to the park. A blanket of gray clouds continued to hang low in the sky, threatening rain. Race slumped down on a park bench and Wynn followed suit.

"Has the fuzz been back asking questions?" Wynn asked as he tossed orange peelings on the ground.

Race shook his head. "Nope."

"Think they be finding them scumbags?"

Race shook his head again. He knew Wynn was talking about Vince's killers. "'Gang-related,' is all those cops can say or think. Five bucks says they close the case before the month is out."

"Gang-related. That they excuse to do nothing?"

"Looks that way." Race stuffed half a banana in his mouth. "I don't much give a flip," he added through the mouthful. "Hate having 'em hanging around. Cops give me the creeps. They can't do nothing anyhow." He started to add, *...because Vince is dead,* but couldn't bring himself to say the words.

"You got that right. In this place, the fuzz be best at doing nothing 'cept causing more ruckus." Wynn finished his orange and wiped his mouth on his sleeve. Jumping up, he said, "Let's find Toon and go get that hot bike you been talking about."

Race didn't move.

Wynn looked at him. "Whassup bro? You okay?"

Race shrugged.

"We can toss that bike in the back of Toon's old car," Wynn said, making a throwing motion with his muscle-bound arms, "and have it down to Sharkey's place in no time at all."

Still Race said nothing, just stared off at a group of younger kids kicking around a partially deflated, much-used old soccer ball. Across the street stood the majestic Cincinnati Music Hall with its twin gables soaring high above the squalor below. The proud lady, so out of place in Over-the-Rhine, had always fascinated Race. Concert nights were the best nights for shoplifting and breaking into cars, as well-dressed patrons strolled into the rose-colored building. While Vince and Wynn made fun of the concert-goers, Race secretly wished he could go inside with them.

"Hey bro," Wynn broke into his thoughts. "You down on Toon or something?"

"Naw. I just…" Race stopped and thought a moment, then looked up at Wynn. "Tell you what, let's just you and me wait'll after dark and get it. No sense snagging the thing in broad daylight. That just invites trouble, man."

Race threw the banana peel as hard and far as he could, then jammed his hands into his jacket pockets. Why couldn't he say what he really meant? Why had plain old talking gotten so blasted hard? So awkward. Awkward because there'd always been Vince between them. Not between them separating them, but between them, joining them. Race had never seen it before now, nor understood it really.

From the time Vince and Wynn were in fifth grade, they'd been tight. The two connected the first time they met. They connected like hot fudge topping melting on ice cream. It never mattered that Vince was white and Wynn was black. When you're in fifth grade, nobody thinks about those things anyhow.

They ruled the playground, knocking the heads of little punks and creaming the bullies. No one dared mess with them. If one got in trouble, both were in trouble—which was most of the time. It was Vince who insisted Race always be included, making it a threesome. Included, but never really a true part of the duo. But now it was just Wynn and Race, like a three-legged stool with one leg missing.

"You be talking crazy stuff, bro," Wynn told him. "We got somebody with wheels, so let's use 'em. We drop you off a block or so away. You go in them woods and grab that bike and tote it down the hill a ways. Toon and me, we come along, whisk that puppy into the car and we be off." He sat back down on the bench beside Race. "Sound a whole lot better to me than hoofing it, man."

Race wanted to tell Wynn that he didn't need him *or* Toon. He could go get the bike all on his own and ride it down to the river easy. But that wasn't entirely true. He *did* need Wynn. When he thought about how much he needed his brother's friend right now, it scared him.

"Besides," Wynn added giving him a friendly punch on the arm, "comin' a downpour."

The skies had continued to darken as they sat there and now droplets were starting to fall. Race wondered since when had they cared about rain. The three of them had been up and down every street and alley in Over-the-Rhine in every kind of weather most of their growing-up years.

Race stood to his feet and heaved a sigh. "Okay," he said. "Let's go find Toon."

Wynn jumped up and flung his big arm around Race's shoulders. "Now you talking, bro. Now you talking."

Toon's old car was a bad excuse for wheels. Rusty body and raggedy interior. Nobody seemed to know where he got it. One day it just showed up on the block. He kept it parked in a vacant lot down the street. Half the time he had no cash to keep it gassed up. Half the time it didn't even run. The faithful old radio, however, never failed to pour out rap tunes at the deepest, loudest rumbling decibel. Today, as it turned out, the car was running and there was enough gas to go get the bike and haul it down to Sharkey's place. And the radio was in fine form.

"Gotcha a little bike, did you Racy boy?" Toon said as they drove up Vine Street out of Over-the-Rhine. He had to shout to be heard over the pounding music. "Whooeee. Big time operator you is."

Toon and Wynn rode in front, with Race in back. He stared out the window at the winos along Vine with eyes as vacant as the buildings they leaned upon. Where would Vince be sitting if he were here? Race wondered. Probably up front, with Race and Wynn in back. Better yet, Vince wouldn't have been in Toon's rattletrap at all. He would have agreed with Race that night was better. Then just he and Vince would have come for the bike—maybe Wynn too—and they never would have told anyone else.

When both Wynn and Race ignored Toon's crack about the bike, he played it cool and changed the subject. "I hope your buddy, Sharkey, has that mangy dog of his chained. I hate that mutt."

"You scared of old Monster?" Race asked, unable to resist the dig. "He's just a pussycat."

Wynn chuckled. "Yeah. Kinda like a wild bobcat be a pussycat."

"That dog'd just as soon chomp off your leg as look at you," Toon went on.

"You don't mess with him, he don't mess with you," Wynn said. "Simple."

Sharkey's dog was well trained; nobody with good sense ever ventured over the fence that surrounded his salvage yard. He'd named him Monty Python after some old movie he'd seen when he was a teenager. But Vince and Race had never called the dog anything but *Monster* Python, or just Monster for short. In the daytime the dog was chained, but Sharkey let him loose at night and let him roam about to protect all perimeters.

Of course anyone with an ounce of common sense was afraid of Monster. When approached, the animal lunged at the end of his chain, growling and baring fangs that proved he meant business. But it was Toon who'd voiced fear. Vince would have hated that. It was the rule. "Never," he would say, "never ever speak the fear. You speak it; you show it. You show it, and you're dead. You don't speak it; you don't show it. I don't care how scared you are!"

Vince and Wynn taught Race how to steel himself from the inside out so that his face became a mask when the bigger thugs approached—at school, in the park, in the alleyways. If you don't show the fear, half the battle is won. It worked with the police; it worked with Mr. Feldman, his PE teacher; it worked with Mr. Jernigan, the principal. Race learned early on how to stuff down fear, and he learned well.

Race hated dragging the bike from its hiding place in broad daylight. Toon parked the car down a ways from the car wash. They waited for traffic to clear then Race hopped out. The plan was for Toon to drive around a while to give Race time to take the bike further down the hill before bringing it out to the street. Like that made any difference, Race thought as he made his way through the underbrush to where the bike was hidden.

Looking around, he wondered how the Looney Toon expected him to get the bike any further down the hill through the tangle of vines and weeds. Carry it over his head, maybe? "Toon has fried mush for brains," he mumbled to himself.

The aroma of damp earth and rotting leaves filled the air. Race breathed it in deeply. Soft rain pattered down tapping the leaves and making them dance. Glancing up the hill he saw the rock outcropping where he and Vince used to sit and smoke whenever there was a break between car wash jobs.

"Someday I'm gonna have a house on a hill like this," Vince told him one hot afternoon as they sat there together. In the summertime, the thick growth of greenness curtained the area so you couldn't even see the houses or the city below. "It'll look like this, but with no city around."

"No city?" Race couldn't imagine a place with no city.

"Nope. Just countryside. Woods and trees and maybe a little stream running through it."

Race wanted to ask his brother how a person would go about finding a place like that. Or how he planned on paying for it. Their mom had been trying for years to get out of Over-the-Rhine and back to Lower Price Hill and it hadn't happened yet. Just when Nealia thought she had a little money saved up, something would happen to wipe out the savings. More often than not, it was her own bingeing.

Race took out the lighter and rubbed his thumb over the intricate leather medallion. To ask Vince *how* questions—to which there may have been no answers—would have destroyed the fragile magic of the moment. It was far better to sit quietly and listen to Vince dream. Listening to him made Race *almost* believe it might really happen. Until now. Until the dream had been blasted to oblivion in a blaze of gunfire; drained away in a stream of Vince's blood trickling down the sidewalk and into the gutter.

Race returned the lighter to his pocket and placed his hands on the cold, wet metal of the blue and silver bicycle. Gritting his teeth, he lifted the bike over his head and pushed his way forward, feeling the vines and underbrush resisting the movement of his legs. The hill was steep and the layers of wet leaves slick. At one point he stumbled and landed hard on his backside. Putting the bike down for a moment, he rubbed his butt. "Stupid deadhead Toon."

Toon had backed the car into a clearing at the edge of the wooded area. It took some maneuvering to get the bike into the trunk, but they did it. Thankfully the older model car had a wide rear end and a mammoth trunk.

"You looks like somebody whupped up on your face," Toon said laughing.

Race didn't reply. The scratches where branches had smacked him across the face stung like fire. To think that after dark he could have carried the bike straight out to the street.

CHAPTER 5

Elevated train tracks spanned over the greater section of Sharkey's sprawling salvage yard and when the trains went over with their deafening roar, you could feel the rumble under your feet and up through your midsection. All talking proved futile till the train snaked on down the tracks toward its lonely destination.

One was going over as Toon steered his old car past the tall fence topped with razor wire, through the rusty metal gate, and up to the small gray building that served as Sharkey's shop and office. True to form, Monster jumped up from his sleeping spot under a rusty dismembered El Camino and lunged at his chain, fangs bared, his barks drowned out by the train's rumble.

Stray car parts and bald tires lay strewn about outside Sharkey's shop. Tattered signs yellowed with age plastered the grime-covered windows. One sign hanging in the window of the paint-peeling door showed a clock face with red plastic hands that said: *Be back at…* But Race never remembered seeing the red hands set at any position other than straight up twelve, telling whoever came that it mattered not at all when Sharkey arrived or left.

Discarded vehicle carcasses, stacked in hodgepodge fashion, lay hollow and lifeless in their open graveyard. They spread out in all directions away from the shop. Tall weeds, still tinged with the green of their summer growth, forced their way up through the open spots in and around the dead cars. Race had never been to the back part of the property, but Sharkey once told them it covered about ten acres.

Race climbed out of Toon's car and let his feet connect with the rumble. As the train passed and the deafening rumbling and clacking faded, the door of the shop opened and Sharkey stepped out. A short man, he was forever stained in grease and motor oil, from his worn leather boots to his faded gray coveralls, to his grimy fingernails. Even his scruffy graying beard never looked clean.

"Hey! What you fellas up to?" he asked. Then pointing to Monster, he ordered fiercely, "Monty. Shut up! Go lay down!" With one last low growling bark, the dog returned to his burrowed-out spot under the El Camino shell.

Sharkey studied them though squinty eyes that seemed to miss nothing. His wooly brows were pulled together in a permanent scowl. He looked up at the tall skinny Toon, staring at him for a time, making Toon visibly uncomfortable. Toon had come with them to the salvage yard only two other times and Sharkey clearly was not too impressed with him. He then looked over at Race and the scowl softened some.

"Hey kid? Ain't seen you since they got Vince." He stepped over to Race and held out his hand.

"*Got Vince.*" In the past few weeks, Race grew increasingly amazed at how many ways people found *not* to say that Vince was dead.

Race returned the handshake and was surprised when Sharkey's firm, solid grasp didn't release right away. "You okay, boy?"

Race felt his face growing hot. It was the same question from everyone—teachers, school counselors, even Wynn's Aunt Ginger and grandma, Mungy. Perhaps if he knew what *okay* was, then possibly he could give an answer. As it was, he usually just nodded. Which he did to Sharkey and started to pull his hand away. But for a moment Sharkey held on. Through a tight jaw, he said in a hoarse whisper, "I hope when they get 'em, they string 'em up by the thumbs and let the buzzards pick 'em clean."

Race could feel that Toon and Wynn almost stopped breathing. They'd none of them ever seen Sharkey display much emotion. The permanent scowl usually kept his face a mask.

As he released his grip, Sharkey added, "That Vince was okay in my book. Real okay."

He turned toward the shop door. "Come on in and tell me what I can do for you."

"I got me a bike, Sharkey," Race said, surprised he still had a voice. He jerked his head toward the car. "In the trunk."

Sharkey motioned to Toon. "Pull that old crate around back. We'll take a look." He motioned for Race to follow him inside.

The inside of Sharkey's shop didn't look much different than the salvage yard itself with car parts and tools scattered everywhere. But Race knew the old guy could rebuild just about anything—from transmissions, to starters, to water pumps, whatever. Although he dealt with hot items here and there, he'd never been caught up in big-time rackets.

The old man walked straight through the cramped office in front to the shop in back, not pausing till he reached the rear entrance. Race followed, stepping carefully over all the stuff so as not to stumble.

Outside the back door, Toon was opening the trunk and Wynn helped him lift out the bike. Sharkey took the bike from them with not a twinge of expression in the squinty eyes. To Wynn and Toon, he said, "Wait out here."

He wheeled the bike inside and motioned Race to follow, closing the door behind him. He leaned the bike over against one of the workbenches piled high with car parts, tools and grimy dog-eared parts catalogs. With barely a glance at it, he muttered, "Good condition." He then made his way to the office and pulled open the drawer of the ancient wooden desk. Race wasn't sure if he was supposed to follow, so he stood still. He heard Sharkey opening his metal cash box. Presently the old man came back to where Race stood.

He held up three twenty-dollar bills. "You take one and give the others to your buddies. You gotta give them fair share I know. Law of the jungle, right."

Race nodded. It was the unwritten code. You stuck tight with your pack. All share the risk; all share the take. It wasn't as though they shared this risk, since Race had found the bike. But the law still stood and Sharkey knew.

Then the old man held out a crumpled hundred-dollar bill in his greasy hand. Race made a noisy little gasp in his throat. Sharkey acted like he didn't notice. "You take this. Them funerals ain't cheap." He shoved the money at Race. "But you gotta promise me you keep this. No splitting this one. Understand?"

Race could only nod.

"I lost me a older brother." The old man's voice suddenly sounded scratchy. "They sent him over to Nam and he came home in a box. I know how it feels. Hurts something awful."

Race had never thought about Sharkey having family. He was just an old codger they talked to, and not that often. Only when they needed to get rid of something they'd lifted. Sharkey was always a ready market. The guy was tough as nails and now here he was getting all weepy. Race shifted from one foot to the other. He just wanted to grab the money and run.

Sharkey pointed at the floor. "Put it in your shoe."

"What?"

"The hundred. Pull off your shoe and stuff it in your sock. At least I'll know you got home with it."

Race did as he was told, his head still spinning. In his mind, he was already walking down the aisles at Kroger's filling the cart.

"Now get on outta here. And try to stay out of the way of the fuzz."

"I'm careful," Race managed to mumble.

Sharkey only grunted. "That's what they all say."

Race wasn't sure how he would keep Wynn from knowing he had that much cash. They knew most everything about each other. He waved the twenties as he got in the car.

"All right," Wynn said grabbing his. "Sweet." He reached into the back seat with his large palm open. "Gimme five, bro."

Race slapped his hand, pleased that Wynn was pleased.

Toon tucked his twenty in his shirt pocket and said, "That old coot'll get more than that outta one measly gear part."

Race settled into the back seat and said nothing. Toon turned up his music and began to rap along, seemingly content that he'd spoiled Race's moment.

Dumb Toon, Race thought as he wiggled his foot to feel the crumpled bill. *If you only knew.*

As they headed back toward Over-the-Rhine, Race thought about what Sharkey said about losing his brother. "Hurts something awful," he'd said. Race had wanted to reply, "Not if you don't think about it."

Lots of people died in his neighborhood. You got used to it after a while. People got shot, or stabbed, or they OD'd, or got sick and didn't get well—like what would probably happen to little Marcus. Homeless people froze to death in their flimsy, barely-protected hideaways. Others burned to death, ignited by a little fire built to warm themselves. Some guys go off to prison and never come back like Wynn's older cousin, Mitchy. And like Uncle Dutch.

Uncle Dutch was probably the hardest, because it happened before Race had learned how to *not think about it.* The man wasn't really their uncle, but he told Race and Vince to call him that. Race never heard him called anything but Dutch. Of all the men his mother had ever hung out with, Uncle Dutch was best. Vince once confided to Race that he thought Dutch was the only man their mother ever really loved. Vince had had one too many beers when he said that, but Race was pretty sure his brother was right.

Race never learned how Nealia and Dutch met, but he knew Uncle Dutch was the one who convinced her to move away from Lower Price Hill where she'd grown up, to his place in Over-the-Rhine. Back then, Nealia lived with an aunt who never gave her a moment's peace, so she may have been thankful for the ticket out.

Living with Uncle Dutch was the happiest time Race could ever remember. Even though he'd been only four at the time, he recalled the laughter, the peace, and the fact that there was never a lack of food on the table. Every day Uncle Dutch caught a bus on Vine Street and went to work, something few other men in the neighborhood ever did.

Nealia still kept a snapshot of the four of them tucked away in her billfold. The photo showed them sitting on the couch in Dutch's mother's apartment—Miss Frieda, they called her. Uncle Dutch, a bear of a man, had his arm around Nealia's shoulders. The way they were situated with Race snuggled on Nealia's lap and Vince on Dutch's lap, they looked like a real honest-to-goodness, all-American family. It was too good to last. At least that's what Nealia always said about it later. "Anything good in my life is doomed to fade away like popping pretty soap bubbles," she'd say—especially when she was drunk.

Uncle Dutch's mother got sick. Miss Frieda lived in the apartment downstairs from theirs. Everyone in the apartment house knew and loved old Miss Frieda. Race remembered being in awe at how neat and clean Miss Frieda kept her place. So different from all the other apartments in their building. Race guessed she was the oldest person he'd ever known. But she got sick.

Uncle Dutch worried about her a lot. For years, he'd resisted the crime and drug dealing in the area, but to buy his mother's medicine, he took the chance of making a few deliveries for the corner druggie. One deal went sour, Uncle Dutch was nabbed and sent to prison. He was killed within his first year there.

Race cried. Vince told him not to cry because it made it harder for Mama. "And besides," he'd added, "men aren't supposed to cry." So four-year-old Race cried with his face in his pillow long after Vince fell asleep.

One of Nealia's friends said that Uncle Dutch wasn't "tough enough or mean enough" to survive prison. At the time, Race didn't understand what that meant. But he understood now. Being tough and mean was the law he'd learned very early. He learned that lots of people in Over-the-Rhine died before their time. And he learned not to cry.

CHAPTER 6

With a few extra blankets to smooth out the lumps, sleeping on the couch wasn't too bad. No matter, it still beat being next to Vince's empty bed every night.

Race lay there watching the pink and green lights do strange things to the room, pondering on how he was going to break that hundred-dollar bill so he could buy stuff with it. He couldn't remember ever even holding one before. At the moment, the bill was safe under his mattress. What he needed was to have it in tens and twenties so he could buy a few things at a time. He pictured himself whipping the hundred out at the corner Kroger's checkout, only to have the clerk panic and call the security guard. Most of the clerks knew him and they knew good and well he never had big bills like that—ever.

While sleep fled, the options ran through his head. He thought about going to a gas station or convenience store outside the hood. But that wasn't good either. People just seemed to know he didn't belong there. The way they looked at him made his skin crawl.

Malone, the owner of the bar where his mother worked, was usually a pretty good dude. Race wondered if he'd break it and be trusted not to blab to Nealia.

Who knew? In the end, none of his wondering mattered at all.

In the wee hours of the morning, he was awakened by a weeping, breathless, Nealia shaking him.

"Kyle, Kyle. Little darlin', you gotta help me. Wake up. Hurry. He's waiting." She was wild-eyed and panicked.

Race flew upward pushing his mother backward and nearly knocking her to the floor. "Help what? Who's waiting? What's the matter?"

"It's Jay-Jay Walker." Her words were thick and slurred and her breath smelled worse than the inside of Mad Malone's. "Before the funeral, he told me I could pay back a little at a time, but now he says different." Her voice took on the whine it always held when she'd had too much to drink. "He's acting real mad. Threatening to hurt me."

Race pushed his hair out of his face and groaned. "Not Jay-Jay. Mama, I told you not to have anything to do with that loser. Especially not to borrow from him. He's a creep."

"And how was I supposed to pay for Vince's funeral? Tell me that, huh? Mister know-it-all. What was I supposed to do?"

She was pulling at his arm now. Race shook her loose and stood to his feet. "We coulda made it, Mama. We coulda done it. We don't need the likes of him." It made him all the angrier because he knew if Vince had told her not to, she would have listened to him. "How much?"

"A hundred."

Race felt his insides wilt. He heaved a deep sigh. A hundred. Poof. Just like that it was gone. Like Nealia always said, "Good things always disappear, just like popping pretty soap bubbles."

"Where's Jay-Jay now?"

"Waiting for me at Malone's. He's awful mad. I never seen him so mad."

"Someone else is pressing down on him, Mama. That's all. He owes somebody else and that's why he needs the cash now. That's how it works."

Race took his mother by her trembling shoulders and sat her down on his makeshift bed. She was small, thin, frail. Looking older every day. "Stay here," he ordered.

She looked up at him through bloodshot eyes. "You gonna take care of it? You got some money?"

"I got some money, Mama. I'm gonna take care of it." He went down the hall, pulled on his clothes, grabbed the hundred and his jacket and came back to the living room. Nealia hadn't moved from where he'd placed her. She'd probably sleep now. Her shoulder-length hair, once dark and shining, was graying and disheveled. She seldom bothered with it anymore, preferring to keep it pulled back and hidden under one of Vince's old ball caps. Whether it was to hide the mussed hair, or to feel closer to Vince, Race wasn't sure.

He stepped toward the door. "Do not leave this place, Mama. Understand? Stay right here."

"I hear. I understand." She pulled up her knees and placed his pillow there, laying her head down on the pillow. "Just like Vince, Race. You're taking care of me just like Vince always done."

He closed the door before she could say another word.

Cold rain hit him in the face as he stepped out of the apartment house foyer onto the darkened street. He pulled his collar up around his neck to keep out the rain and wished he'd grabbed his knitted ski cap. The dimly-lit bars along Fifteenth belched warm, stale beer smells as he walked by.

When he came to Malone's, he thought for a second about telling Malone about Jay-Jay's threats to Nealia. He quickly changed his mind. He could handle it himself. No need getting the whole neighborhood in an uproar.

After his eyes grew accustomed to the dim interior, Race spotted Jay-Jay sitting hunkered over a drink in a back booth. The place was nearly empty. Malone had probably gone home. The barkeeper scowled at him. "Hey kid, get outta here. I don't need no babies bringing the cops down on me."

"I got business to tend to," Race said, without glancing that direction or slowing his step. He didn't stop till he reached the booth. Jay-Jay looked up at him. He looked worse than Nealia. "What're you doing in here, kid? You got my money?"

"Here's your money, creep," Race spat the words, dropping the crumpled bill into his drink glass. "I'm warning you—don't ever threaten my mother again."

"Then you make sure she pays up what she borrows."

"Don't worry, she'll never borrow from a creep like you ever again."

He waved a hand. "Yeah sure. I'll believe it when I see it. That souse will always need dough for something or other."

In a split second, Race felt the white-hot anger boiling up and his hand slipped to his pocket and held tightly to his knife. But before he could pull it out, the barkeep yelled at him again. "Your business is done, kid. Now get on outta here. I mean now."

Race released the knife and felt it drop back to its resting place. He turned away. That scum wasn't worth dirtying up his knife.

"And stay out!" Came the last words from the bar as Race opened the door to the cold, slishing rain.

"Oh why don't you just shut up?" he said evenly and slammed the door.

So much for having extra food for a few weeks. But that's how it always happened in Over-the-Rhine. He'd seen others try to get ahead only to be slammed flat on their backs. Happened every day. Why should he think he'd be any different?

"Toon's moving."

When Wynn said that, Race was hoping he meant Toon was moving to Siberia or someplace like that. He didn't let his inner reaction show. "That right?" was all he said.

They were hanging out in the living room at Wynn's Aunt Ginger's place. Race was still pretty steamed about losing the hundred and had no one to even talk to about it. It made him feel tight and jittery inside.

Ginger Hawkins, mother to Hawk—whose real name was James—kept a fairly clean place. Her stove usually held a pot of something simmering, like stew, or chicken soup, or ham hocks and beans. Race liked her stew best. Big chunks of beef, with lots of chopped up potatoes, carrots, onions and tomatoes. Sometimes at night when he was real hungry, he dreamed of having a whole pot of Aunt Ginger's stew all to himself. As it was, he tried to be polite and only eat one bowl when Ginger offered, and say, "No thank you," when she offered more, and only took another if she really insisted. Aunt Ginger wasn't in the habit of boozing up all her welfare check like Nealia did, so they usually had more food on the table.

It was a good thing too, because she also rode herd on Pinky, who was her sister's son. Cortisha Pinkerton skipped out on them when Pinky was in first grade and they hadn't heard from her since. Just walked out, leaving Pinky behind. No one even knew if she was alive. Pinky's given name was Ross, but certainly no one ever called him that.

Ginger Hawkins was a no-nonsense, in-your-face, African-American mom who took no guff off the boys. She tried her dead-level best to keep them off the streets, while Wynn tried his best to keep them *on* the streets in order to teach them to survive.

Wynn lived down the hall with his very tired, very grumpy granny whom they all called Mungy. The older lady still grieved over the loss of her wandering daughter and her two sons—Wynn's father, who still languished in prison, and his uncle Mitchy who'd died in prison. Mungy's meager welfare check had to stretch thinner than either Aunt Ginger's or Nealia's. She would often wonder aloud why she'd been so cursed as to have to bring up another no-count manchild—namely Wynn.

That October afternoon when Wynn announced that Toon was moving, Hawk and Pinky had just come in from school. They were in the middle of the living room floor scuffling like two cub bears.

Pinky, lighter-skinned than the rest of his family, could almost hold his own against the more muscular Hawk. Last summer, Hawk had hit a growth spurt, plus he'd been lifting weights at the rec center with Wynn. Pinky, on the other hand, was wiry and thin and somewhat of a crybaby. Wynn confided to Race more than once that he was going to "knock the whine outta that boy." Of course he never did.

"If you was in the Deuce Dragons," Wynn told Pinky one day, "you'd have to get jumped in by letting all them punks beat on you at once." Shaking his head, he added, "They'd mangle you."

The words never fazed Pinky who knew he was safe as long as Wynn was there to watch over him.

Ginger yelled from the kitchen for the boys to "cut that out, right now," while the television blared out the piteous story of love gone wrong on Ginger's favorite soap.

In the midst of the noise, Race acted like he was watching the soap. He tried to ignore the fun Hawk and Pinky were having, and acted like he didn't give a rip if Toon moved or not.

Finally Wynn said, "Yeah, he be moving all right. He met up with a dude with digs on Fifteenth. They be splitting the rent."

Just then, Pinky landed on Wynn and Wynn shoved the younger boy back into the fight on the floor. Ginger yelled again for them to cut it out or she'd tan their hides and hang 'em out to dry. They ignored her.

"Toon'll be a lot better off," Wynn added.

Race thought surely Toon would be happier in Siberia and wished again that that had been the answer. "Anything's better than that hole he lives in now," Race offered.

"You got that right."

Race had been to Toon's place only a couple of times, and didn't care to go back. Toon paid a few dollars a week for a basement room—barely a hole in the wall that stunk really bad. He slept on a shabby mattress on the floor. Race was pretty sure rats could get in there. Race's apartment was a palace in comparison. Rats might have the run of the alley, but he'd never seen one in their apartment.

"What's the dude's name?" Race asked, trying to keep the conversation going. Talking with Wynn felt as stiff and unnatural as the cheap leather shoes his mother had bought him to wear to Vince's funeral.

"Kind of a funny name–Savastano or something like that. Goes by Savvy."

A new thought snapped in Race's mind. If Toon had him a new running partner, maybe he'd split from their pack. What a piece of good news that would be.

Hawk had finally pinned Pinky and the smaller boy was yelling for mercy. Ginger came in then and made them go to their room. "I bet you clowns got homework. Get to it," she ordered like a drill sergeant. The two jumped up and fell all over each other getting down the hall to their room.

It was a marvel to Race how the little woman could speak and the guys obeyed whether they wanted to or not.

She turned her dark eyes on Race and Wynn. "And if you two wasn't so empty-headed as to be dropping outta school, you'd have homework too."

"Now Aunt Ginger don't you be raggin' on me and my homie here. We be doing all right."

"Yeah, you think all right. You need somebody to bang your empty heads together and knock some sense in you. You could at least get your lazy carcasses out and finds you a job."

Wynn jumped up and put his arms around his aunt who was about half his size and kissed the top of her head. "Now sweet little Aunt Ginger, all me and Race here really need is some of that apple cobbler you been fixin' there in your little kitchen. You got any that yummy stuff left?"

"You overgrown grizzly," she said wrestling free of his grasp. "Help yourself to the cobbler, but see to it you leave enough for the boys. They be hungry too."

As they followed her to the kitchen, Race was still withering under her stout words about school. Dropping out didn't seem to bother Wynn. He'd known all summer that he wasn't going back, and didn't even bother to enroll in the fall. "I don't need them jokers telling me what to do," he'd say.

But Race never planned to drop out. It just happened. One guy too many came up to him with the same old line, "You that kid whose brother got himself shot and killed? Man that's a shame. I'm really sorry." The dude who said it that last day had probably never in his life heard gunshots ring out in his neighborhood in the late night hours.

Race had always been pretty content just to be Vince's younger brother, but now he was the kid whose brother got shot. People looked at him funny. Especially the girls. Pitying looks. He couldn't stomach it another minute. He went to his locker, grabbed his stuff and walked out. It happened barely a week ago. Nealia still didn't know. Part of him was relieved; part of him longed to be back. He wasn't even sure which was which. Or why.

CHAPTER 7

Nealia was angry when she finally wised up that Race had quit school. Or at least she acted angry. Race knew she was too out of it to really care much. He'd been staying away from the apartment as much as possible during the daytime, just kicking around the neighborhood.

As chance would have it, a phone call came from Mr. Jernigan, the principal, on a morning when she was both awake and not hung over. A rare combination. Race was in the kitchen spreading the last of the peanut butter on the last slice of bread and he could hear her all the way from her bedroom with the door closed.

"Not been there? What do you mean he's not been there? Of course, he's been there. Where else would he be every day?" There was a pause and then her voice rose to a higher pitch. "Why, that's the most ridiculous thing I ever heard of."

Race threw the empty jar into the trash. He knew the pattern. First she would do the angry, indignant part, then switch to the poor me, pity-party, whiny part. The transition that day was quicker than usual.

"Well, Mr. Jernigan," he heard her say, "I can't be everywhere, you know. I have to work late every night. Late. I mean real late. Like to the wee hours."

Work late, yes, Race silently corrected her, *but then booze it up into the wee hours.*

"After I get a little sleep, it's time to get up and get going all over again. Now you tell me how I'd be able to keep track of that boy every single day? Would you just tell me that? I'm doing the best I can, for heaven's sake."

By the time she came out of the bedroom to where he was slumped on the couch finishing the bread and peanut butter and watching television, she was really into the whiny part.

"Why didn't you tell me, Kyle, darlin'?"

"Race. My name's Race."

She sat down in the overstuffed chair, perching barely on the edge. He didn't look at her.

"I'm your mother, for heaven's sake. Why didn't you tell me? I can't believe you didn't tell me."

"Nothing to tell." He shoved the last of the bread in his mouth and suddenly he could hardly chew. He jumped up to get a soda from the fridge.

"Don't walk away from me when I'm talking," Nealia said, but without much conviction.

"Just getting a soda, Mama. I'm listening. Keep talking."

By the time he came back in the room, her face was buried in her hands, her stringy hair draping sadly. "What will become of you, Race? You gotta finish school. You just gotta."

He wasn't sure where this reasoning was leading. "I'll be okay, Mama."

"But what will become of you? Where will you end up with no education?"

He wanted to say he'd end up at the same place no matter what he did. That place was right here, rotting away in this slime ball apartment. Or in prison with Wynn's uncle. Or dead like Wynn's uncle Mitchy. Like Dutch. Like Vince.

She looked up at him now, her eyes red and puffy. "You're all I got left, Kyle darlin'. You gotta do this for me. You just gotta."

He drained the soda. He wanted to run. To not have to listen to this.

"If you just hang around the streets, you're gonna get sucked into one of those gangs." Her face twisted painfully. "It was probably one of those gang bangers that shot your brother."

"I'm not gonna join no gang, Mama."

"They can push you, Race. They can push. I hear the talk at Malone's. I know something about how that works. I'm not dumb. I hear. I know."

Race didn't like how the conversation was going. Crunching the can in his hand, he took it to the kitchen to throw it away.

"I'm going to the school and talk to Mr. Jernigan. I'll find a way for them to *make* you go back."

But her voice was getting softer now—empty of any resolve. Race knew she'd never in a million years be able to force herself to board a bus that would take her to his high school, located blocks outside OTR, let alone walk into the school and actually sit down and talk to the principal. She just couldn't do it. And she knew he knew. So her voice went soft.

Suddenly, Race felt sorry for her. Usually he was angry with her. But not now. He grabbed his jacket from the hook by the door and went over and touched her shoulder. She didn't move.

"I'm not gonna join no gang, Mama. Vince didn't need them and neither do I." He gave her shoulder a little pat, then moved to leave.

As he went out the door, he heard her say, "But Race—you're not Vince."

As if she had to remind him.

They didn't meet Toon's new buddy, Savvy, for a quite a while after Toon moved in with him. But did Toon ever talk him up, big time. It was "Savvy done this and Savvy done that. Savvy say this and Savvy say that." In a few short weeks, Toon had made him into some kind of superhero. Race got sick of hearing it real quick.

It was close to Halloween and the night air held a new bite to it. They'd pulled off a quite a few successful car heists since the fumbled one in Clifton. Toon was the one who handled all the follow-up transactions and doled out the take—because he knew the connections. Race was pretty sure Toon didn't divvy up fair, but who was going to accuse him? Not Race. Nor Wynn either, evidently. Wynn appeared to be along for the ride, never once countering Toon. Race could hardly believe Wynn was the same guy who'd ruled supreme with Vince by his side.

"Vince the Invincible and Wynn the Winner," was how they were known. "A Vin-Wynn deal," Vince would say. "Double trouble," Wynn would add.

The titles fit. They had turned the head of every girl in school and could have had any one they wanted. Together or single-handedly, they could take apart any bully who stood in their way. Even the teachers feared them and gave passing grades just to get them out of their classes. And Race followed along, content to float in their wake, thankful simply to be included.

Where had Wynn the Winner gone? Had his life's blood trickled down the gutter along with Vince the Invincible's?

Toon's relic Bonneville was on the fritz again. It sat forlornly in the vacant lot looking not at all out of place beside an old couch that was throwing up its insides. Great nesting place for rats, Race thought, as he stepped carefully through the trash and overgrown weeds.

It was just growing dark when they all piled into the car. Toon ground the ignition a few times but other than giving a weak dying groan, it refused to spring to life. Toon had been bragging about how they were going out to the mall and work the parking lot.

"Guess that was a loser idea," Race mumbled as he got out.

"Hey, cool it, child," Toon said. "Nothing here that can't be easily fixed. I'll work on it tomorrow and we'll head to the mall then."

"Yeah, right," Race mumbled. Turning to Wynn, he said, "Let's go to Mad Malone's and shoot some pool. At least it's warm in there."

Malone ran a junky poolroom and video arcade next door to his bar where minors could hang out.

Hawk and Pinky crowded in to hear what they were saying, not wanting to miss a beat. "Yeah, man," Hawk agreed. "Malone has the best video games."

"Hey now. What you pansies talking about?" Toon loped around the car. "Nobody gonna play no pool tonight. I told

Savvy we'd snag another set of wheels and that's what we gonna do."

Race bristled and held his breath, waiting for Wynn to protest. Hawk and Pinky froze.

Toon jabbed a thumb toward downtown. "They's a Bengals game tomorrow. Downtown'll be brimming over with classy wheels tonight. Let's head that direction."

He didn't wait for a response, but headed out of the vacant lot, taking a leap onto the dead couch and off again as he went, his dreads flying, laughing his hyena laugh. No telling what kind of high he was on.

Race looked at Wynn. Wynn shrugged. "I could use the scratch," he said.

"You babies comin' or not?" Toon called back.

Mutely they followed.

Toon be-bopped and rapped his way down Vine Street like some kind of wound-up pied piper. They'd gone only a few blocks when Race felt Wynn tense up beside him. Race slowed when he saw what Wynn saw.

"Check it out," Wynn said softly.

Up ahead, clustered on a corner they'd claimed as theirs, were the Deuce Dragons. They wore royal purple doo rags and look-alike jackets with their dragon emblem airbrushed on the back. Last time Race saw the Dragons they didn't look that slick, and their numbers had been smaller. Something was in the air. And it wasn't good.

Even Toon slowed till Wynn whispered harshly, "Keep walkin' just like you was. Stay cool. And don't say nothing. Hear me? Nothing." The last words were slow and emphatic—almost like the old Wynn would have talked.

There's no way they could turn off now; that would not look good. Race slipped his hand into his pocket and located his knife. Wynn did the same. Wynn also slowed a beat to station himself between the Dragons and his two young cousins.

A needle of pain moved through Race's midsection as his gut tightened. Funny, it'd never occurred to him till this moment—he'd never been in a fight in his life without Vince by his side. He trusted Wynn, but nothing like he'd trusted his own brother. Quickly he forced his mind into no-think mode. Into auto-reflex. Steel the face, loosen the arms, cradle the knife, all nerves on *ready*. But the stomach screamed. It always did, but not this much.

The space between the two groups shrunk gradually. The Dragons weren't steeled at all. They were talking low, turning heads, checking them out, making the study. Race didn't know who was the leader. He wouldn't allow himself to look that way long enough to determine. A couple girls were in their midst. Their high giggles filled the night air.

Tension in the air snapped like live electricity. More shuffling of feet, rustling of low talk as they came closer. The Dragons were to their left. Now Race could smell the beer and the weed. His fingers snugged up on the knife. He struggled to control steady breathing as they paralleled the gang.

Suddenly he flinched as a voice called out, "Hey Toon, whassup?"

"Everything cool, man. We be trucking down to lights of the city." Toon never slowed his pace.

Race forced his head not to look their direction.

"Cool," came the voice again. "Catch you later."

"Later, man," Toon shot back. And by that time, they were past them.

Race's wrenched insides simply switched gears from one stimulus to the next as it sunk in what had just happened.

Toon just talked to a Dragon. How could that be? Especially after Wynn had ordered silence.

None of them spoke until they'd covered the last few blocks before stepping into the glittery lights of Main. Then Race said, "How'd you know that dude?"

Toon shrugged. "Juvie. Plus I done a couple deliveries for his brother. He's okay."

Race waited for Wynn to step in. To protest violently. But all Wynn said was, "He a leader?"

Race knew the dude had to be a leader or he'd have had no permission to speak to them.

Toon just nodded as he started singing another rap song, acting as though what he'd just done didn't amount to a hill of beans. Race thought he was going to be sick. He'd wondered for weeks if the Deuce Dragons were responsible for Vince's murder and here Toon was chatting with them all chummy like.

"Just a bunch of little wannabes is all they are," Race said softly, not trusting his voice.

Toon stopped singing. "Don't look now, bro, but them wannabes is starting to *be*."

Race would not even allow himself to ask Toon what he meant by that remark. Then Hawk said, "Cool jackets, man."

"Studly," Pinky agreed.

Race shoved his hands in his jacket pockets. He had to make some movement to mask his shock. If Vince were there he would have knocked heads together for so much as glancing at the Dragons, let alone speaking to them. But Vince was not there. Not now. Not ever. Nothing could bring him back. And nothing would ever be the same again.

CHAPTER 8

Toon and Toon's new-found bro, Savvy, lived in a made-over loft in Over-the-Rhine. One of those places that some "do-gooder"—as Aunt Ginger called them—had refurbished in an attempt to improve the neighborhood. Race figured it was the best place Toon had lived in a long time. Maybe ever.

It was Hawk who finally had his fill of Toon's raving about Savvy. "You goin' on about him like he some kinda god. If he so great, why you keep him under wraps?"

At first Toon came back with, "Aw, he don't wanna meet you two-bit chumps. He gots better things to do with his time."

But Hawk kept pestering. In the void left by Vince's absence and Wynn's clammed-up silence, Hawk grew more and more mouthy. Race didn't like it. The kid had a lot to learn and he needed to keep quiet and watch and listen.

But the effect of a mouthy fourteen-year-old ragging at him finally wore Toon down. One cold, gray day in November, Toon announced that Savvy was ready to meet them. Whatever that meant.

The front of the place had undergone a facelift, making the building appear out of place in the midst of her decrepit sisters on either side. The lobby was litter-free with new tile on the floor and painted walls. Unlike the other apartment buildings in the area, this place actually smelled good.

The pack clumped up the wooden stairs to the fourth floor. Toon led the way. He stepped forward, opened the door, and ushered them in, then grinned his empty grin at the shocked looks on their faces.

"Whoa!" Pinky said, bug-eyed and staring at the over-stuffed black leather couch and chairs and the glossy hard-wood floors. Oriental rugs scattered randomly added their subtle colors. A massive black-lacquered entertainment center, complete with big screen TV, graced one wall. The room was open and airy with skylights that let the light pour in. "Didn't know they was nothing like this in OTR," Pinky added, not attempting to disguise his awe.

Even Hawk lost his toughness. "Me neither," he said, sounding a little out of breath.

Wynn never let out a peep. Race held back, keeping his hand in his pocket, fingering his knife. He didn't like this place and he didn't trust Toon as far as he could throw a dump truck.

Just then Savvy strode out of the back bedroom. Now Race had another surprise. All along, he'd assumed Savvy was black, else why would Toon team up with him? Or rather, why would a guy like Savvy team up with a black crank like Toon? It made no sense. Race tried to catch Wynn's eye to see if he registered the same shock, but Wynn was still ogling over the nifty digs.

Toon was in all his glory as he introduced his new buddy to the pack.

Savvy stood about five nine, but he was built like an ox. Good-sized biceps stretched out his blue turtle-neck sweater.

Now the name Savastano made more sense to Race, because Toon's buddy looked Italian with neatly combed thick black hair, a trim dark mustache and piercing dark eyes that roamed over each one of them with apparent distain.

"Hey, Toon. Brought your babies up to see me, did you?" He nodded, unsmiling, as he shook hands with each of them.

Race's every nerve came to immediate alert. His gut told him Savvy was a bad news dude, and because of Toon, they were somehow connected to him.

He had no intention of releasing his knife to shake hands with this total stranger, but then, how could he not? His hesitation wasn't lost on Savvy, whose lip curled up in a smile that bordered on a sneer.

"This must be Vince's brother," he said reaching out his hand.

Race shook Savvy's hand and released it quickly. "You never knew Vince."

"Everyone's heard of Vince Paloma."

Savvy didn't elaborate and Race refused to give him the satisfaction of asking what he meant. Savvy waved at them to sit down, then instructed Toon to grab beers from the fridge and pass them out.

When Toon handed Race his, Race just shook his head.

"Racy, baby," Toon said acting incredulous. "You turn down free beer? That's a new one."

Savvy's dark eyes turned on him. "My beer not good enough for you, Race?"

The boys were settling in and tipping bottles. Even Wynn seemed to let his guard down. Race didn't want to sit. Everything in him wanted to bolt and run—now. Nerves churned and rocked in his stomach. "Not thirsty," he said, shrugging.

"Sit down, Race," Toon said from where he'd plopped down in front of the giant TV. "You making me nervous."

Pinky waved him over to an empty spot beside him on the black leather couch. Reluctantly, Race moved that direction and perched himself on the edge of the soft cushion, his nerves still taut. His shame and disgust mounted as he realized he'd just obeyed the youngest baby of their pack.

Savvy had accepted a bottle from Toon, but he remained standing, continuing to assess with a critical eye. No one said anything. Presently, Savvy said, "Toon here's been bringing me your work." He paused. "So far, not too bad. But the market is growing. Law of supply and demand, right? I got outta-town contacts. Classy contacts. That means we need more product. More product, more dough. You fellas do right by me, I make sure your percent goes up."

Race knew that the past few weeks, the heists had been going pretty good. None of them knew where Toon took the wheels after he dumped off the pack. Race didn't want to know. The cash was nice. Hard to complain when his stomach was full and the bill collectors weren't screaming. They'd been lucky so far. How far their luck could stretch, no one knew. And the subject of risk factor never came up.

Back in their shoplifting days, Vince always warned not to work too fast, too much, or too often. "When you feel safe, you get cocky," he'd say. "You get cocky, you get caught. Simple as that. We ain't looking to get caught. We're looking to survive."

Race could see the more they succeeded with each heist, the more cocky they felt. Especially with cash in their pockets. All Vince's wisdom was cast aside.

Toon gazed up at Savvy, seeming to drink in every word along with his cold beer. "You want we should bring you more wheels? That what you be saying, Savvy?" he asked in his empty way. His spray of dreads bounced with each move of his head. Savvy smirked. "You catch on fast, Toon. You're really quick."

Toon grinned, totally oblivious of the diss he'd just received.

Across the room, Race could see Hawk rising to the bait. Hawk loved money. Every time he got a few bucks, he bought more new threads. Aunt Ginger was half frantic over her two charges. The more she clamped down on them, the more they snuck out and stayed out all hours of the night.

Wynn, on the other hand, remained a blank slate, staring at something off over toward the kitchen. Vince had taught him well. He skillfully masked all emotions.

"Cincinnati's big," Savvy went on. "Plenty of work here. I'm ready to up the percentage when you up the scores you're making."

He took a long drink from his bottle, looked at each of them, then said. "Once you get production up, the only way more scores can be made is to split into two teams."

The room went deadly silent. Even Toon's bouncing dreads froze in mid-air. Split the pack? Everything inside Race screamed out *Never. Never in a million years would we ever split up.* But his throat closed tight and dry. He didn't care if he had to starve to death and be put out on the street, splitting the pack was absolutely out of the question. Race stared at the fancy Oriental rug on the floor and said nothing.

In his mind, he sent messages across the room to Wynn: *Tell him no. Tell him no. Tell him no.* Wynn Jamison's receptors, however, seemed to be out of commission. For a split second, Race allowed his eyes to flick up and take in his brother's life-long friend. What he saw scared him. The panther's eyes weren't simply steeled to mask his thoughts, they were lifeless. A cold chill swept over Race as he realized the Wynn he'd always known was now as lost to him as Vince.

Race had known fear—lots of times. But that fear came and went. This was different. Deeper. More terrifying. What would happen to them if some two-bit, out-of-town jerk like Savastano could split them up?

Savvy finally cut into the stone-cold silence. "It's a new idea. I'm in no hurry." His voice was cool and even, with no emotion. "Let it grow on you."

"A new idea, but not a bad idea." Toon put in too quickly—like he had to say *something.* "The more teams we gots, the more work we gots. More work; more dough." He laughed his hyena laugh. "We like the dough, right homies?" Toon was sitting close enough to kick at Hawk's foot, which was stretched out in front of him, nudging Hawk out of his trance.

"Oh yeah, man. We do like the dough," Hawk admitted as a smile spread over his dark face. He then looked up at Savvy and grinned even bigger. "We do like the dough."

Savvy nodded smugly, his dark eyes turning to small slits. "I know you do, Hawk."

A purple twilight was settling over the city with a few snowflakes drifting down as they emerged from Toon's fancy loft. Race could barely control the anger boiling beneath the surface. He stomped off ahead of the pack not even knowing where he was going—just going. He needed to be alone. To think. To figure this mess out. God, how he wished Vince were there.

The others followed in his wake, but it was Toon who caught up to him. "Hey bro, slow down. You act like you be pissed or something."

When Race didn't slow down, Toon reached for his arm to stop him. Wrong move. Race jerked away, then in a lightning move swung out with his fist hitting Toon square in his skinny chest. The satisfying feel of contact and Toon's subsequent gasp for air only served to stir Race's anger more. "Keep your hands off me, Toon!"

"Race!" came Wynn's stern voice from behind. "What's that gonna solve?"

Race whirled to face Wynn. "Hey, you tell me. We been listening to some loco talk about splitting us up and you act like it's all cool."

Wynn moved in closer, his sheer size taking control of the situation. In a more rational moment, Race knew he was no match for Wynn's muscles or his moves, but in his present state, he'd loved to have tried. He stood there clenching and unclenching his fists.

Then Hawk, like a young stud sensing a break in the herd leadership, inched a little closer to the action. "Hey man, that Savvy guy's okay in my book. I likes the way he thinks. He thinks big and I wanna think big like that." He gave a shrug. "So what's the diff if we do a few jobs in two teams 'stead of one. We still be a pack. Like the man say, more work mean more dough."

Race glanced over at Hawk. Now Hawk he could pulverize easy. "Butt out, Punk. Nobody pulled your chain."

"Hey, you the one all hepped up, not me," Hawk answered with a shrug. He started to say more, but Wynn took another step between them.

"Shut up both of you. You acting stupid."

"Stupid?" Race spit out the words. "You want to talk about stupid? Stupid is all of us sitting there listening to some dude we don't even know telling us where to go, what to do, and how to do it. Now *that's* stupid."

With that, he spun around and let his legs do his thinking as he began to run as hard and as fast as he could go. Because if he hadn't, if he'd stayed in that spot a second longer, something really bad would have come down.

CHAPTER 9

Race ran blind. Not thinking; just running. Toward down-town. Past downtown. Down toward the river. At first, he thought Wynn would chase to catch up with him. To stop him. To talk. First Race wished he would, then he prayed he wouldn't. Race knew that Wynn wouldn't talk; he'd take him apart limb from limb. Race had never dissed Wynn like that, ever. Everything had gone crazy. His mind screamed inside his head and soon his lungs were filled with fire.

He sped through a deserted industrial district, jumping fences, running through deserted weed-infested freight yards, passing old warehouses with jagged broken windows. Huge shells of factories now closed. Nothing in this part of the city lived or breathed any more. Dead. All dead. People used to work here. His great aunt had told him that once. People went to work in factories here and earned paychecks and then went home each evening to watch TV and play with their kids. Now winos, junkies and baseheads took up residence in the hollowed-out tombs.

By the time Race came to the end of his strength, he wasn't too sure of his location. And he didn't really care. Maybe some cop cruiser would see a wild kid running, think he'd done something real bad, and grab him and lock him up. Funny. He didn't care about that either. Maybe he just needed an excuse to scream and fight and punch and kick.

His breathing was short and ragged as he stopped to try to catch his breath. Snowflakes fell more thickly now. Night was closing in and this wasn't the part of town where the city paid for bright, shiny streetlights.

He made his way across a series of train tracks, down a slight grade to where a high fence, with razor wire at the top, strung along down the incline closer to the river. The other side of the fence appeared to be a field of thigh-high weeds. Slowing some, he jogged along following the angle of the fence, worrying about what he'd just done and what he might do next. His mind was a muddle.

All his life, he'd looked up to Wynn, very nearly worshipping him, and now he'd dissed him bigtime. Maybe he could just walk down to the river and not stop walking. *Wonder how long it takes to drown? Or how much it would hurt?* Surely it couldn't hurt any worse than the pain that tore up his insides day and night.

For a moment, he strained to remember what it'd been like before. Before Vince's death. The pack operated so smooth. Smooth as soft butter. No one questioned it. No one tried to figure it out. Certainly no one bucked it. Vince and Wynn had all the respect of the younger ones. No one dissed them. Unwritten rules had grown out of the strength of Vince and Wynn. Their own workable system.

Race stopped and bent over with his hands on his knees, sucking air into his burning lungs. Questions banged around in his head like ricocheting bullets in an Over-the-Rhine showdown. Would the pack still be strong if it had been Wynn who caught the bullets in the back? If Wynn were gone and Vince still there, would the pack be splintering like it was now, with Hawk all mouthy and disrespectful and Loony Toon calling the shots? Those were questions he didn't want to ask, nor did he want to answer, but they were questions that wouldn't go away.

Wearily, Race slumped down in the tall grass with his back against the fence, his face in his hands, mindless of the wet snow. The answers seemed pretty clear. Obviously, Vince had been much more of a force than Race had ever given him credit for. He'd just been too close to see it. In spite of how it had appeared at the time, evidently even Wynn had followed the charismatic Vince Paloma.

Suddenly something slammed hard against the fence, snarling, barking, snapping. Race sprang to his feet, yelping in fright. The fence shook and rattled as it was hit again. Then in the shadows, Race saw Monster's ominous dark snout growling and snarling, as he continued to lunge at the fence like he wanted to rip Race into tiny pieces. Race was already completely out of breath, and the scare very nearly did him in. He pressed his hands against his chest in an effort to stop his heart from pounding clear out of its place.

"Monster, you ugly old dog. You nearly scared me out of two years' growth." Again, he fell down to the grass, this time a few feet away from the fence.

But the truth was, Monster wasn't really ugly at all. In fact, Race often noticed when the dog lay quietly near Sharkey's office, how shiny black his coat was and how peaceful he looked when sleeping. Race had often wished he could pet the animal.

After a few more noisy lunges, Monster gave up and trotted off through the tall weeds, satisfied that his job was completed. At least Race now knew his location—he was on the backside of Sharkey's sprawling salvage yard.

Looking down the way, he muttered, "Sure hope there're no holes in that fence."

The fence wasn't new by any means, and in places the razor wire at the top was completely detached and falling to the ground. Not that it mattered. Who in their right mind would want to go in? Even if you wanted to steal something you'd have to heave it over the fence. But first you had to be chewed up by a bad monster dog.

By this time, Race was so exhausted he could have curled up beside the fence and gone to sleep. Had it been summer, he might have considered it. But now his clothes were getting wet and he was chilled to the bone. At least the anger had drained out—along with all his strength.

Walking the entire circumference of the salvage yard, he came around to the road he knew. Back on familiar ground, he dragged his way slowly homeward.

The streets of OTR pulsed with its usual nighttime rituals. A low-slung car with smoked windows rumbled slowly by on Vine. The windows were cracked open just enough to allow the music to spill out into the cold night air. Baseheads nodded in the doorways of vacant buildings. Daylight panhandlers were replaced with restless groups of kids trying to find out where it was happening, so they wouldn't miss out. This was the time of night the baby gangsters ran their deliveries, darting in and out of shadows, trying to make it through alive for one more day.

Race couldn't begin to count the number of times he and Vince were hit up to make deliveries for the big boys. No matter the pressures coming down, Vince never wavered.

His answer was always no. "It's a trap," he'd explain to Race alone in their small room. "You think the money's good, and it is. But just one time, and they think they own you."

Lying in his bed barely an arm's length from Race's bed, propped up on one elbow, Vince'd go over it again. Carefully, thoroughly. That's how Vince did everything. He thought about things a lot. In grade school, they called Vince "gifted." Race was never sure what that meant, but he knew up until sixth grade Vince got mostly A's in every subject. That was the year he and Wynn hated the principal and seemed to have a run-in with him most every day.

That was also the year that Nealia's drunken binges came with more regularity. And different men following her home also happened with more regularity. Cooped up in their room, Race and Vince made feeble stabs at spreading their homework out on their beds. However, the obnoxious, mouthy men-friends made their efforts almost impossible. That's when Vince stopped trying. "I ain't taking nothin' off nobody," became his byword. Then he'd look at Race and add, "And don't you either." They took to the streets a lot after that—the three of them, Vince, Wynn and Race, with a string of younger stragglers in their wake.

Maybe it was because Race was so tired that he dropped his guard. Or maybe because he was lost in thought—like he always was when thinking about Vince. Whatever it was, Race didn't notice the guys kicking back in the alleyway just ahead until he was almost on top of them. He had but a few seconds to get his wits about him and slip his hand into his pocket and locate the knife. To set his face hard and keep his eyes ahead. But the knot in his stomach screamed. The flash of purple out of the corner of his eye indicated they were Dragons.

"Well, well, homies. Would you take a gander there," said the biggest of the three. "If it isn't one of Toon's babies. Wandering 'round OTR all alone."

Race recognized the guy as the one known as Piston—the Dragon with the juice. Just his luck. Mentally, he was kicking himself. Stupid, stupid, stupid. Carelessness is what got Vince shot. Gotta be on guard every blessed second. The pounding of his heart echoed in his throat and his breath came tight and short.

"Who be so dumb to do a thing like that?" came a retort. "Prowl about them wicked streets with no protection?"

"Dunno," came the third voice. "How's about we ask and find out."

Race kept walking at the same pace. The third voice definitely sounded higher and younger. If Race had to take them on, he'd throw the younger one and cut him first, in hopes spilled blood would scatter the other two. Not much of a plan, but it gave life to his right hand. When the time came, the wielding of the knife took on a life of its own. Vince had spent hours teaching him.

Race was almost even with them when they made their move. Emerging from the shadows, they stepped directly in front of him and turned to face him. Piston in the center, flanked by his two smaller, younger homies—three black brothers guarding their turf.

"Stay cool," Race could hear Vince saying. "Never make the first move. Better to calculate your move by what they do. Let them make their mistake. Puts you in control."

Race swallowed the fear and worked to control his breathing down to steady. "You kiddies out playing awful late, ain't you? Your mommas know you're out this late?" The solid sound of his own voice pumped a new surge of adrenaline.

At that Piston hooted. "You hear that, bros? This little guy's the one messing 'round and got no colors. And he dissin' us."

"Maybe he need that we should teach him what protection colors can give." The smaller guy stepped forward half a step and Race tightened his hold on the knife. Ready.

"We could," Piston said real slow. "But let's let the baby talk. He gots no big old brother to nurse him now. Maybe he need friends."

At the mention of Vince, Race flinched. But Vince never caved when words were thrown. Fists moved Vince; words seldom did. So let 'em throw their words.

"Whatcha say, baby?" the smaller kid echoed the diss as though he could hold his own, which Race knew good and well he couldn't. "Ain't no safety when you kicking 'round solo."

"I manage," Race said evenly. The danger seemed to have diffused. All they wanted to do was jack around with him.

"Tell you what." Piston's arms moved from being folded across his chest to hanging loose by his side. "How 'bout we jump you in? Dragons be cool, man. We watch each other's backs real good. They no sense you roaming 'round here all by youself." He shook his big head like he was talking to a little kid. "Just way too dangerous. We could set it up next week easy."

"Never needed gang banging. Don't need it now." Race stepped off as though to pass by them. Piston stepped over to stop him.

"Tell you what," Piston continued. "Make you a deal. You come in with us, they be no jumping in for you like regular. How about you just go heads up with our big man?" Piston paused as though he wanted to evaluate the wise decision he just made.

If there was another Dragon bigger than Piston, Race hadn't seen him. Piston was almost the size of Wynn.

"And tell you something else. I do the same for you big black buddy. Sound fair?"

"I don't think for Wynn. Ask him yourself." Race winced as he remembered his run-in with Wynn earlier in the evening. The way Wynn had been acting lately, who knew what he'd do? Race stepped out again. "Now move out of my way."

Piston gave a fake laugh and put his hands in the air and took a step back. "Hey man, we be cool. You moves right on through the dark all by your little self, home to your beddy-bye—this time. You be warned. You be invited. Next time be different. Way different. You remember that."

Race walked on still fingering the knife just in case, the blood pounding in his ears.

Dumb jerks. It took several blocks before his breathing evened out. He thought his stomach would never calm down. Even after he was bedded down on the couch, the burning in his midsection continued to keep him awake.

The thing he hated most was that the Dragons were dead on about one thing. Race *was* alone. Very alone.

CHAPTER 10

The incident between Race and Wynn was never mentioned, but it hung in the air like a stale foul odor. The effect was worse on Race than if Wynn had beaten him to a bloody pulp. If talking had been hard before, it now became impossible. The pack functioned like so many empty-headed wooden puppets and Savvy held the strings.

One cold weeknight in late November, they stood inside the entrance of a deserted building slapping their hands against their arms and stamping their feet to keep warm. The place stank with stale urine, an obvious sign of a junkie hole. Savvy had them wait in different places to be picked up by Toon before a job. In the past two weeks, he'd come for them in a different car every time. Not flashy new cars, but better than his antique Bonneville.

Two more babies had begun to tag along. Brothers, Worley and Zip Crider. Black boys Hawk knew from school. Hawk and Worley had started kicking together, so Hawk suggested they be included. "Why let Savvy decide who be comin' on board? Let's do it ourselves," was his strategy. Pinky openly resented the addition. Because Worley mirrored Hawk in word, action, and size, Pinky felt left out.

Zip, the younger of the two, rarely spoke and rarely smiled. Moody, sullen, and angry, he seemed ready to smash something—possibly somebody's face—for no reason. To this new change of events, Wynn said nothing.

Race's stomach burned like fire most all the time now. He finally gave up trying to eat a hamburger he'd just bought. He wrapped it up and stuffed it in his coat pocket. His favorite too. Maybe he could eat it later. He shifted from one foot to another and rubbed his hand over his stomach, applying a little pressure, willing it to stop hurting.

"Wish Toon would hurry up and get his booty over here," Hawk complained. "I'm 'bout to freeze to death in this rat hole."

"Hope this car has a heater," Worley put in.

Worley had only been with them on one other heist and the pick-up car had had no working heater. Race wondered if that gave him griping rights at the outset. Bigtime bad man—one job.

"You don't like it, you can ditch now," Pinky told him. "We don't need no pansies."

"Cool it, smart mouth," Hawk shot back at him. "You the one that be's a pansy most all the time. Whining 'bout ever' little thing. Ma always did call you 'little whiny pants.'"

Pinky gave his cousin a hard shove. Caught off guard, Hawk stumbled into Wynn. Like being awakened from a trace, Wynn grabbed Hawk by the scruff of the neck and shook him like a cat with a mouse.

"Stuff it, both of you. We gots a job to do and we ain't doing it worth a flip if you be scrabbling between yourselves."

The timing of Toon's arrival couldn't have been more perfect. Wynn opened the door and shoved Hawk through, pushing Pinky after him.

They all crammed into the mid-sized, nondescript Mazda.

"'Bout time you got here," Hawk said to Toon, as cocky as though he'd never been slammed by the Panther. "We was about to freeze in there."

"Aw you bunch of little sissies. Ain't even cold," Toon said over the sound of the rap music pouring from the radio.

"Not when you be cruisin' the streets with the heater blowing all cozy on you," Worley added.

Now, instead of one cocky smart-mouth, they had a pair.

"Hey, now," Toon said, "tell you babies what. You smarten up and you could all be wrapped up in warm purple jackets. Matching. Your names stitched just so." He swirled a skinny finger in the air like he was writing. "Real cool-like. My old juvie buddy, Piston, say he can make it happen easy. For each and ever' one of you."

The car got quiet except for the jumbled pumping pounding music. Suddenly the heater was blowing air so thick and warm, Race thought he might be sick. The same queasy swimming-sick he'd felt riding in the police car following the ambulance after Vince was shot. He shoved on Pinky who was practically in his lap to get the window cracked open. He had to have air. The blast in his face did it. He stared out the window for a minute at the huge orange moon hanging down in the sky.

The guys griping about the cold wind blowing in on them broke the silence.

Finally, Race managed to say, "Tell your old buddy he can take his suggestion and shove it."

Toon laughed his hyena laugh and the matter dropped. But not before Hawk said under his breath, "Them jackets is way cool."

Toon dropped them off at their designated spots. Wynn with Pinky and Hawk; Race with Worley and Zip. Race, now the expert, taught the new recruits how to pick and choose. How to move fast. How to signal the others. How to get it popped open. To keep gloved at all times. No prints. How to split and run if the fuzz showed up. "Never follow each other," Savvy instructed them.

Fine with Race. He never wanted to be caught with these deadheads anyway.

The location tonight was a dark street near downtown. As dark as it could be on a bright moonlit night.

"Find something in this block," Toon said with his new air of importance. He pulled to a stop and they jumped out quickly. The rule was, you found nothing, you walked home—even on a cold night. They always found something.

Race located the late-model Buick and had it open almost before the babies got their legs under them. His signal brought them running.

"Cool," Worley breathed as he scooted in. Zip dove into the back. "I'm gonna be that fast real soon. Savvy already likes me and says I is gonna be a main man."

Yeah sure, little man. Keep on dreaming. Race shoved it in gear and peeled out. He'd not even gone a block when the sirens sounded behind him. He swore. How could they have been so close?

He cut the lights and twisted into a side street. "Hang on," he ordered. "When I tell you, split and run."

Suddenly the little hotshot had nothing to say. Race could almost smell the fear in the car.

Race knew this area pretty well. Gunning it, he swung around two corners which took him down under the viaduct, back up on the other side and across a grassy median to the highway. Down the highway as hard and fast as he could take it. They'd be calling for another patrol car soon, then he'd be trapped. Didn't want that. But the flashing lights had disappeared. Couldn't be too careful. One more time he pulled off the highway and down a slight embankment and cut the engine.

"Bail," he ordered.

"Where we supposed to go?" Worley whined

"Shut up and run, stupid," his younger brother yelled at him as he took off like a flash.

Race knew his exact location. Back up over the highway he ran, down the other side, across the railroad tracks. There it was—the high fence. Now he heard sirens. They'd caught up. Faster. This was probably the dumbest thing he'd ever tried in his life. But it was this or iron bars. Now voices yelled behind him.

At the point where the razor wire hung down loose, he made a flying leap grabbing the chain link fence and vaulting his body over, landing hard on the cold ground on the other side.

Within a matter of seconds there was Monster's snarling face coming straight at him. In his most Sharkey-sounding voice, he ordered, "Monty, you hush now. Go lay down." To his everlasting amazement, the dog obeyed his order. His heart pounded in his ears and his head was spinning. Maybe he was dreaming. As the dog sat, his tail was wagging.

"I don't believe it," he said under his breath. From his pocket, he pulled out his partly eaten hamburger. "Here boy. Got something for you." The food disappeared in one gulp.

"I always leave him a little hungry," Sharkey used to tell them. "He works better that way."

The voices were closer now. Crouching down in the high weeds, he pointed Monster to the fence. "Sic 'em, Monty. Go get 'em, boy!"

Race's voice had evidently become the voice of authority, because Monster did exactly that! He couldn't help but chuckle as Monster bared his menacing fangs and lunged snapping and snarling at the fence as he had at Race only a few days earlier.

He could hear the officers swearing loudly. "Nobody but an idiot would go in there," he heard one of them say. "That dog means business."

Another voice replied, "Come on, let's get out of here. We've lost him."

The voices faded into the night and were gone.

Monster came back to Race, tail wagging as though to ask if he'd done a good job. Slowly, carefully, Race reached out his hand. Monster sniffed the fingers, then lowered his head for a pat. As Race rubbed his big head, the dog pushed against him like a puppy wanting attention. "This is nuts. I don't believe it. You're all blow and go on the outside, and a little weenie on the inside. Who'd have guessed?"

Race's ragged breathing began to even out. He got up off the cold ground and looked around to survey his surroundings. Nothing but acres of old dead wrecked cars and trucks lined up in the weeds, and probably a lot of little critters. Then he noticed off to his left sat an old wrecked travel trailer illuminated in the bright moonlight. A little bunged up, but sitting on all its wheels.

Curious, Race pushed his way through the tangle of undergrowth to check it out. The facing side looked good as new. He peered around the back and saw that it was rusty and bent up on the top and side. Possibly it had rolled on that side.

"Funny what people throw away," he said as he stepped up on the first step. Monster was hard by his side now.

He reached up and pulled at the door. It resisted. "Stuck because it's sat for so long, I bet." He pulled again. And again. "May need a crow bar or something." Instead of pulling he tried wiggling and shaking it, then pulling. This time it swung open with a loud creak.

Behind him, Monster gave a little whimper. Race stood staring at him for a long moment. He could hardly believe it was the same dog. Reaching down to pet his wide, soft head, he said, "Good boy. You saved my life. Wish I had more food for you."

He turned and entered the trailer. "But I'll make it up to you. Maybe next time," he said as he looked around the little enclosure. Not too bad. Just neglected for a time. A few years, maybe. He pulled the door closed and opened it again a few times. It worked better each time he tried it.

"Always wondered what one of these little dudes looked like on the inside. Pretty nifty."

To his right, a sofa spanned the width of the trailer below a wide window hung with faded curtains. He pushed back the curtains to let in more moonlight. Soon his eyes adjusted to the dimness. The kitchen to his left had a sink and stove on one side, with a little booth-like dinette and fridge on the other. Past that he could see a double bed from which the mattress had been removed. Guarding his movements lest he disturb any little creatures that had made this their home, he stepped toward the bed and opened the door to the left. "It's the john," he whispered to Monster. "These things have everything." Monster was directly behind him pushing at the back of his knees. Cupboards lined the walls above the kitchen and above the bed, with a small clothes closet tucked in beside the stove.

Returning to the sofa by the door, he reached down to feel the light-weight foam cushions. He smiled inwardly. Still soft, not brittle. And in all his moving around he'd not heard any scurrying of little feet. Perhaps it'd been tight enough to keep out the mice. The whole thing could stand a little cleaning, but he'd spent the night in worse places.

Monster took his pause as an invitation and approached, his toenails clicking on the linoleum floor. Again, Race reached out to pet the softness of the big head, then rubbed a silky ear.

"Well, boy, I guess I can't hardly call you Monster no more. You just don't act like much of a monster. Guess I'll have to call you Monty. Is that all right?"

Now his tongue lopped out and in the dim moonlight he looked to be almost smiling.

Right. The dog's smiling and I'm going loco right here in this deserted trailer. Maybe I'm just dreaming all this stuff and it ain't really happening at all.

But when his hand got a wet lick, it sure enough seemed very real.

"Maybe you're just lonely. Is that it? Roaming around this place all by yourself all night long. And being tied up all day with Sharkey never paying much attention to you at all. No wonder you warm up to a half-eaten hamburger and a little attention."

One by one, he pulled the sofa cushions from the seat and the back, and took them outside, knocking them against the side of the trailer to get off the worst of the layers of dust. He then took them back to the bedroom and laid them out side by side on the bed. Making sure the door was closed tight, he sat down on his makeshift bed and sucked in a big breath. Sitting still like this, he could sense the cold begin to creep into his bones. Especially after that bad scare and running hard – his sweaty body was now chilled.

He never even thought about whether to leave or stay. It seemed natural to pull his feet up on the bed, pull his coat around him and curl into as small a ball as he could make. If there were mice, they'd just have to give him room.

"Maybe I'll bring some candles here," he mumbled. "A little food. They got some of them little heaters at the Army Surplus. Toon used to have one in his hole-in-the-wall place. That'd be pretty neat. What do you think, Monster? I mean, Monty?"

Monty's reply was to take a leap and land up on the bed. He then snugged up as close to Race as the space allowed.

"Well, can you beat that?" The warmth felt wonderful against his back. "Vince and me always wanted a pet. Mama never would let us have one. Wish old Vince could see me now." Almost instantly he fell into a deep sleep with no nightmares.

CHAPTER 11

Race awakened before dawn. He knew he needed to be out of there before Sharkey arrived and noticed that Monty wasn't at the gate to greet him. At this moment, Race didn't want anyone suspecting anything.

With Monty at his heels, he inspected the length of fence to see if there was a better way to enter and exit. Not finding any, he gave Monty a hug and scaled back over the way he'd come. Somehow he needed an easy way to get stuff inside. But if he had to throw stuff over the top, so what? He'd think of something.

The sun was just coming up when he entered his apartment building. At the top of the dim stairway, he almost fell over Marcus who was in his usual spot.

"Up awful early, ain'tcha, little buddy?"

"You be comin' in awful late. I been waitin' for you."

Race sat down beside him. "Now why would you be waiting for me?"

"I heard stuff last night."

"Stuff?"

"Them cousins of Wynn…"

"Hawk and Pinky?"

"Yeah. Them two. They was here."

Race felt his heart sink. "Stupid, stupid, stupid, punks," he said softly.

"I heard 'em knock on your door. Mama was sleeping, so I came out and asked what they want. They say to tell you Wynn be picked up."

"Wynn picked up," Race repeated dumbly. That wasn't possible. Not Wynn. He was so smart. So careful.

"They looking real scared, Race. They been running real hard." After a moment Marcus said, "Whatcha think they do to him, Race? What them cops gonna do to Wynn?"

"I dunno, buddy." He stood to his feet. A few minutes earlier, he couldn't wait to get home to get some food, but now his hunger had fled. "Go on back in now. Remember Wynn's a big boy. He can take care of himself."

"Even the big guys get beat up when they take 'em in, Race." His big eyes were wet. "I knows all about that."

"You don't know squat, little buddy. That's just a bunch of bunk. That's all it is. Now get on back inside before your mama wakes up and gets worried."

Race let himself into his apartment and sunk down on the couch. He knew Marcus was right. Getting roughed up by the cops was all part of the game.

When Uncle Dutch's mother died, the authorities allowed him to come to the funeral. Heavy chains held his cuffed hands in front of him; chains on his feet reduced his walk to a shuffle. Race was only five at the time, yet he could remember every detail as if it were yesterday. So clear. He'd never seen Uncle Dutch sad before. At the cemetery, the men with uniforms, guns and badges said that Vince and Race could go up to Uncle Dutch before they loaded him back in the patrol car.

Looking down at them with sad eyes, Uncle Dutch said, "Boys, don't ever come here." They knew what he meant. He was talking about prison. "You hear me? No matter what, don't ever come here. Promise me."

Vince's voice was strong when he answered. "I promise, Uncle Dutch."

But Race's throat closed. He couldn't speak.

"Promise me, Graham Kyle. I gotta hear you say it."

The words finally squeaked out thin and scratchy, punctuated with a little sob. "Promise, Uncle Dutch."

The chains gave an eerie rattle as he climbed awkwardly into the car. The door closed and Uncle Dutch mouthed, "Don't ever forget. You promised."

They never saw him again. No one ever said how he died. He just died. In that place. That place where they lock people up. Uncle Dutch had no one to watch his back.

Now the cops had Wynn. Race hadn't been at all happy with Wynn of late, but none of that mattered. Because they still watched each other's back. Race shivered as he realized he now had no one to watch his back. No one.

"How comes you both get followed in the same night?" Toon wanted to know. "Something kinda weird 'bout that. Don't you think? What you two dudes been up to?"

They were sitting on a bolted-down metal picnic table in the playground near where Vince died. The wind was sharp with cold and the sky hung low in a steel gray color.

Race mulled things over in his mind. He had no idea why the police would have been hot on them so fast in a single night.

Toon lit up a cigarette and released a cloud of blue smoke into the cold air. "You know Wynn was packing?"

Race struggled to mask his shock. Wynn never carried a gun. Always a knife, never a gun. Where would Wynn have gotten a gun—and why would he want one?

"How would I know that?" Race kept his voice steady.

"You his bro and you don't know important stuff like that? How tight you be, man? Hmm. Not very, I guess. Maybe he don't trust you no more."

Everything inside Race wanted to jam Toon's stupid head down into his shoulders. He clenched his jaws and waited. He had to know what was coming down now. The only way to find out was to let Toon rattle. Auto theft and caught with a gun—bad news for Wynn.

"Savvy say we gonna cool for a few days, seeings how you both mess up in one night."

Race waited for Toon to say what was happening with Wynn, but then he realized Toon wasn't going to tell anything without Race prying it out of him. He should have known. Now he wondered why he'd even agreed to meet with him. He needed to get over to Aunt Ginger's right away.

Toon stood up and stretched as though he were bored with the whole mess. "You babies better get you some protection, that's all I gotta say." He turned to go. "You know them cops is shooting at anything that moves in OTR. Them Dragons watches each other's backs real good."

"So go get jumped in," Race said, his voice low. He'd love to see them pound Toon into the sidewalk.

"I'm thinkin' hard on it, bro. Might come sooner than you think."

"Be my guest."

As soon as Toon loped away, Race headed toward Wynn's apartment house the back way, through the alley and up the fire escape. He and Vince had come into Wynn's room this way countless times so Grandma Mungy wouldn't know. But now he was headed for Aunt Ginger's apartment in the same building. Hearing music blaring, he knew Hawk and Pinky were in their back bedroom. It took several taps on the window before they heard him above the bee bop. Pinky pushed the window open and Race climbed in.

"You get our message?" Pinky wanted to know. "They gots Wynn."

"I got the message. Kinda dumb, you coming to my place. I got fingered too, but I outran 'em. We're all pretty hot right now."

"You right about that." Hawk sat on the edge of his bed, not bothering to get up. "Like they was just primed and waiting for us." He shook his head. "Like the cat waiting for the mouse."

Race didn't want to hear their whiny chit-chat. "What do you know about Wynn?"

"Mama's bad upset," Hawk told him. "She been down to Juvenile Hall most all night."

"They gonna hold him?"

"Oh yeah. They gonna hold him all right. Mama say he messed up real bad this time. Real bad. It's some big time trouble."

Pinky came over to Race, his face full of worry. It seemed the bigger Hawk grew, the smaller Pinky looked. Now his face looked like a small child's. "Race, why you think he be packing a gun? Wynn ain't never had no gun before."

"And he say if he ever catch us with one," Hawk added, "he be rearranging our faces."

Race's gut tightened and burned like fire. "Where'd he get it?"

"You asking us?" Hawk said. "How we supposed to know?"

"You're with him almost every second. How could you not know?"

"Used to, maybe," Pinky said. "Not no more. Not since he don't have Vince."

"He go off without us now—a lot," Hawk agreed.

This was news to Race. "Since when?"

Pinky flopped down on the bed. "A little bit ever since August, but more the last few weeks," he said, then looked over at his cousin.

Hawk nodded his agreement. "You best not stay around here too long now," he said. He stood up and moved around the bed to their cluttered dresser to pull out another CD. "Mama and Mungy both be fighting mad like a coupla wet cats."

"I'm going. No more jacking for a few days, Savvy says."

"We figures as much," Hawk said. "I'm thinking we be needing them Dragons for sure now. When Wynn's gone..."

Hawk didn't get another breath out. Race closed the space between them in two strides and had Hawk slammed up against the bedroom wall. "Don't even think about it. Steer clear of those Dragon creeps or I'll rearrange your face myself."

Hawk squirmed and pushed, but he was still no match for Race's strength. "Let go of me."

Pinky jumped up from the bed and was by his cousin's side. "Yeah, Race. You can't push us around."

Race held on a minute longer. "Don't *ever* let me catch you hanging around the Dragons. If I do, I'll beat you within an inch of your lives." He released Hawk with a shove that sent him sprawling.

Aunt Ginger's voice came from down the hall. "What's going on in there, you two?"

"Ain't nothin', Aunt Ginger," Pinky called back. "Hawk's just pushing me around again."

"Well cool it! And I mean now."

"You got it, Aunt Ginger."

Race pushed up the window, letting in a blast of icy wind. As he climbed out onto the fire escape, Hawk said, "Just 'cause Vince is gone and Wynn is gone, don't make you no leader." His voice held a sneer that Race had never heard before. "We's following Toon and Savvy! They the ones that's got it going on, man! Not you!" And with that the window slammed shut.

Over the next couple of weeks, a little at a time, Race stocked his new hideaway. His shoplifting took a new turn, as he grabbed up hand warmers, fuel sticks, Sterno lamps, candles, flashlights, batteries, and even a small portable CD player. He removed the blanket off Vince's bed, stuffed it into a backpack and took it in. In every way, he made himself look as inconspicuous as possible as he transported needed items to the abandoned travel trailer. He took care to avoid areas where he thought the Dragons might congregate. The last thing he needed was another run-in with the likes of Piston and his thugs.

On this particular night, his backpack was filled mostly with food. Early darkness of winter provided excellent cover as he made his way along the fence line to where he vaulted over to the other side. As soon as he hit the ground, Monty trotted up to greet him, his tongue lolling out.

"Hey, boy. C'mere boy." He knelt down to give the wriggling dog a hug. "Got a special treat for you tonight." He patted the backpack where he'd stuffed in a package of doggie treats. Monty's favorite.

From his coat pocket, he pulled out his small penlight flashlight. The smaller the light, the less chance of anyone seeing him. Although he couldn't imagine who would ever be on the backside of a salvage yard, guarded by a dog like Monty, still he tried not to assume anything.

Inside his little hideaway, he lit a candle and set it in the center of the table. The windows were now insulated with newspapers secured with masking tape. That kept the cold out, and the light—and what little bit of warmth there was—in. Even though it was still mighty cold inside, he preferred this place over his apartment. Monty's heat helped some as well.

It would be foolish, he knew, to come every night. Much too predictable. Too easy to follow. So he chose the days at random, only allowing himself to come a couple evenings a week.

The week earlier, just before dark, he'd walked all the way across the salvage yard up to Sharkey's shop, in the hopes he could find water. Bingo. Not only did he find an outside faucet and hose, but located several plastic buckets sitting in among the tools, car parts, and old tires. Most were coated with oil and grime, but one sitting nearer the building looked to be fairly clean. He didn't plan to drink it. He'd stocked bottles of water for that. He used it to scrub off the filth of neglect.

For the first time in his life, cleaning became fun. A thing to be enjoyed. Because *he* would enjoy the results. No one but him. And Monty.

CHAPTER 12

The cooling off time didn't last long. Not near long enough for Race. Savvy had them heisting cars again shortly after Thanksgiving. Race went along, saying very little. He did what was expected of him, took the money and stashed it in the back of a dresser drawer in his room.

Wynn's sentence came down two weeks before Christmas. A year in juvie. A *year*. When the word got back to him, Race was stunned. Wynn would be gone from him for an entire year. A lot could happen in one long year. The very thought sent unbidden jabs of fear all through him.

Life without Vince was already the worst nightmare he could have ever imagined. Now Wynn was gone. The emptiness clutched and grabbed at his midsection and made his heart feel like it was bouncing all over his chest till he wanted to scream.

Race had never been the other half of a pair; he had *followed* a pair. *The* pair. Vin and Wynn—the duo known, respected, and feared in all of Over-the-Rhine. He did have Vince to himself sometimes. At night in their room. Good times, kicking back with him. Talking with him. Soaking up his vibrancy, leaning on his strength, taking in his street smarts. Pushing back the furniture in the living room for intense bouts of wrestling. So many times in the past year, Race had *almost* pinned his brother. Now he'd never know. The shock of the loss still hit him at times. Like ice water slung in his face.

You get cocky; you get caught. If Race had heard Vince say it once, he'd heard him say it a million times. But no one ever told him that if you get distracted, you could also get caught. That thought never occurred to him. Because lifting the items needed for his hideaway wasn't done to prove anything to anybody, or even to get money, so being cocky wasn't even involved. He just wanted to get the place—*his* place—fixed up.

For the first time since Vince died, Race had something to look forward to. He liked his hideaway in the salvage yard. It was his—all his. It gave him a smug feeling that no one else knew about it but him. He stocked it with books and magazines to read, CDs to listen to, and plenty of food. The intense cold had become a problem the past couple of weeks as the temperature dropped to the teens. But even that small problem would be solved very soon.

The trailer was the only place where the hollow emptiness didn't follow him. There was something complete there that he couldn't explain, nor did he try. No one to explain it to anyway, except for Monty Mutt.

And then there was this thing about that crazy dog who wanted to be with him the moment he vaulted over the fence. Go figure that one out. Race had never known a dog like that, especially since he and Vince had never been allowed to have a pet. It was like some old *Lassie* movie. The Mutt seemed to sense the nights Race was coming, and he'd be standing at the fence dancing around crazy-like with his tail almost wagging off his backside.

The money piling up in his dresser drawer was enough to actually buy the things he needed for the hideaway. But why use it when it was so easy to lift what he needed? This particular night he was anxious to get there, but he'd heard that the temperature was to drop below zero in the night. He really needed a down-filled vest and thermal underwear.

If he'd been thinking at all, he'd have realized he should have gone to the mall, or the old army surplus store. At either of those places, he would have blended in. But no, he was in too big a hurry. Instead, he opted for the sports store downtown, which was right on his way. Downtown where he stood out like a sore thumb. He'd always hated downtown Cincinnati. The people there looked at him like he'd just stepped out of an alien space ship. Snooty folks who drove shiny new cars and didn't have to wonder where their next meal was coming from, or if the landlord was going to fix the broken windows or turn on the heat. But here he was, stepping out of the freezing wind into the warmth of the sporting goods store right on Main Street.

About an hour remained before closing time and the place was elbow-to-elbow people. That was great because the busier the store, the easier it was to be ignored.

Race proceeded to stroll casually up and down the aisles till he located what he wanted. Deftly, he stuffed the items under his oversized coat. He then selected two flannel shirts, which he held out in plain view and then made his way to the dressing room, going into the last stall. In the dressing room, he pulled off his coat, put on the down-filled vest and stuffed the packages of thermal underwear into the back of his jeans. Once his coat was back on, he returned the two shirts to the fitting room attendant. "Too small," he mumbled. She glanced his way with a look of distain. Snooty broad. If she only knew he had more money stashed at his house than she made in a month.

Oh well, who cared about the all the snobs, anyway. He turned his thoughts to how warm he'd be that night at the little trailer. With these last things—the down-filled vest and thermal underwear—his place would be nearly perfect. Now he couldn't wait to get out of the dazzling lights of downtown and get to his own little dark corner of the world.

Hey, Monty Mutt. I know you know I'm on my way. Calm down, boy. I'll be there in just a minute.

Race hadn't taken three steps out the front door when someone yelled, "Stop that kid!" Before his mind could tell his feet to run, he was grabbed from behind by someone much taller and heavier than he.

"Let me go!" Struggling wildly to yank free from the hold, Race's hand automatically pulled his knife to defend himself.

"Oh no you don't, you dumb little jerk," came the low voice very close to his ear. Race's left arm was caught and twisted behind him. One more slight twist and he yelped from the pain. People were stopped now, watching the scene unfold. One bystander took it upon himself to jump in to assist. As he approached, Race slashed at him with the knife, making the man jump back. Suddenly Race's legs were knocked out from under him and he hit the sidewalk with a thud. A kick at his hand sent his knife clattering down the concrete. Hot pain shot through his hand where it'd been kicked and he again let out a surprised cry of pain.

His knife. He couldn't lose his knife. He'd be lost without his knife. In one last violent desperate attempt, he jerked and pulled with all his might, but his captor only twisted his arm more tightly behind his back sending sharp stabs of pain up through his shoulder.

"You don't learn too well, do you kiddo?" Now there was a knee in his back and his free arm was pulled behind him. He had no strength left to even hold his head up. All he could do was lay his face against the icy cold, rough, dirty sidewalk. His coat was lifted from the back and he felt the packages being pulled out of his waistband. The harder he struggled, the tighter the grip on his arms, and more the pain screamed inside his head.

"If you'd be quiet, I'd let you up," said the voice, still disgustingly calm. "Cops'll be here in a minute. We'll let them take over."

Stupid, stupid, stupid. How could he have been so stupid? Vince would *never* have made such a stupid mistake. Just a few more minutes and he'd have been back at his hideaway all quiet, warm and comfortable. With Monty Mutt snuggled close by his side.

In a matter of minutes, a cop car pulled up with sirens wailing and a frenzy of lights whipping around, sending flashes of blinding reflections in the store windows. Two officers climbed out as the oversized store detective who'd apprehended Race hauled him up onto his feet. The bear-like detective explained briefly about the shoplifting and that Race had pulled the knife. Race watched as the store dick handed the knife and the unopened packages over to one of the cops.

The taller of the two officers sized him up with a look of pure disgust. "Hey pretty boy, you into expensive underwear?"

"Aw, stuff it."

"Smart mouth," the officer said. He grabbed at Race's arm and jerked it hard before twisting it behind his back to snap on the cuffs. This time he was ready. He bit his lip and didn't make a sound.

They read him his rights and searched him. Not very easy to hide an expensive down-filled vest when you're wearing it. From that moment, everything happened at lightning speed. The next thing he knew, he was being pushed into the back of the patrol car, heading straight for juvenile hall. Visions of Uncle Dutch filled his head as he squirmed around to try to get comfortable and ease the dull throb of pain in his back and shoulders. *"Don't ever come here,"* Uncle Dutch's stern warning echoed in his brain. *"Don't ever come here."*

Sorry Uncle Dutch. Looks like I screwed things up big time.

It was a busy night at juvenile hall, and it was still early. The halls were jam-packed with bleary-eyed parents and grandparents sitting on hard benches. Race kept his eyes down as the cops led him through the crowded area. His ID was checked and confirmed before the officers could turn him over to the juvenile authorities.

Before they left him, one cop put his hand on Race's shoulder and said, "Why don't you wise up, kid, and keep your sticky fingers to yourself."

Race avoided eye contact and simply tuned the voice out. What did he care what some dumb cop said or thought? Vince's rule was simple. *Don't take nothin' off nobody.* And he wouldn't. Not now. Not ever.

The chances of the authorities finding Nealia at this time of night were pretty slim. This was her night off, and she could have been in any one of a half dozen bars along Vine Street. Race was torn between desperately wanting to be released into her custody, and not wanting to cooperate in any way with those who were questioning him about her whereabouts. In the end, it didn't matter either way. By midnight, it looked fairly certain that he'd have to be locked up for the night.

When that realization hit him, the room started swimming crazy-like, as though he'd had too many beers. Every time he stood as they moved him from place to place, his jelly-knees took on a mind of their own. He had to struggle to keep them from buckling. There must have been people talking to him, telling him stuff, but later the entire night would be just a blur in his memory. Nothing seemed real: the questioning, the paperwork, the fingerprinting, the booking.

At the showers, he was told to strip and place all his clothes in a black trash bag, even his brand-new shoes that he'd paid for with his own money. His sharkskin wallet, the neat watch he'd lifted in the jewelry store in the mall last summer. All of it went into a plain old black trash bag.

Eyes were on him every minute, the cold, glaring eyes of bored people. He hated every one of them. Concrete walls, concrete floors, all gray, bare and cold. As he shivered beneath the prickly stream of barely-warm water, his mind kept going back to the down-filled vest. The softness and the warmth of it against his chest and back.

He could barely remember dressing in the *other* things he'd been handed. The socks, underwear—old stuff that someone else had worn before him, threadbare from countless launderings. Old beat-up shoes, two sizes too big.

Clown shoes. Disgusting. Then the orange jumpsuit. The clown suit. Everything in him wanted to scream and swing his fists at those gaping faces.

Don't take nothin' off nobody. Don't take nothin' off nobody. Always before, those words were packed with power, especially when Vince said them. But here, in this rotten hole, they only rang hollow.

So Vince, old buddy. You forgot to tell me. How exactly do you take nothin' off nobody, when you're trapped and surrounded with guns, metal detectors, and glassy-eyed guards?

That tiny thread of doubt sobered him worse than being watched by stone-faced, armed guards. At this moment, he had to have the *solidness* of Vince to lean into. No room for doubts.

"Everyone cries their first night in juvie," Toon had said a jillion times.

Either Hawk or Pinky would inevitably reply in an astonished voice, "Everyone?"

To which Toon would reply, "Even them bad old tough dudes. Them that says they don't is liars."

But Race didn't cry. He almost lost it right at the cell door. "Hate to have to do this to you kid," the guard said as he unlocked the door. "But with no legal guardian available, I don't have much choice."

"Yeah, right," Race said between his teeth. "Save it for the babies who need it."

"Have it your way." With that, he gave Race a shove forward through the door.

That shove was too much. He whirled around cursing and swinging, but he was a hair's breadth too late. His flailing fist made painful contact with the edge of the door as it slammed shut with bone-chilling finality.

CHAPTER 13

From time to time, Race had tried to imagine what it might be like to be locked in somewhere and not be able to get out. His mother once threatened to lock him in a closet when he was little. His screams after she shut the door were enough to make her relent. But in his most vivid imaginings, he never even came close to the horror that the reality held.

Oh man, Vince. You only thought you knew drab. Feast your eyes on this joint. This drab is by far the most drabbiest of drab.

Cold, empty, bare, and drab, drab, drab. Even his cockroach-infested apartment with the stained ceiling, broken windows, and leaking faucets was better than this place. At least the stain patterns were interesting.

The bed wasn't a bed at all, but only a ledge made from the same concrete as the walls and floor. On it lay a thin mattress, a pillow and one blanket. And, of course an open toilet and a sink which appeared to be plumbed right into the toilet. Disgusting thought. Up in the corner near the ceiling, the single eye of a surveillance camera stalked his every move. If that wasn't enough, every fifteen minutes or so, a face appeared at the window in the door. Evidently someone wanting to see if he'd slit his wrists yet. Although it didn't seem possible that anyone could commit suicide in such an empty place, Race knew it happened. Toon had told him so.

He yanked the blanket off the bed and wrapped it around his body Indian-style to see if it would stop the shivering. But it didn't help. Then he wondered if the shivering came from being cold or being scared. Yet another unsettling thought.

Race rubbed at his sore throbbing fist where he'd hit the door. The pain in his shoulders and back seemed to grow worse because his body was tied in such tight knots. Until now, he hadn't realized that his chin had been scraped as he landed on the sidewalk in front of the sporting goods store. He rubbed at it and it burned like fire. But nothing was as bad as the burning in his gut, which never seemed to let up. It only flamed with more intensity whenever he was uptight. Tonight, however, was the worst he'd ever experienced.

His roll of Tums had gone into the trash bag with all the rest of his possessions. He wasn't sure how he'd get through the night without them. Maybe he could ask for just that back. After all, it was something he really needed. But then, after thinking about it, he knew he didn't want to give those jerks even one opportunity to say no to him. He didn't need the Tums that bad. Or did he?

One thing that had not gone into the trash bag was Vince's lighter. If he had one thing to be thankful for in all this mess, that was it. The lighter was safe in his dresser drawer. He was sure if it had been on him tonight, he would never have laid eyes on it again.

He had to pee really bad, but kept putting it off because of that stupid camera and the geeky guy who gaped at him through the door window. Eventually he had to go so bad it hurt. Pretty stupid to think he could hold it forever. Where else was he going to go, for heaven's sake. Not like they were coming to open the door and escort him down the hall to a restroom somewhere. He finally decided he'd go right after the geek appeared at the window. At least no one would be peering in at him. After that pressure was relieved, he relaxed some. But his stomach still hurt.

As the minutes ticked slowly by, he began to wonder if maybe his whole stomach was just rotting to pieces inside him. What could be happening to make it hurt so bad? Maybe he had some dread disease and didn't know it.

As he paced back and forth his thoughts swirled and tumbled, making his head feel like it was going to burst. The night lay long and endless before him, but then he began to wonder what tomorrow was going to bring. And the next day. What if they couldn't find Nealia? Or what if she was so drunk, they couldn't trust him to her custody? There couldn't be two nights like this. Not two in a row. But then, what if he were sentenced to six months or a year? That down-filled vest had been a very expensive one, so the charges against him could be steep.

That thought alone—the idea of endless days of being trapped in a cage—set off a fresh wave of shivering that wracked his whole body. His knees turned to mush. And even though he'd told himself previously that he'd never *touch* that mattress, he now had no choice. He was forced to sit down on the ledge-bed. Then fearing he was going to puke up his guts, he found he had to actually lie down to stop the spinning sensation. As soon as he did, the walls began to move in on him, and he was sure they were going to crush him to death. He clenched his teeth to keep from yelling his head off.

The place was light as day and noisy as well. No chance that sleep would ever mercifully take over. No wonder guys found ways of checking out of this place—permanently.

Curling up in a ball, he wadded up part of the blanket and pressed it tight against his midsection to relieve the pain. As he did so, he remembered the first night Monty Mutt jumped up to lay beside him in the travel trailer. The warmth that emanated from the animal onto his back was like a little oven.

Thoughts of that friendly old dog somehow made him relax a little, and he began to whisper to Monty Mutt under his breath. Because it made him feel just a little better, he decided to force himself to think only of Monty Mutt and his travel-trailer hideaway. Then he actually pretended he was there. It wasn't easy because he was still cold, he still hurt, and it was still light and noisy in his solitary cell. But he didn't give up. It was a matter of survival. And Vince had taught him a lot about survival. After a very long time, he actually fell into a merciful, though fitful, sleep.

By mid-morning of the next day, Nealia had been located. The guard who came to fetch him, first shackled him in belly chains. He was taken down an elevator to a lower level, then down a long hallway lined with offices.

Race could hear his mother long before he arrived, in his rattling chains, at the office where she was talking—to use the word loosely—with a juvenile probation officer. Wretched though it was, his mother's high whiny voice was the first familiar thing he'd heard for many long hours. And in a weird way, *familiar* felt good.

At the sight of her son in the cuffs and belly chains, she went off at an even higher pitch. She wailed about him being her only son left, and what did they think they were doing to him, and how could they treat him like a common criminal, and what was this world coming to when innocent little boys were snatched off the street and no decent mother could even trust someone to get hold of her before he had to spend the night in this hell-hole. And on and on with hardly a breath between sentences. At one point, she actually jumped out of her chair and ran at him to try to hug him. But Race gruffly told her to go sit down. He didn't look at her when he said it.

"Kyle, little darlin', don't talk to your mama like that. I was worried sick about you this morning when they called to tell me to come down here."

Yeah right. That'd be a first. Part of him was glad she was there, but he also knew the more she acted like a ditz, the less chance of these morons releasing him into her custody.

With some deft maneuvering, he managed to shuffle and rattle to the chair indicated by the probation officer who was sitting behind a desk piled high with papers and file folders. As Race managed to sit down, Nealia went into a fresh wave of sobbing.

A few minutes elapsed before he realized the skinny PO was actually talking to him. A moment earlier, as he shuffled down the hallway with the guard, he'd been steeled and ready for anything, but Nealia's dramatics had disarmed him. He was caught short and it took a moment to pull himself together.

The guy was looking at him and introducing himself and saying something about the fact that Race was in a great deal of trouble. Race glared at him while trying to remember the guy's name. But there it was written right on a nameplate on his desk, *Dan Goforth.* Dumb name. Dumb guy. Another dode. Another moron.

Race merely waited to hear what he needed to hear: would he be released or would he have to endure another night of hell in that cage? Breakfast that morning—such as it was—had helped some to ease the burning in his gut. That relief alone was enough to make him want to shout for joy.

The skinny guy named Goforth kept taking off his glasses and hooking the earpiece over his shirt pocket. Then when he picked up another piece of paper to read, the glasses went back on his smallish face. When he was done reading, they went back to being hooked on the pocket. *The guy can't even make up his mind about his glasses, and he's gonna tell me what to do and where to go?* Race was no good at judging age, but there was a smattering of gray in the guy's dark hair. Maybe late forties.

Finally, the guy said it. The words Race needed to hear. He was being released into Nealia's custody, but she was given a very stern warning that she would be held responsible if Race didn't show up at the detention hearing in two days.

Then Goforth stood up. He was pretty tall, but much too skinny to be any threat. Race was sure he could pin him if it were just the two of them. That thought, plus the thought of being set free, put his feet back under him again. The queasy feelings disappeared as though they'd never been there.

Goforth came around to the other side of his desk and leaned his skinny frame against it. He began to read from a paper in his hand—after once more unhooking the glasses from the shirt pocket, that is. Race's release from that moment until he appeared in court, Goforth explained, was to be entangled with a long list of rules. Goforth proceeded to read them: a 10:00 PM curfew, reporting daily to his probation officer, no hanging around with any of the *gang members* he'd been hanging with before his arrest.

Lamebrain assumption. Race wanted to remind this dode that he'd not been with any *gang* when he was brought in.

"Your records show that for the most part, you've kept your nose clean," Goforth was saying. His monotone voice made Race know he'd parroted this stuff a million times before. Maybe Wynn had sat in this exact same chair in this exact same office only a few weeks earlier. "Because of that, the judge will most likely be lenient."

"And I see you've not been attending school," Goforth went on, "but your grades were pretty good when you did go."

This was Nealia's cue to jump back onstage. "I tried and tried to get him to go back. Honest I did. But he just wouldn't listen to me. You know how they get at this age, don't you Mr. Goforth. Headstrong and stubborn."

Goforth ignored her. "You'll have to be in school." The tone was firm. "But now that you've been arrested, you can't return to a regular classroom setting just yet. We'll arrange something with an alternative school."

Race cringed. Street school where all the creeps and misfits wound up. He'd have to figure out a way to avoid that place. It might not be easy, but he'd find a way. Vince would have found a way.

Looking at Nealia, Goforth said, "Ms. Paloma, I'm going to put together a program for Kyle that will, hopefully, keep him out of long-term juvenile detention."

Nealia's eyes were dry now. She pushed her stringy hair out of her face and moved to the edge of her chair. "Oh, that's real nice of you Mr. Goforth. You don't know how much I thank you for that."

"I don't do this job because I'm nice. And before you get too excited," Goforth warned as he replaced the glasses on the pocket for the umpteenth time, "keep in mind that your utmost cooperation will be required. Or else this will never work. And if it doesn't work, he *will* be locked away from you for a very long time."

"Oh, no problem there, Mr. Goforth. I promise to give my *utmost* cooperation."

Chains rattled as Race rolled his eyes and slouched further down in his chair. Utmost cooperation? What a royal joke.

Now Goforth looked directly at Race. He was closer now, and Race could almost feel the eyes boring through him. "Okay, Kyle, what about you?"

"He likes to be called Race," Nealia interjected, probably trying to give her *utmost cooperation*. "He don't usually answer to nothing else."

"All right, Race, how about you? Are you willing to do what it takes to stay out of lockup?"

Race continued to gaze right past Goforth as though he weren't there. He didn't want to say a word to this creep. But neither did he want another night in that nasty, skanky cell.

"I'll give you one more chance, Race. Are you willing? Or are you ready to chuck it all and be put away for a while? The rules I'm talking about are nothing compared to the rules you'll be living under on the inside. It's tough in there, in case you haven't heard."

But he had heard. Of course he'd heard. He sat frozen for a few minutes more. Waiting for Goforth to say something else to try to persuade him. But there was only silence. Even Nealia was quiet. Where were her drama-queen antics when you needed them?

The silence dragged on, and Race began to feel a trickle of sweat run down his chest. He wanted to rub it hard to make the itch go away, but that would have meant a horrible rattle in the midst of this crazy silence.

Finally, Goforth simply said, "Well?"

Still not looking at the PO, Race said, "Whatever."

"Sorry, buddy. That's not the answer I'm looking for. I'll need a firm yes or no. Surely you're capable of making one clear decision in your life. Are you willing to do what it takes to stay on the outside or not?"

Don't ever come here, Uncle Dutch's voice whispered in his ear. *Don't ever come here.*

As low as he could and still be verbal, Race forced out the needed "Yeah."

"I heard that, and I trust your mother heard it as well. Now we'll see how good you are at keeping your word."

CHAPTER 14

Race learned that Aunt Ginger had driven Nealia to Detention Hall, then dropped her off. That meant Race and his mother had to catch a bus home. Nealia talked non-stop the entire way, patting him as she talked. He wanted to shove her away, but it would have only caused a scene. Actions like that provided the "on" switch for her wailing, and he didn't need that kind of attention on a bus full of people.

He had his own clothes back on—his own watch, his own sharkskin wallet, his own underclothes, his own shoes, and even his roll of Tums, which he chewed several at a time. Even the Zippo had not been lost. With his own stuff returned to him, the burning gone from his gut, and being free *free free*, he could have run *alongside* the bus and kept up. The only thing missing was his knife. Of course, he'd get another one right away, but it'd never be the same. He'd spent many years in the company of that knife. He had no idea how long it would take to get used to a new one.

When they stepped off the bus in Over-the-Rhine, three Deuce Dragons decked out in purple jackets were kicking back on the street corner. If only he'd thought to get off a few blocks earlier. They spotted him the moment he hit the sidewalk. He didn't look, but he knew they were having a good laugh. No cool homie in OTR ever rode the bus, and *never* with your mother. He couldn't herd Nealia to the apartment door fast enough. Bummer timing. Every Dragon in the city would know before the sun went down.

Back at their apartment, Race made plans to slip away to the salvage yard just as soon as Nealia left for work. She gave him a pathetic little lecture before she went out the door. Actually, it was half lecture, half begging. He tuned her out.

Race had learned long ago that the whole PO thing was a lot of empty yammering. They seldom followed up like they said they would.

"They be so many bad little kids in this city," Toon used say, "them POs is just so busy they can't never takes care of all of us. Know what I mean?"

Chances were, Goforth would call him late tonight. So he'd wait for that call and then he'd leave. The way he planned it, he wouldn't even go out the front door anymore. But always out the back window and down the fire escape— just in case. He and Vince took that exit many times when they were younger. The last section of the metal fire escape folded up to prevent intruders. The hinges had grown rusty through the years. Vince never cared. He taught Race to leap the last ten feet or so. And taught him how to scale the wall to reach it when going back up.

Race had been right about Goforth. His call came shortly before midnight. Race felt pretty smug that he'd figured it out and hadn't left too soon. The worst part was that on the phone, he couldn't work his steel glare, and he actually *had* to talk—*had* to engage in a conversation with that dode. What a drag.

Goforth again warned him that he was under close surveillance and that any slip-up could land him back inside juvie. When Race didn't answer, Goforth pumped him. "Do you have that clear, Race?"

"Yeah."

"You got a lot hanging over your head, kid. So keep your nose clean."

When Race didn't answer, Goforth finally signed off. As soon as he'd hung up the phone, Race grabbed his coat and was out the window, down the fire escape—taking a big leap at the bottom—and headed toward the salvage yard.

He decided he'd make a game of finding how many different routes there might be and he'd take a different one each time. His ski mask, pulled full over his face, not only helped as a disguise, but also shielded him against the zero temperature. Man, what he wouldn't give for that long underwear and the down-filled vest. And he'd been so close...

He'd forgotten to grab his flashlight, but by the time he left the railroad tracks and followed the fence to where he could leap over, his eyes had become accustomed to the darkness. He could hear Monty's high whine as he approached.

He took a running leap and vaulted the fence easily. Monty was there almost before he hit the frozen ground. Race knelt down and hugged the animal and felt the warm life force emanating from beneath the black fur. "Hey boy! How ya doing? Miss me?" For the briefest of moments, tears burned in Race's eyes. Now that was stupid. Just plain stupid. He pulled up the ski mask and pressed at his eyes with gloved hands.

"You're just an old mutt, aren't you, boy? Nothing but a dirty old junk-yard dog. But hey, you wanna hear how you helped me get through a hellish night?" Race jumped up. "C'mon boy. Let's get inside and get a little warmth going."

Everything was just as he'd left it. Well, why shouldn't it be? After all, he'd only been away from it a few days. But it'd seemed like a lifetime. How could that be? Strange.

After lighting candles and turning on his battery-operated hand warmers, he dug around in his food stash and pulled out a can of soup. The guy at the Army Surplus store had told him about the little Sterno stove which he now unfolded and set up on the table. He lit the Sterno fuel under it. The hot soup, heated in a small saucepan, tasted like a feast for royalty. And, of course, there were doggie treats for Monty Mutt.

The place was still cold, but not unbearably so. The nightmare of being locked up in detention seemed far, far away. In fact, when he was here, everything seemed far, far away. His stomach was full and wasn't burning with pain. He was cozy and safe with Monty Mutt pushing close by his side. Even if someone tried to approach this place, he figured Monty would tear the unsuspecting jerk to pieces. For the briefest of moments, Race allowed himself to imagine what it might be like to feel like this all the time. Normal. Ordinary. Just an ordinary kid with an ordinary life and an ordinary family, instead of some OTR trash who'd been arrested for shoplifting and headed for a court date. But it was such a dumb thought, he extinguished it as quickly as he had the Sterno lamp.

That night he dreamt about Vince. He could see his brother so plain, walking along with that confident air he possessed every moment he was alive. Deftly, he dribbled the basketball as he walked. He was almost to the playground where the hoops were, then Race saw the shiny barrel of a gun. He tried to scream. Tried to warn Vince to duck. To hide. To run. But Race couldn't move; his voice froze in his throat. Then the blaze of fire from the gun barrel and Vince falling in slow motion and blood splattering everywhere.

His own screams awakened him. He sat up and poor Monty went flying. For a few minutes, he was confused and disoriented, unable to think where he was. Monty Mutt came whimpering back up on their makeshift bed. Race put his arms around the warm strong neck.

"I shoulda been there, Monty. I shoulda been there to watch his back. He asked me to go shoot hoops with him, but I told him no. Didn't want to go. If only I'd been there..."

Monty whined and licked his face.

Race suddenly realized he was shivering. His little hideaway was much colder than when he fell asleep. The temperature must have plummeted. Not even Monty's warmth was enough. He'd heard stories about people dying from hypothermia. Probably could happen pretty easily.

He turned on his big flashlight, which he saved only for emergencies, and checked his watch. Almost five.

"I better get home, Monty Mutt. Some freakin' mess I'm in. Too cold to stay here, too dangerous to go home. My life just sucks."

Race made certain he never got on or off the bus in OTR and never with Nealia. In spite of his mother's whining and arguing, he insisted that he catch a separate bus from her at another stop and meet her at Detention Hall. Of course, she could have chickened out altogether, which would have meant bad news for Race. But there she was, sitting on one of the hard, wooden benches in the hall outside Goforth's office—she'd arrived before he had. Surprise.

She motioned for Race to knock on the door. Race sucked in a breath and took a moment to steel himself before rapping on the door. He dreaded this confrontation; Goforth was a real weirdo. From inside he heard the invitation to come in.

The skinny PO stood and pocketed his glasses as Race and Nealia entered. His gaze toward Race held steady. "Hello, folks. Good to see you again. Glad you kept the appointment." Glancing at his watch, he added, "And on time. That works in your favor." He stepped out from behind his desk and extended his hand, which Nealia shook enthusiastically.

Race hesitated, wondering whether to give him the limp fish shake or the bone-crusher. He figured the fish would work here, but it was totally wasted. Goforth gave no reaction, just kept on talking, pointing them to the same chairs they'd sat in previously when Race was chained from stem to stern.

Nealia chattered on as gaily as if this were some party she'd been invited to. Race figured she must be pretty proud of herself for getting up, getting on the bus alone, and actually getting herself to this destination. That, plus the fact that she was only a smidgeon hung over, was a major accomplishment for her.

When Goforth could wedge a word in, he began to talk about the *program*. In the coming days, Race would become sick to the teeth hearing about the *program*.

"Mondays, Wednesdays, and Fridays," Goforth explained glancing at the paper he'd fetched from his desk, "you can attend alternative school. I've talked to the principal and there's space."

Race groaned inwardly. *Loser school. Creep school. Hanging with the creeps and losers. No way can I stomach that three days a week.*

"One of the classes they offer will be a life skills course," Goforth added.

Was he serious? Life skills? *Oh goody. Now that'd make it worth my time for sure. Maybe I'll learn to tie my shoes.*

Goforth didn't even look at him, just continued reciting: "Monday nights will be family counseling—six o'clock to seven."

Now he had Nealia's attention. Hooking a strand of unruly hair behind her ear, she let him know that that commitment would be impossible to keep. "I gotta be to work by four-thirty, sometimes five. And I gotta be there on time, too. And I work late. Way into the wee hours of the morning."

"I understand you have work hours, Ms. Paloma, but you now have a son in serious trouble. If you can't make it for family counseling, then this program will be trashed. Do I need to review the alternative?"

Nealia grew pale. "No sir." It was obvious she was terrified of that alternative. "Well, I guess I could talk to Mad Malone." She gave an embarrassed laugh and ducked her head. "That's what they call him, Mad Malone. That's my boss. I been working for him for almost two years now. Maybe he'll work it out with me."

"Good. You find out and let me know before the court date."

Nealia ducked her head again, but she nodded.

Goforth continued to go down the list as he alternately took his glasses from his pocket, placed them on his nose, then pulled them off again and hooked them in his pocket. "Never be out after ten o'clock curfew. That's a biggie. That'll get you a one-way ticket inside quicker than anything."

His droning dragged on and on. The longer he talked, the more Race's gut burned. Never had he been forced to remain steeled for so long. Even a trip to the principal's office took only a few minutes, and a run-in with the coach less than that. Vince never taught him how to hold out for more than just a few minutes. Just when it seemed Goforth had finally run out of steam—and out of rules—he dropped the bomb.

"And we've got a job lined up for you," he said as easily as though he might say it was raining outside.

Race wasn't sure he'd heard correctly. "A job?" The words slipped out before he could stop them. Goforth gave a little half-smile.

Nealia also rose to the bait. "You got him a job? Now that's real nice. A job. You hear that, Kyle darlin'? They got you a job. Ain't that nice?"

Goforth ignored her, choosing rather to focus his gaze on Race, who was now quite weary.

"What do think, Race? Would you like to have some honest employment?"

The emphasis on the word *honest* made Race wonder if he'd been suspected of anything other than the shoplifting. Suspicion of car theft had never been mentioned. Could they know and now they were trapping him? You couldn't trust these dirt bags. That much he knew for sure. Now the gut-burning cranked up big time.

"Kyle, honey, the nice man's offering you a job."

"How about it, Race? You interested?" Goforth's gray-green eyes were not angry eyes, but they sure were unflinching eyes. He could hold a gaze much longer and steadier than Race.

Race slouched a little further down into his chair. "Depends."

"On what?"

"What it is." He sure as heck wasn't gonna be flippin' greasy burgers.

Goforth stood to his full skinny height. "Well that's a start. Ms. Paloma, please wait for us outside my office. Race, you come with me."

Reluctantly, he followed Goforth out the door and down the hall to a room that was just a little larger than the PO's office. A large oval table surrounded by upholstered chairs filled the room. In one of the chairs sat a squat man who was facing toward the center of the table. He didn't turn or look at them as they entered. Goforth led Race closer to the man.

"Race, I'd like you to meet Stanley Crosslin. Stan tunes pianos and he's in need of a trustworthy driver. Stan, this is Race Paloma."

The man turned a little in the swivel chair and extended his hand. "Glad to meet you, Race."

Now Race could see that the man's eyes were *dead*. Dead eyes that saw nothing. Too spooky. Too, too gross. He'd known a blind man once who hung out in OTR. Everyone laughed at him and played tricks on him. He'd burned to death one winter while trying to stay warm in a deserted building. Nobody even cared. Vince had nailed it when he said, "Nobody cares about a freak."

The soft pudgy hand hung in the air in front of him. Race didn't care. Fourteen Suma wrestlers couldn't force him to shake that gross hand. He'd rather die first.

After a moment, the blind man slowly lowered his hand. But then it got worse.

"Come around here, Race," Goforth instructed, "so Stan can *see* you."

Race gave the PO his best cold stare. "*See* me?"

"Touch your face. That's how he sees people, by touching."

Race pulled out the chair on the other side of Goforth and practically fell into it making it scrape against the tile floor, then slouched low. "Tell him to feel his own stupid face. He sure as heck ain't touching mine."

Goforth patched up the awkward moment by noisily pulling out his own chair, and sitting between Race and Stan, then outlining what would be expected of Race in this new job. As Goforth talked, Race stared at the wooden table top, catching bits and pieces of the speech about getting Stanley Crosslin to his appointments and getting him there safely and on time.

"Mr. Crosslin has agreed to work his appointments around your school schedule," Goforth explained. "You can drive for him on Tuesdays, Thursdays and Saturdays."

Everything was coming too fast. Thoughts swirled and churned through Race's head and he wanted to burst out that door and keep running till he got far away from this freaky fat man. No way could he do this; he could never bear to be shut up in a car with this man. He wouldn't last one minute. Not one second. The tabletop swam before his eyes. He was having trouble holding his steeled expression.

Goforth was now saying something about taking the bus to Stanley's house and something about "...not always working in the metro area..." There was quiet for a moment, then Goforth added, "This might give you a chance to see more of the world than just your own neighborhood, Race. How does that sound?"

Race continued to stare. What was he supposed to say? How the heck was he going to get out of this mess?

"Of course," Goforth went on, as he shuffled a few papers he'd pulled from a file folder, "we do have other jobs available. What I mean is, if you don't think you can *handle* this. After all, you've probably not driven very much."

"I've driven plenty," Race defended himself too quickly. He didn't add that they were mostly stolen cars.

"Well then...?" Goforth tapped his glasses steadily against the tabletop. "I need to know whether or not you feel you're up to this level of responsibility."

Suddenly Race broke out in a cold sweat. The sweat of fear. What Goforth was asking him stretched far beyond anything he'd ever learned from Vince, or Wynn, or any of the encounters he'd ever had in OTR. The fear was as thick and as strangling as what he'd felt when they pushed him into that cage.

Now the blind guy was saying something about how his appointments took him to different places—sometimes homes, sometimes churches, sometimes schools. "Even a concert hall or two," he finished, as though that juicy tidbit of information clinched the deal.

Suffocating silence once again filled the room. These two men were expecting Race to answer, but his throat closed up tight.

Finally Goforth spoke, his voice calm and steady. "What about it, Race? If this is too tough for you, we can always look around for something a little easier. Like a burger place..."

Race didn't for a second want them to know how scared he really was. Swallowing over the dry spot in his throat, he said, "Heck yeah, I can handle it. No sweat." As soon as the words fell from his mouth into the stuffy air of the room, he knew he'd stepped into something much bigger than he was.

CHAPTER 15

If there was anything worse than riding a freaking bus, Race wasn't sure what it'd be. He detested getting on the stupid thing, always having to make sure he was in an area where no Dragons hung out. Never knowing if he was being tagged. People looking at him as he got on.

He was frozen to the bone, walking in the snow to an out-of-OTR bus stop and then standing there waiting for the stupid bus to arrive. When he stepped up into the bus, stale over-heated air hit him in the face like a furnace. Miserable. No knife, no baggy pants, no chains—he felt naked. He sat as far toward the back as possible so he didn't feel as though everyone in the place was gawking at him.

He'd spent the better part of last evening studying the bus schedule from a flyer Goforth had given him. It was one confusing mess—worse than figuring out a math problem. But he had no choice. He had to be at the fat man's place on time. Another one of the jillion new rules in his life.

Goforth knew immediately that Race didn't have a driver's license. That little detail had to be taken care of before he could start. Plus, Goforth came down on him about his clothes. Race had to get a pair of pants that *fit*, as the PO put it. So what the heck did it matter what he wore? The guy couldn't see him anyway. In his pocket was the folded note with the blind man's address on it. He kept pulling it out and looking at the directions Goforth had scribbled. The place was in Covedale, Goforth had told him—west of the city. Race had never had to look for an address before. And, other than the few weeks he and Vince had detailed cars together, he'd never had a job before either. Way too many new things thrown at him at once. His stomach felt like someone had lit a bonfire in it. He should have grabbed breakfast.

Race knew before he ever got off the bus what the neighborhood would look like. Disgustingly neat little houses all in a row. Shoveled walks. Cutesie, phony little Christmas decorations on the lawns. Not as ritzy as Clifton Heights, but head and shoulders above OTR. People who ate three squares a day and no broken windows. Race had heisted a few cars in this area, but you don't have to look for addresses when you're stealing cars.

The blind man's walk was shoveled just like all the rest. Can a blind man shovel snow off a sidewalk? What *can* a blind man do, Race wondered? Other than tune pianos, that is.

The house was just as neat as all the others on the block. Dark red brick with green trim. Even green shutters at the windows. Real cute. He turned up the sidewalk to the front door, then stopped and took a breath. How was he ever going to get through this? *Vince, you big dummy, you never told me how to use the steely look on a guy who can't even see! In fact, I been meaning to tell you, bro, there's a whole bunch of stuff you never told me ...*

Before he could think about moving his wooden legs another step, the front door opened and scared him silly.

Stan stuck his head out the door. "Race, that you? I heard footsteps."

Heard footsteps? Race wasn't even halfway to the door. Cripes. He thought this guy was going to be creepy, and now he knew he'd been right on.

"Yeah, it's me."

"Oh good. And right on time." He opened the door further. "Come on in here and get warm. Really cold out there this morning."

"Yeah," was all he could think to say. If the little fat guy only knew …

Stan Crosslin's house was as neat on the inside as it was on the outside. The warmth wasn't stifling like the bus, but comfortable and sort of cozy-like. Smelled good too. There wasn't a whole lot of furniture, and not a lot of junky stuff sitting around. The room was the color of a fall day, all tans and golds with a little scarlet added in. A tan couch and matching chair were flanked by a gold-colored recliner circled around a massive fat-legged coffee table. The pictures on the walls didn't look like cheapy stuff, but were encased in heavy frames. While Race knew nothing about art, he had sense enough to know you don't put the shabby stuff in glitzy frames.

A cool stereo in the corner caught his eye. He wondered how much that'd bring on the street. He knew several contacts who handled hot stereos. Neither Vince nor Wynn was ever big on house break-ins, but on a few occasions, they'd been middlemen for hot items like stereos. Not much cash, but an okay take if a guy was hungry. And they usually were.

As Race stood awkwardly looking about the place, Stan closed the front door and pointed a pudgy finger toward the kitchen. "We still have a few minutes. I know guys your age are always hungry. Help yourself to the cinnamon rolls on the cabinet. Edith—that's my housekeeper, Edith—made a fresh batch yesterday. You can't beat homemade cinnamon rolls, right? Especially on a cold morning."

Race hesitated, dumfounded. He'd just walked into a strange house and now he's being asked to help himself. How weird is that?

Stan waved him off. "Go on. Go on. Get yourself a glass of milk while you're at it. Milk's in the fridge, glasses in the cupboard to the left of the sink."

Homemade cinnamon rolls sounded too good to be true. Race managed to mumble some kind of agreement and went into the kitchen, which was so clean it dazzled the eyes like those funky ads on TV. The cinnamon rolls were whoppers. Two of them sat crowded together on a dinner plate covered with a clear plastic wrap. Just as he was wondering whether to take one or eat both, Stan called to him, "They're both yours!" Spooky. Then he added, "Bring your breakfast in here and I'll take a few minutes and show you my toolbox before we go."

Yippee skippy. Can't wait to see the blind man's toolbox.

When Race returned to the living room, Stan was sitting on the edge of the recliner with a very large toolbox standing open on the floor by his feet. The thing was filled with more strange tools than Race had ever seen. Stan motioned to the couch opposite. "I think you can see me if you sit over there," he said.

Race did as he was told while he wolfed down the rolls. He couldn't remember ever eating anything that tasted so good. When the milk was gone, it seemed to have quenched the fire in the pit of his stomach.

"There'll only be a few things I'll need for you to lay out for me each time, Race," he explained, feeling around in the box. "The tuning fork, of course, and these wrenches and the hammer." As he named them, he laid each one out on the table. "Always place them on the bench or on a nearby table. Don't put them on top because I'll be taking the lid off the piano. And always lay them on this cloth." He waved a chamois-looking cloth in the air. "That way we don't scratch the customer's furniture."

The blind man kept on talking just as though Race were comprehending; all the while Race was wishing he could get out of there. He'd never last a day with this guy. Who was he kidding? He wondered what other jobs Goforth had on his list. Anything would be better than hanging out with this freak.

"The toolbox," Stan explained, "will be your responsibility to take in and out of each place we go." He looked over at Race with those creepy dead eyes and smiled. Race looked away quickly. "I can still carry this titan," he said, patting the gray metal box, "don't think I can't. The trouble is, it messes up my balance—especially in the snow and ice. What I don't need is a bad fall."

Yeah right. The little fat man can lift the heavy toolbox all by himself. Not!

"Keep in mind these people are my customers, and we're guests in their homes, or churches, or schools, or concert halls. They deserve our utmost respect. After the tools are laid out, you may wait where I'm working, or wait for me out in the car. Your preference."

Race's preference was to be back in his little hideaway with Monty close by his side with nobody bugging him, ever.

Stan paused a minute, possibly waiting for Race's input. But Race had nothing to say.

"You can bring your studies along, if you'd like. I'm sure you'll have homework to do."

Race had no clue if there'd be homework. He didn't even know his schedule yet, except for counseling sessions. Oh yeah, and *life skills* class. Big whoopee.

"One other point to remember. When I'm tuning, if you're there, I must have absolute quiet." Stan paused again, waiting while thick silence hung in the room. "Okay, I guess we're ready for our first appointment." He returned the tools to the box and shut it, closing metal clasps with a loud snap. Just then the phone rang. Since it was sitting on the small lamp table, it was within Stan's reach.

"Stan here," he said. Then, "He sure is. Just a sec."

Handing the phone across the coffee table, he said, "It's for you, Race."

For a moment, Race was dumbfounded, then it hit him. Goforth. Checking up on him. Dogging his every step. Sickening.

"Yeah," he said stiffly into the phone.

"Hey there, Race. Just wanted to see if you made it on time. Chalk one up for you. Keep up the good work."

There was silence, but Race had nothing to say.

Goforth went on as if Race had answered. "Have a great day, and just remember, you can expect my calls anytime!"

Even if Race had planned a response, he wouldn't have had the chance. Goforth hung up.

Now Race wasn't sure what to do with the phone. How do you hand something to a blind guy? But Stan reached across for it as normally as a sighted person, and plunked it back in the holder.

"My car's out back," he said. "I'll get my coat and we'll be on our way."

Race stifled a groan when he stepped out the back door and saw Stan's car—a Chevy dinosaur—at least mid-eighties or older. Not as old as Toon's Bonneville, but close. Didn't he just have all the luck.

Their first appointment of the day was in a home. Stan gave him the address and the general directions. Great combination, Race thought as he put the old crate in reverse and backed out of the drive, a blind man and a guy who's never looked up an address in his life.

Even though Stan's car was old, it was surprisingly clean, both inside and out. Somehow the old guy had been able to care for it. Race wondered how a blind man did such things. Or had them done—whatever.

Race succeeded in getting lost twice before he located the house. Stan kept giving the directions, but Race didn't listen and no way was he going to ask for clarification. It wasn't easy to drive and look for house numbers at the same time, especially maneuvering such a boxy, unwieldy car that cornered like a Mack truck. He nearly curbed the old crate twice. When he finally found the street, then he had to figure out which way the numbers went—did they get bigger going east, or smaller? When he finally spotted the house number, it was like a rush. He'd done it! "That's it," he blurted out. The little shot of pride he felt immediately embarrassed him. He felt his face burning. He'd have to be more careful.

"Good job, Race," Stan fairly crowed. "I knew you could do it. Just takes a little practice."

As Race pulled up in the drive of a one-story bungalow in an older subdivision, Stan said, "This is Adelaide and

Clarence Dotson's place." Then added, "I've known them for years."

Race went to the trunk and pulled out the ten-ton toolbox. That thing was a whole lot heavier than it looked. Much more of this and he'd be the Incredible Hulk.

Stan went on ahead, feeling his way up the walk by tapping his cane. That infernal sound ate away at Race's already jangled nerves. He could just imagine these people taking one look at him and throwing him out on his ear. Stan Crosslin might be blind, but the rest of the world sure wasn't.

CHAPTER 16

"**H**ello, hello, hello. You come right on in here now and get yourselves warm," Adelaide chirped at them, skittering around like a little bird, while taking their coats. Race had to set down the toolbox as she practically pulled his coat off him. He'd planned to keep it on and escape to the car as quickly as humanly possible.

"My, my, Stan, you got you a fine young man for your new driver. Isn't that so nice."

This lady was some kind of *old*. Older even than Grandma Mungy. Race was sure if he touched her, she'd just crumble like aged yellowed paper. She barely came up to his shoulder, a little stooped, and her wispy gray hair was brushed back from her narrow face. Her eyes, too, were like a little bird's, hardly blinking, but intensely studying till it made Race very nervous.

Stan just stood there smiling, not even trying to get a word in.

"I'm Adelaide." She stuck out a thin little hand to Race with skin so delicate you could see almost every vein. If she noticed his hesitation, she masked it well. What could he do but return the handshake? He'd never had to shake hands with anyone like this before. All he knew was the limp fish shake or the bone crusher. What was a *real* handshake supposed to be like, anyway? He took the thin little hand and the moment he did, her other hand came up to pat the back of his hand. The clasp was so warm and so gentle it made his breath catch in his throat.

"Now what was your name?" she asked looking right up at him with those dark little eyes.

"The name's Race," he said. "Race Paloma."

"Race? Hmm. Race. Fine name. So much meaning." Adelaide finally released his hand and it immediately felt cold again. She closed her eyes a moment, then began to recite:

"Life's race well run,
Life's work well done,
Life's victory won,
Now cometh rest."

She reached over to pat Stan's arm and chuckled. "Learned that as a schoolgirl and still remember it after all these years. Can't remember the author though."

Turning back to Race, she added, "So Race, make sure your life's *race* is well run, and your work well done!"

Race had no clue what he was supposed to say to that. He wasn't even sure what life's race meant, but he darn sure felt he was being chased—and in a mad race to escape, to be safe. Somewhere—he had no idea where.

Stan grabbed that pause in the conversation to announce that he'd better get busy.

"My, my, here I stand around chattering like an old magpie and you need to get busy. Mercy, I act like I'm the only person you have to see today." Tsking loudly, she waved toward the piano in the corner of the large living room.

"Have at it," she said and then added, "Clarence is out in his workshop. When you're finished, I'll call him in and we'll have some pie and coffee. That is, if you have time."

Stan chuckled. "For your pie? We'll *make* time."

When she left the room, Stan whispered, "Wait'll you taste her pie. Better than Edith's cinnamon rolls." He patted his middle. "No wonder I can't lose weight."

Meanwhile, Race was taking in the piano, the top of which was cluttered with framed photos in wood, silver and brass. Some were so old they were black and white. Pictures of graduations, weddings, babies, families, people frozen in time. Did people really have that much family?

Stan felt his way to the instrument and moved the bench out of the way. "What about the top? Does it have a few things on it?"

Race released a noisy sigh. "About a million pictures."

The blind man cocked his head and smiled. "Sometimes she remembers to clean it off for me, other times she forgets. I guess she just forgot. Get them out of the way the best you can."

Race looked around for a place to put them and spotted a nearby plant stand that was partially empty. Carefully, he took the photos and stacked them going from left to right and laying them down in the same order in which he picked them up. Beneath the photos lay one long lacy doily thingy, which draped over the edges of the piano like snow. This he folded up and placed over the stack of photos.

After the lid was cleared, Race opened the toolbox and took out the cloth, spread it on the piano bench and arranged the tools as Stan had instructed him at the house. Meanwhile Stan felt the top and removed the lid, then removed the front of the piano below the keyboard—the kickboard, Stan called it—and started to work.

Race's plan to hide out in the car and make himself as inconspicuous as possible had quickly fallen apart. Now he'd just have to sit around and be bored out of his gourd.

And boring it was. Across the room from the piano sat a burgundy couch covered with more little lacy thingies on the back and arms. He made his way that direction and gently sat down, terrified he was going to break something. On the coffee table in front of him were scattered little glass figurines of angels, kittens, and ballerinas.

The bookshelves flanking the stone fireplace were jam-packed with books and two full shelves of old *National Geographic*. He really wanted to look at the magazines, but no way was he going to touch a thing in that room. So he just sat. Laying his head back, he considered a short nap, but then began the incessant *plunk plunk plunking* as Stan worked his tuning hammer up and down the pins. *Plunk plunk plunk. Plink plink plink.* Sleep was impossible. At the next stop, he'd have to devise an escape plan ahead of time.

How could a blind man do that? Race watched for a time as Stan felt—obviously counting—from peg to peg, then pinging and plinking and plunking, pausing to cock his head, listening intently. Then more turning of pegs. Without question, the guy sure knew what he was doing.

Minutes stretched out endlessly, almost like the night Race had been locked up. Well, not quite that bad. Nothing could even come close to that terrifying experience.

After about forty-five minutes, the plunking changed to running the scales. Later, Race would learn that meant the job was nearly over. Stan then replaced the kickboard and the lid, after which he pulled up the bench and sat down and began to play.

Race was stunned. It was one thing to tune the thing, it never occurred to him that a blind guy could play.

Well goofus, ever heard of Ray Charles? He plays the piano and he's blind.

Yeah, but he's famous. This is just a little fat guy who tunes pianos for a living.

The melody began with Stan dinking around a little with his right hand. But soon the chubby hands swept over the entire keyboard and the music swelled to fill the room, moving like a fog to encompass Race as he sat there, bored no more. It was as though the room were too small to hold the fullness of the sound. The chords swirled and danced and played around one another, catching Race in their heated intensity and lifting him up in a lightness and yet a strange and inexplicable fervor till his eyes burned hot and he had to squeeze them shut tight—like he had at Vince's funeral.

At that moment, Adelaide appeared at the doorway to listen. Smiling, she looked over at Race and said, "When you hear him play like that, it usually means he's finished. I bet you're starved." The sound of her voice broke the sweeping spell, and then he was sure it had never happened at all. Just his wild imagination going off again.

In a few minutes the lacy thingies and photos were returned to their rightful positions on the piano, and they joined Clarence in the kitchen where Adelaide was filling mugs with coffee and cutting wide wedges of cherry pie.

"Coffee for you, son?" she asked.

Race hesitated. Coffee worked on his stomach like a blowtorch. Luckily Adelaide caught his expression.

"Rather have milk? We have plenty."

He nodded, feeling his face redden.

Adelaide's kitchen glowed in yellow, with the pale winter sunshine filtering through yellow curtains at the windows behind the table. On the cabinet sat a white dish drainer in which four yellow plates had been placed in a neat row. Behind the plates, four bright yellow tumblers also stood in a neat row. Race wondered what Nealia's life would have been like if she'd ever had a little yellow kitchen with plates and tumblers all sitting neatly in a row in the dish drainer.

Adelaide set a white mug on a large saucer in front of her husband, who was already seated at the yellow Formica table. Not much hair grew on top Clarence's balding head. What was there had been combed over the bare spot, but most of it just stood straight up. The sleeves of his green flannel shirt were rolled up and bits of golden sawdust clung to the hairs of his forearms. "Come on in here, Stanley, and set a spell," he said with a wave of his long arm. "Rest your bones."

Stan easily felt his way to the table, pulled out a chair and sat down, chatting with Clarence about his latest woodworking project.

The pie looked good, but the thought of eating in front of strangers petrified Race. Manners had never been a priority in the Paloma household.

But nobody paid any attention. He could either sit and eat, or stand and watch. He sat. And he ate, being careful not to let any bright red cherries roll off his fork. The pie was as good or better than the cinnamon rolls. And the cold milk washed it down just fine. His stomach felt fine too.

Clarence proceeded to pour a little coffee into his saucer and slurp noisily from the saucer. Adelaide laughed at him as though it embarrassed her.

"Learned that little habit from his German grandpa," she said to Race as though she had to apologize. "I tell him he sounds like a baby pig when he does that, but it never stops him."

"What's a feller to do, Mama?" Clarence said reaching over to gently pat his wife's hand. "I'd rather slurp like a baby pig than scald my poor old mouth. Gotta cool it off somehow."

When Clarence's plate was nearly clean, he pressed his fork over all the piecrust crumbs and ate them till the plate was spotless. You couldn't tell there'd ever been a piece of pie sitting there. Then he put his arm around Adelaide's shoulders and patted her. "Perfect, Mama. Just perfect." Then he looked over at Race's plate, which was also clean. Not as clean as Clarence's, but clean.

"So what'd you think, boy? Isn't my wife's pie just the best ever?"

Race nodded as he sat down his empty milk glass. "Yes," he answered. "Yes, sir, it is." At any rate, it sure beat those frozen pies in the cardboard boxes he and Vince used to buy at Kroger's. They were tasteless compared to this. But then, he couldn't tell Clarence all that. He was surprised he said as much as he did.

Stan's next appointment was across town in another middle-class subdivision. On the way, he had Race stop at a hamburger place where he bought them both lunch. Only now, Stan ordered a salad and got Race fries, a shake and a burger.

"See," Stan told him once they were seated, "I can eat right once in a while."

Like Race even cared what the guy ate. Made him no difference. He wolfed down the burger because now it didn't matter. The blind guy couldn't see if he was messy or not.

As they ate, Stan explained about the next appointment: a single mom, a nurse's aide, who scheduled the piano to be tuned on her day off.

"Shelly bought the piano used a couple years ago so the kids could take lessons," he explained as though Race were interested—which he definitely was not. "Thankfully, there were no cracks in the soundboard, or loose seams in the bridges, and most of the keys still worked. It was considerably off-pitch, but it wasn't worth it to raise the pitch. Shelly couldn't afford it."

Stan felt for the small container of dressing. Race caught the move and found himself pushing it toward Stan's hand before he even realized what he was doing.

"Thanks," Stan said, poured on the dressing perfectly, and continued his dissertation. "Even the highest and lowest notes were low, but if I attempted to push it up to concert pitch, what would be gained? And besides strings might break if I did. So I left it. Neither she nor the kids know any different, and I doubt they'll be tuning with an orchestra anytime soon. So I tuned it as is and everyone's happy."

Stan wiped his mouth with his napkin and pushed his empty bowl back. "That's the way I help people. I discern each client's instrument individually." He paused then. "You finished? Ready to go?"

"Yeah," Race replied. Somehow, he didn't feel quite as reluctant as he had just a few hours ago. He didn't have time to think about it, however; the next appointment awaited.

Within twenty minutes they arrived in Shelly's neighborhood and Race had to turn the old crate around only twice before he successfully located the address.

Shelly, a hefty woman with dark curly hair and dark-framed glasses, opened the door to let them in. She was a woman of few words. She showed them to the den in the back of the house where she reminded Stan of the two steps down. He thanked her.

"I'll be in the kitchen," she told them, "cleaning out cabinets." She sighed. "Seems like I try to get everything done on my one day off."

The long narrow room looked as though it'd been added onto the back of the house as an afterthought. The room definitely had a lived-in look—very hodgepodge compared to Adelaide's house. A small table held an older-style computer with a folding chair pulled up to it. The printer rested on the floor beside it. An oversized entertainment center held the TV, stereo, and, Race noted, even a PlayStation. He'd like to get his hands on that jewel. He guessed this mom couldn't afford a good tuning for the piano, but could still give her kids a PlayStation. Good priorities, Race was thinking. A low couch, covered with a rumpled red plaid throw, faced the entertainment center. The piano was snugged up against the wall at the opposite end of the room from the television.

The top of the instrument was strewn with piano lesson books and sheets of paper filled with scribbled notes and instructions—perhaps from a piano teacher.

Race hesitated a moment as he surveyed the mess, then thought, what the heck. He scooped it all up and put it on the floor, opened the case and laid out the tools as he'd done at the Dotson's.

Before he could tell Stan he'd wait in the car, Shelly asked if either one wanted a soda. Stan turned down the offer. "But Race here would probably like one," he added as he turned back to his work.

Race was beginning to like all this free grub, so he said, "Sure," thinking he'd grab the can and head for the car. Instead Shelly handed him a tall flowered glass complete with little half-moon ice cubes floating in the foamy soda.

"There're coasters in the drawer of the coffee table," she told him.

He muttered his thanks and went to the couch to wait.

Before Stan was barely half finished, Race heard the front door open and slam shut. From the sound of the ruckus, he guessed Shelly's kids were home from school. Voices sounded from the kitchen, then two boys, about eight and ten, tumbled into the room, pushing and shoving and laughing. Stan greeted them, then asked them to please be quiet so he could finish.

"Hey man, we got stuff to do in here," the older boy insisted.

"Yeah," said the smaller boy. "You're not our boss. This is our house, we can do what we darn well please."

Race looked over at the scene. The boys hadn't yet realized Race was sitting on the couch at the other end of the room. Stan stopped what he was doing and patiently explained that he needed silence in order to tune the instrument correctly. "I'm almost finished," he said, "then the whole room is yours."

"We don't give a flip if it's tuned *correctly*." The smaller boy used a mocking tone that didn't set well with Race.

"Jason's right," agreed the older brother. "We don't wanna take stupid lessons anyhow."

At that point Race, in one smooth move, was off the couch and standing over two wide-eyed little boys. "Hey, you little twits," he said in a low, steady voice. "You heard the man. Now get your skinny carcasses outta here or I'll knock your heads sideways and ugly."

All he saw was heels as the pair sped out of the room and into the kitchen to tell their mother. Race heard Shelly saying, "You got what you deserved. You know better than to bother the tuner when he's working. Now stay in here till he's finished."

Race returned to the couch, smug as a bulldog.

At the conclusion of Stan's work, he ran scales, then launched into the lively theme from the Charlie Brown TV shows. At first Race was a little disappointed. He hated to admit it, but he was somewhat curious to once again hear the music Stan had played at the Dotson's. But then who cared what the blind man played anyhow? It made no difference to him one way or the other.

As they were driving back to Stan's place, the blind man was quiet most of the way. When they were within a few blocks of his house, Stan said, "I appreciate your helping me with the kids back there at Shelly's." He paused a moment. "But next time, could you be a little more polite about it?"

Race didn't answer.

Then Stan added, "Sure wish I could have seen how fast they moved."

Race looked over and the fat guy was smiling.

All in all, it'd been an okay day, Race told himself as he rode the bus back to OTR. He guessed he could possibly keep this up till probation was over. Tomorrow was his first day at creep school. He dreaded that like the plague. The pits for sure.

He boarded the bus near Stan's house, then got off well outside OTR. He chose the long way to his apartment in the fading light of day, shivering in sub-zero cold. But there at the corner of Liberty and Fifteenth stood Hawk and Pinky, kicking back like it was a balmy summer day. They still had their baggy pants and cool chains. Remembering how much he'd lost in the past couple weeks – much of his freedom and his right to wear whatever he wanted – Race felt hot anger rising up, and immediately the burning in his stomach was back.

"Yo bro. We been waiting for you," Hawk said, striding toward him.

"Yeah, man," Pinky echoed, "Where you been hanging? Toon be needing see you. He say now!"

CHAPTER 17

Stupid punks. Hawk and Pinky were nothing but stupid punk babies. Race wanted to smash their faces in. To think he and Vince and Wynn had taught them everything they knew, but were they grateful? Nada. Zip. No shred of loyalty. Still thinking Toon and Savvy were the end all.

Race ignored them and kept walking.

"Toon say you done been slapped on the wrist for a little shoplifting jag," Pinky said in his whiny voice. "Thought you's better than that, bro."

"Sheesh! Nabbed lifting," Hawk said. "How wimpy is that."

At that Race whirled, his hand automatically going for the knife that wasn't there. "You little creeps. Get outta my face or I'll turn you both inside out and feed you to the pimps."

Hawk instinctively leaped back out of the way. But Pinky didn't move, his eyes bugging out in disbelief. "You wouldn't, would you, Race?"

"Hide and watch." Race knew he had to get out of there before he hurt one of them. How would he explain that to Wynn? "Go back to your mama and grow up," he said as he stalked off, trembling from cold and from anger.

"Toon say he gotta see you, Race," Pinky called after him. "Tonight. At the picnic table by the hoops."

Race kept walking. First on his list was to get home and get warm, then he'd worry about Toon.

He hadn't been in the apartment long enough to pull his coat off when the phone rang.

"How was your first day at work?" It was Goforth in his ever-dull and boring style. Even his tone was blah.

"Okay." How Race despised this cat-and-mouse game.

"First day of school tomorrow, remember."

Like he could forget. "Yeah."

"Starts early. First class at 7:30."

Surely nobody in his right mind got up that early. "Yeah."

"No breaking curfew, and no hanging with any of the old pals. Keep your nose clean and it'll all look good to the judge."

"Yeah."

Goforth barely waited for the answer. He was gone. Probably had three zillion other bad little boys to call tonight.

Race moved over by the radiator and tried to soak the heat into his frozen bones. He'd have to go talk to Toon. No choice. And the longer he waited, the worse it'd be.

He took a minute to go get a sweatshirt from his bedroom and pulled it on over his shirt. Zipping up his coat, he went out the front door and realized he was hungry again. It'd been a few hours since the burger.

Even though two big lights flooded the basketball court at the playground, Race hated being there after dark. He sure didn't want to be picked up and thrown back in that monkey cage.

As usual, Toon was perched on the edge of the metal picnic table. Probably too stoked to feel the cold.

"Hey, Racy baby," Toon called out when he spotted Race. "They is talk that you sit in the slammer for a night."

"Yeah, so?"

"So now they gots your head in they noose? They jerk you around, you follow. You nothing but a little pussy cat."

Race clenched his fists and shoved them in his pockets. "I was told you wanted to talk. That all you got to say to me?"

"They is also talk that you gots you a little job. And you gonna go to they little school? I shoulda brought you a box of Crayolas."

Race stood still and said nothing.

"Those popo boys say that stuff to me and I tell 'em where to put it, man. Ain't nobody gonna jerk Toon around on the silly string. Besides that, can't never learn nothing outside like you can on the inside."

"Yeah, well, you live your life and I'll live mine."

"You keep walking like you walking, Racy boy, you life be in the gutter like Vince's."

At that Race flared. "You want to flap your jaw, fine, but you leave my brother out of this. You're not good enough to lick the bottom of his shoe, let alone mention his name."

"Hey cool it. What I be telling you, man, is that the popo done gone on a killing spree in OTR. They shooting first; asking later. You think you safe cuz you skin is white, you gots another think coming. Savvy say we all gotta stick together through the heat."

Toon pulled a reefer out and lit it and pulled a drag. He held it out for Race to take a puff. Race shook his head. He wanted out of there. He was remembering all over again why he despised Toon so much.

"Savvy got wind you playing kiddie games, sucking up to the JPO and all. He say you need to quit the kiddie games and come on over with us."

"Over?"

"Yeah man. You dense? We gotta watch each other's backs and for that we need force. That mean we hook up with the Dragons. When we be tight with them, it be all us against all them gun-happy fuzz."

Race reeled like he'd been hit. He should have known it was coming to this. "Not me. I don't want any part..."

"Hey it's all set, man. Door's wide open. You be the leader of our group. They say we be a set inside of a set. Nobody gets jumped in. Just you and one of theirs go at it. Piece of cake for you, homie. After that we all in. Even Wynn's little babies. It's the way OTR's going, man."

Toon jumped down off the hard table, pulled one last drag on the reefer and threw it in the dead grass. "Plus Wynn wants it."

"Wynn?"

"Yeah, your buddy who's sent up for a while. Remember? He be like me. He don't let nobody lead him around neither."

"Wynn was packing. They didn't give him any choice. And for all I know, they didn't give you any choices either."

"True, man. You don't know. You don't know nothing." Toon reached in his pocket and pulled out a folded piece of paper. "This be from your homie. Look like he side with Savvy."

Race took the paper, unfolded it and held it up to the light to read. It was without a doubt Wynn's handwriting.

Race, watch them babys backs till I get out. It be drab here, man. Terrible drab.

"How'd you get this?"

Toon laughed his hyena laugh. "You gotta ask? Once you been in juvie, you connected, man. No problem. You'd know too if you wasn't such a pussycat."

Race wadded the paper, stuffed it in his pocket and turned to go.

"Do I tell Savvy you in?"

"Tell Savvy he can shove it."

Race didn't go to his hideaway that night although he desperately wanted to. He tossed and turned on the lumpy couch clutching the note from Wynn, looking at it periodically by the blinking pink and green light coming in through the window. Why couldn't he have written more?

Just because Wynn asked him to watch the babies didn't mean he agreed about crossing over to the Dragons. But how could Race find out for sure? And what if Wynn did mean he was ready for them to make the move? Would Race really do it? Vince always said they'd never be sucked into a gang. And that was his final word on the matter.

And how was Race supposed to watch Hawk and Pinky and their baby buddies when all they could do was diss him? Can't watch somebody's back when there's no respect coming at you.

What with the Dragons down on him, Savvy, Toon and the remnant of their pack lined up against him, a probation officer breathing down his neck, and the cops shooting everything that moved, what chance did he have?

First thing he had to do was get a new knife. At least then he'd have a fighting chance. But how? And when? And where?

Creep school was about a hundred times worse than Race had imagined. It was where the scabs and maggots hung. He didn't want to be associated with any of them. He kept to himself, sat at the back of the classroom and kept his mouth shut. When addressed, he answered with a shrug.

At lunch, a couple slime balls tried to approach him, asking if they could sit with him. He gave them his special ice stare and told them to "beat it or he'd have to mangle them." They complied. Quickly. Creepy little wannabes.

Goforth's calls became fairly predictable. At least for the present. Race didn't want to trust that pattern. No matter what Toon said about juvie, Wynn's message shouted the truth—*terrible drab*. It had to be hell. And no matter what he had to do, Race still wanted to stay out of that place. He might be in a noose now—as Toon put it—but he was still breathing free air. That's more than Wynn could say. Wynn wasn't in a noose; he was in a straightjacket.

A dusting of snow had fallen in the night, so the sidewalk to Stan's front door wasn't as clean as before. Race wasn't going to be surprised this time by the old guy opening the door before he got up to it. He'd be ready this time. But he wasn't ready at all.

He got all the way up to the door and had to knock. When the door opened there stood a girl about his age. Brown hair feathered softly around her face, and light hazel eyes crinkled as she smiled at him.

Race's mouth went all dry and for one terrifying second he wondered if he'd gotten off at the wrong street.

"You must be Race," she said pleasantly. "My name's Ellie. Come on in. Uncle Stan's almost ready to go."

Stepping back suddenly, Race nearly slipped on the slick step and had to do a little fancy footwork to keep his balance. Now he was more embarrassed than before. "I'll just wait out here."

The girl laughed. Not a giggle, not a sneer, just a soft laugh. "No need in that. Come on in and get warm. He'll only be a minute." She moved back, opening the door wider for him. Race felt the warm air on his face. It was another one of those weird moments where he seemed trapped. Like at the Dotson's when he'd planned to stay out in the car, but couldn't.

Reluctantly, he stepped inside and then just stood there awkwardly, not knowing what to do. Maybe she'd just go away and leave him alone so he could get out without talking to her.

No such luck.

"So you're Uncle Stan's new driver," she said.

She seemed friendly enough, but Race knew her kind. If she'd ever met him on the street or in the school hallway, she'd pass by with her nose in the air.

Race nodded slightly. "Yeah." *Come on blind guy. Where are you when I need you?*

Ellie sat down in the easy chair and waved him to the couch. She had a nice enough figure, made evident by the sweater and jeans. Not too tall, maybe about five three or four.

"So is Race a nickname?"

Race wasn't sure whether to sit or keep standing. Surely Stan'd come and he'd be out of here. He saw the tool case strategically positioned by the kitchen door.

When he didn't answer, she said, "Well, Ellie is definitely a nickname." She looked up at him and her hazel eyes didn't seem to be judging. "You can sit down. I promise I'm harmless."

At that, Race decided he felt stupider standing. So he sat.

She continued as though he really were keeping up his end of the conversation. "Ellie's short for Eleanor. Really dumb name."

She paused, but he had no idea what to say. Ellie didn't really sound dumb. He'd heard a lot worse. Especially some of the street names in OTR.

"Years ago, my mother did a college paper on Eleanor Roosevelt and was so ga-ga over the woman that she declared she'd name her first daughter Eleanor." Ellie put out her hands palms up. "So, guess who? I'm the first and only daughter."

Race looked down the hall to see if Stan was coming, but the place was quiet. He swallowed over the dryness in his throat. "That's nice," he managed to mumble.

"Nice?" Ellie said. "Have you ever *seen* a picture of Eleanor Roosevelt?"

Race wasn't sure. Maybe he had. Maybe in some far off past history class. In some part of his past life when he still studied and received fair grades.

"Well, the woman was *some kind of ugly*, let me tell you."

Suddenly, something about the cute way Ellie wrinkled her nose made Race smile. It made him want to laugh at the thought of this cute girl being named for some ugly woman out of a dry history book. Pretty ironic.

"You mighta got the name," he said, "but you missed all around on the other. I mean, the ugly part." The words just sort of tumbled out. He was shocked he could even say something coherent.

She turned to look at him and when she did, the feathery hair swung softly around her shoulders just like on those corny shampoo commercials. "Why, thank you," she said. "What a nice thing to say."

Race stood quickly because Stan chose that moment to enter the room, pulling on his heavy coat.

"Sounds like you two are getting to know each other."

"Well, sort of," Ellie said. "I was doing most of the talking."

"Sounds normal to me," Stan quipped, and then gave his low chuckle.

"Uncle Stan, that's not nice." Ellie jumped up, walked over to him and pretended to hit his arm. Then put her arms around him and gave him a hug.

"Ellie comes over every couple of weeks to handle my accounting records," Stan said to Race. "She's the math brain in the family."

"Uncle Stan," she joked, "your accounts are so simple a grade-schooler could do them."

"So you're saying, right here in front of Race, that I'm not an entrepreneurial tycoon? Of all the nerve."

"Well, if you were, I'd have to demand a serious hike in pay." Ellie glanced at Race and winked as though he were in on their little game.

"You already *had* a serious hike in pay," Stan shot back.

"Pray tell when that happened? I must have missed it."

"Well, there are two missing frozen Snickers bars, and I know I didn't eat them. Now that is a bigtime added expense."

Now Ellie laughed out loud, covering her mouth in mock surprise. "Caught in the act." Then to Race, "I *love* frozen Snickers. My weakness."

"I'll try to remember that," Race said, unable to resist adding his bit of humor to the silliness.

Stan leaned toward his niece in a pretend whisper. "Oh ho. Would you listen to that. Man of few words speaks clearly. You'll have to keep an eye on him."

Ellie laughed, but now Race could tell she was the one who was embarrassed, and he knew he'd gotten the upper hand. That felt good.

Stan motioned to the gray tool case. "Grab the tools, Race. Miss Maudie awaits us."

"Is she the lady by the church?" Ellie asked.

"That's the one," Stan replied as he headed toward the back door.

Now Race had to walk right past Ellie as he followed Stan.

"You'll like Miss Maudie, Race," she said to him as he passed. "She's one powerful little lady."

As Race loaded the tool case in the trunk of the Chevy, he wondered why Ellie didn't say something *normal* like "Good-bye, have a nice day, nice to have met you." Instead she talked about a client as though he might possibly be interested in her. Which of course, he absolutely was not. But still it was strange. And not a little confusing.

CHAPTER 18

Maudie's house was simple to find. Race almost laughed when he saw it. The yellow frame house sat between a large church on one side, and the church's activity center building on the other. A chain link fence enclosed the generous yard, which displayed obvious care. Dormant flowerbeds, visible through the melting snow, neatly lined the walk and spread out on either side of the front entrance. Trimmed shrubs grew close to the house. Several large trees, the names of which Race had no clue, filled both the front and back yards. The property perched like a little oasis in the middle of a desert of concrete since the snow-cleared parking lots came right up to the fence on all sides.

When Race pulled up and stopped the car, Stan said, "Not too hard to find this one, eh?"

"Stands out like a zit on the nose."

Stan chuckled. "Apt description."

"So what's it doing here?" Race's curiosity had gotten the best of him.

"When the church decided to build their activity building, they started buying up houses and bulldozing them, but Maudie wouldn't sell." Stan unfolded his white cane and waited a moment while Race fetched the tool case. "Said it was her place, it was paid for, and she wasn't leaving."

"Did they give her a bad time?" Race couldn't imagine that anyone wanted a house sitting in the middle of their parking lot.

Stan felt for the gate and opened it. "They did, sorry to say," he admitted, lowering his voice as they approached the front door. "You can see who won."

Race wasn't sure what he was expecting to see on the other side of that door, but the trim, gray-haired, black lady was not it.

"Good morning, gentlemen," she called out in a sing-song voice. "Isn't this a lovely day?"

Maudie was decked out in a brightly colored sweater, dark slacks and loafers—like an old-fashioned schoolgirl. Her graying hair, twisted up into a knot in back, sported a long yellow pencil stuck into it. Escaping gray wisps gave her small face a halo effect.

When Stan introduced Race to Maudie, she looked up at him and said, "What a privilege for you to get to travel with this fine man. But you may not know that yet."

"Now Maudie," Stan protested as he handed her his coat. "Don't get carried away." He gave his soft low chuckle, a sound that Race was becoming very familiar with.

The rather large front room was divided into three areas: a sitting area in front of a fireplace at one end; a play area strewn about with children's toys, bookshelves full of chil-dren's books, a kid-sized table and chairs and a toddler-sized blue and red slippery slide; then the music area with the piano at the other end with several straight-back chairs clustered nearby. Race soon learned that Maudie served as the neighborhood piano teacher and the room was designed to accommodate her business. The piano itself was in much better shape than that of either Adelaide's or Shelly's.

Not much on top of this piano—a metronome, a class roster book, a smattering of sheet music and a magnet board with a music score across it, decorated with black magnetic notes. Race had the instrument cleaned off and the tools out in no time.

"So what's the problem, Maudie?" Stan asked.

"Two of my older students have become quite serious in the past few months." She patted the instrument with hands that were wrinkled, but with straight tapered fingers. "They're giving this old thing a run for its money."

"That must make you very proud."

"Indeed I am. And I want to do right by them. Some of the wider-range keys are a little sluggish. Nothing you can't fix, though." When Maudie smiled, every part of her face lit up.

"I'll give it my best shot," Stan said and turned to his work.

As they were talking, a tawny-colored cat strolled into the room and began rubbing against Race's leg. It surprised him at first. He'd never been around cats much.

"Well, would you look at that," Maudie said. "Shug likes you."

Stan snorted. "Lucky you. That cat never has liked me."

Miss Maudie laughed. "That's true. Shug keeps her distance from Stan. I say it's because she has an ear for music and she doesn't like all that plunking noise he makes."

"Well, Race," she went on, not waiting for Stan's reply, "Stan doesn't need us in here. Come on out to the kitchen. I think I can rustle up something for you to eat. You look to be a growing boy."

Once again, Race had been corralled. The weird thing was, it didn't seem as bad as it had at first. When Goforth first explained this job to him, Race simply assumed all of Stan's clients would be called ahead of time and warned that a wild, dangerous juvenile delinquent would be intruding into their safe little homes and to lock up the silverware and hide the stereos. But nobody seemed to take any thought of him at all, except that he was Stan's driver. And that he needed to be fed. That was it.

Maudie had a thing for apples and her kitchen was proof. In front of the stove was an apple-shaped rug, an apple cookie jar sat on the cabinet, and the cabinets themselves had apples stenciled on the doors. Apples echoed into the curtains and the wallpaper. Instead of looking like overkill, it seemed to fit Miss Maudie perfectly.

She smiled as she saw him looking around. "You know what they say—an apple for the teacher. But I needed a few more." She laughed and waved at him to sit on a high stool at the counter.

Opening the refrigerator, she said, "Coke or Sprite?"

"Coke, please."

"Potato chips or tortilla chips?"

"Tortilla's fine."

"Then I bet you'd like salsa with it. Or shall I make you nachos? I think I've got some cheese in here."

"Salsa's okay." Then he remembered to thank her.

Meanwhile, Shug jumped up on the stool beside him and sat there looking at him. Hesitantly, Race reached out his hand to her and she rubbed up against the outstretched hand. The soft feel of her fur and the warmth of her breath made him miss Monty Mutt. When he was busy throughout the day, he could almost forget about his snug, private hideaway. Then, just like this moment, it all came rushing back to him and he detested the mess he was in.

Maudie started puttering around her kitchen while Race devoured the chips and salsa. "My papa built this little house in 1931," she said as she rinsed off a few dishes and placed them in the dishwasher. It wasn't as though Race had asked her anything. She just talked.

"He and Mama raised eight kids in this old house. When Floyd and I were married, it was deeded to us. Then one of my sons became a builder and he helped us remodel and fix it up from roof to foundation."

She began to point out where this wall had been removed and this one added to make the kitchen more open. And how the deck had been added onto the back and on and on and on. Race only half-listened as he alternately ate and petted the cat, slipping her a chip or two which she ate right off the counter. That made him smile. Animals were so cool.

Then she talked about the church's acquisition of the properties. That subject commanded his attention. "Every house in these two blocks was filled with the people I'd grown up with. They all pressed on me to sell out and let 'em bulldoze the place. Floyd had already passed on, you see, but I knew what he'd say about giving up the house.

"Then those church folk started in on me. The pastor and his deacons. Whoooee." She shook her head. "You talk about determined. Now there was some determined people. Dead set on getting rid of me and my property. I told them one day, I says, 'You must not serve the same God I serve. My God is loving, kind, gentle and forgiving.'"

She looked over at Race. "Too bad they don't serve a loving God like I do. They didn't have an answer for that one."

Race nodded toward the church building. "That your church? Your pastor?"

She shook her head. "No. That was one blessing in all of it. I'd always attended a little church way over there on the other side of the highway."

Maudie stopped a moment and gazed out the window above her sink. Her voice sounded as though she'd left the room. "I had to do it. Wasn't easy. But I had to do it. For Mama and Papa. For Floyd and the kids. For me. For God. If I had it to do all over again, I'd stand just as firm or a little firmer."

Pretty amazing that this lady had had to stand alone against so many people. Even people she'd known and been friends with. But Race had no time to mull it over further, because at that moment Stan was running the scales, letting them know his work was almost done.

Maudie wrung out her dishcloth and laid it carefully over the edge of the sink, then wiped her hands on a towel that was decorated in, what else, apples.

"Hand me your plate, Race, and come on in here now. You got to hear this," she said as though she were letting him in on a little secret. "Come hear Stan and me test his work."

In the front room, Stan had replaced the lid and kick-board. "Come on, Maudie," he said. "Let's take her for a spin."

Race wasn't sure what to do with himself. Was he supposed to stand up? Sit down? Lean against a wall? Shug curled herself round and round his legs. So he just plopped down cross-legged on the floor near the piano and allowed the cat to crawl into his lap, which she did. He could feel her purring against his legs.

He was then witness to one of the funniest sights he'd ever seen in his entire life. Maudie sat her tiny backside on the piano bench next to Stan's broad one, and the two of them began to play a duet of "Coming 'Round the Mountain." The crazier part was that they actually sang the verses. Loud.

She'll be coming 'round the mountain when she comes.
She'll be coming 'round the mountain when she comes.
She'll be coming 'round the mountain,
She'll be coming 'round the mountain,
She'll be coming 'round the mountain when she comes.
Then the rest of the verses.
We will all go out to meet her when she comes...
We will kill the old red rooster when she comes...
We will all have chicken and dumplings when she comes...

Race had never seen two adults act like this in his entire life. Before they ever reached the last verse, they were laughing so hard they could hardly sing. He wondered if Stan was going to fall clean off the bench. Now that *would* have been a hoot.

Stan's afternoon appointment was at a small, nondescript church north of Winton Woods Park. They grabbed sandwiches at a drive-thru and ate on the way. Race hadn't been in very many churches in his life. He remembered his mother taking him and Vince to a little storefront church in Lower Price Hill a few times. He couldn't have been more than three at the time. He remembered the folding chairs, the singing, and the kindhearted, friendly people. Kinder than the church people Maudie described.

This particular church sat at the edge of a small community. The pastor greeted them and let them in, commenting on how sad it was to have to lock church doors because of vandals. They followed him through a dim hallway and into the sanctuary where he left them to their work.

All Race had to clear off this piano was two hymnals. While Stan did his plinking and plunking, Race strolled up and down the aisles looking at the colors in the stained glass windows, wondering why churches always had colored windows. He had nearly decided he'd go outdoors and walk around when Stan called to him.

"Can you come here a minute? I need your help."

"My help?" Now there was a weird statement.

"There's a buzz in this piano."

"A buzz." Race wanted to give his shoulder shrug and his *I-don't-give-a-flip* look, but all that was wasted on a blind guy.

"I can't find the cause in here." He tapped the piano. "So it has to be in the room somewhere. I want you to walk around and listen. I mean really listen."

"What am I supposed to hear?" This was dumb. He'd already been walking around and he hadn't heard anything.

"It's some kind of sympathetic buzz somewhere in the room."

Sympathetic buzz. Yeah right. So a buzz can be sympathetic. Now that'd be something to see. It could go into the world book of weird facts.

"Race?"

"Yeah."

"The quicker you move, the quicker we can get out of here."

So he started walking again. Up and down the aisles, between the pews, across the back, feeling more stupid with each step. But suddenly at the furthest corner at the back of the sanctuary, he stopped stock still.

"What is it?" Stan said, sensing his stillness.

Race looked up at the ceiling where a plastic grate covered a fluorescent light. It was giving off a definite buzz. "Could this be it? The grate over the light?"

"Let's find out. Get the pastor and ask if he has a ladder."

The pastor kindly produced a stepladder from a storage closet and Race climbed up to the light, not even sure what he was going to do when he got there. But once he started fiddling with the thing, he simply firmed it into place and the buzzing stopped.

Across the sanctuary, Race could hear Stan's audible sigh of relief. "That's it. Thanks, Race." After a moment, he added. "I knew you'd find it."

CHAPTER 19

"If they only knew," Race said to Monty Mutt as they sat together on the bed in the back of the hideaway. "But of course they don't. None of those people have a clue who I am."

He dug into the bag of chips, ate a handful and fed a few to Monty. The temperatures had risen some in the past week or so. Without the challenge of the miserable cold, the temptation to steal away to his refuge had become overpowering.

"They're all nicey-nice to me. And they even feed me. But if I ever met them in OTR as they were on their way to their nice cars from the Music Hall after a concert, they wouldn't give me the time of day. In fact, they'd walk a little faster to get away. You can count on it."

Race handed Monty another chip, then reached over and fiddled with the dial on the radio. At first, he searched for jiving rap or bee bop, but after it came on, it made him think of Toon. If there was anything he didn't want to think about while he was in his special place, it was loser-Toon.

One night while running the dial, he came across a classical station and left it there. Then he laughed as he thought what Vince would say if he ever witnessed his own brother listening to such off-the-wall square stuff. "Nothing pumping in that," he'd say. Before any heist, the pack always had a few beers and pumped the hip hop at a fever pitch to psych them for the job. No need for that here. So he left the dial on the classical stuff sometimes. Just because he could. Without taking flak from anyone.

Some of it he liked. Some of it bored him to tears. Once he even caught a snippet of the melody that Stan had played at Adelaide's house. In a momentary rush, it came back to him how strangely the music had affected him that day. But before he could get the station tuned in clear, the song ended. The thought left as quickly as it had come.

"Yeah, Monty, you should see how I've been eating lately. Snacks at every house, and then the old fat guy buys me lunch to boot. It's a trip, I tell you. And my stomach's not burning so much now." He pulled gently on Monty's silky ear.

"The cafeteria at creep school is pretty much a sad joke, but it's take-it-or-leave-it 'cause bad little kids like us have to stay on campus all day. Sheesh. The only good part is that I'm only there three days a week." He took a drink from his Coke can. "I mean it, Monty, I couldn't stomach that place any more than three days."

But Race had to admit he'd sort of settled into the routine of the school. Unlike regular school, there weren't a lot of wild, noisy, interruptions. You fight, you sass a teacher, you make a scene, you're outta there fast. The next step takes you face to face with a judge. Nothing to do, really, but just do the work. So he did.

Before, in regular school, following Vince and Wynn, Race was constantly distracted just keeping up with them.

They marched through the halls pushing people out of the way. When someone looked at them, they glared back, hissing threats and obscenities.

Wynn's favorite thing was to step into a classroom and slap the person closest to the door on the back of the head as hard as he could. He was lightning fast—incredible footwork—stepping in and back out again before anyone even knew what had happened. No matter how many times he did it, it was still uproariously funny.

It was a matter of honor to never be in class on time. The point was to arrive late enough to disrupt the entire class with a noisy entry. They grew to love the look of dread on the teachers' faces, and felt disappointment if they had not produced it at least two or three times a day. Completing assignments became impossible, because they never bothered to find out what the assignments were.

Race locked his hands behind his head and stretched his long legs out, disturbing Monty's comfortable position. He sighed as he remembered those days that were now gone. Forever.

"None of that kind of fun and games at creep school," he confided to Monty. "Zero fun in that place."

Monty turned around a couple of times, then rested again across Race's legs.

"But you know what, Monty? I did an algebra problem the other day—all the way through."

Monty gave a throaty little whine.

"I mean *all* the way through. With *no* help. And my answer was right. That was really wild. Listen, Monty, I couldn't tell this to anyone else—especially not that Goforth nerd—but it felt kinda cool. Weird, huh?"

Coming and going from the hideaway had become a science for Race. Late at night, he'd go to a convenience store, or Kroger's, or even into Mad Malone's. He'd hang out a while, then slip out the back way, maneuvering through dark alleys to get out of OTR.

Just before dawn was the best time to get home. The street people were soused and sleeping off their highs. So far, so good, but he knew his luck could run out at any second. He was blatantly breaking curfew. That was the price he was willing to pay. Because without the hideaway, he was certain he would have lost it before now. He'd have blown into a gazillion pieces. Not a pretty thought.

The first time Stan's work took him out of town, Race had to get permission from Goforth. Stan told him about it a couple days in advance, explaining that Race would have to make the call.

"I'm working for you and you're the one who needs the appointment," Race countered. "You call Goforth."

It was the most he'd said to the guy since the two of them started working together. Oftentimes Stan would just start off talking about things as they drove along—about people he'd known, his clients, and sometimes even about his childhood growing up on a farm in Nebraska—but Race did nothing more than grunt monosyllable replies. What did he care about any of it? It had nothing to do with him.

"You're partly right," Stan replied. "I do need the appointment, but you're the one who needs permission, not me. If you can't get permission, it means I have no driver and I'll have to turn down the job." Then he added, "It's in a concert hall up near Columbus."

Driving around Cincinnati had become sort of a lark for Race. Getting out of the city entirely would be way cool. It'd be a waste to miss out over one little phone call.

"I'll ask," he told Stan.

"Good."

Calling Goforth was tough. It was bad enough talking to the guy when the nasty check-up calls were made. It was as though Race's voice had almost forgotten how to be gruff, cold, and authoritative. How could that be? After all the years of Vince and Wynn whamming that stuff into his head. But somehow it didn't make sense to be gruff, cold, and authoritative when you call somebody to ask a favor. So what was he supposed to do?

He picked up the phone several times before he was able to dial the number. Once he punched in three of the numbers and hung up again.

"This is so stupid," he muttered into the empty living room. He was sitting cross-legged on the couch with the phone in his lap. Across the room, the television blared out a mindless game show. "It'd be easier to knife the guy than talk to him. What's up with that?"

He took a deep breath. "Okay, man," he said, "let's talk it straight. Do you wanna drive up to Columbus or not?"

He knew he did. No question. Even with the fat blind guy, he wanted to get out of town.

"Then make the freakin' call and get it over with."

Sucking in another deep breath, he didn't let it out until all the numbers were punched in and the line was ringing.

"This is Goforth."

Race froze. He'd never addressed the man before. Mr. Goforth? Officer Goforth? Plain old Goforth?

"Uh. Hey," he plunged in. "This is Race."

"Hey yourself, Race. How's it going?"

"Going okay."

"I'm hearing good things about you from the school. You're quickly becoming one of their better students."

The unexpected compliment completely undid him. Part of him wanted to hear more. To know more. Who would say such things about him? And what made him any different than anyone else in the creep school? But he had to stay cool.

He'd learned it from Vince over and over again. He could still hear Vince's voice. "You drop your guard and you're dead in the water, man. Don't ever drop your guard."

But he'd already dropped his guard so much …

Goforth finally spoke into the silence. "How can I help you, Race?"

"Uh, it's about Stan."

"Is there a problem?"

"No. No problem. At least, I don't think there's a problem. He needs me to drive him up to Columbus. I need permission to leave the city."

"I don't have any problem with that as long as you're with Stan and you're back before curfew. If you'd been gonna take a hike, you'd have done it before now. At this point, it looks like you're fairly trustworthy."

There was an empty silence. Race's throat had closed up again.

"Call me when you get up there and when you leave to come back. Okay?"

"Okay." Race started to hang up, then jerked the phone back up. "Uh, thanks."

"You're welcome, Race."

Race sat on the couch for a long time, thinking. *One of their better students?* So what was that supposed to mean? He already knew he was better than the creeps that hung out at creep school. But Goforth had said *better student* ... What did he mean? The idea made him feel good and then scared all at the same time.

And then he'd said *trustworthy*. But Race knew he wasn't trustworthy. If he'd been trustworthy, he'd have been watching Vince's back the night he was shot. If he'd been trustworthy, he'd have known Wynn was packing a gun and he'd have made him get rid of it. If he'd been trustworthy, he'd have been able to lead the pack and keep them going strong—apart from Savvy and Toon's interference. If he'd been trustworthy, Hawk and Pinky would still respect him.

The blaring television moved from game shows, to stupid sitcoms, to the empty talk shows. By the time Race fell asleep, he'd convinced himself that Goforth knew nothing. Absolutely nothing. Just another con man blowing hot air.

In fact they were all blowing hot air. And they were all intent on bringing him down: the wimpy, mousy counselor he and Nealia met with on Monday nights; the teachers at creep school; goofy Goforth; and yes, even the fat blind guy and all his customers. More than ever, Race needed to keep his guard up. The problem was, he'd almost forgotten how to do that.

As he tossed and turned on the too-small couch, he kept seeing a dish drainer with yellow plates and tumblers sitting in a neat row, and through his brain ran a rousing rendition of "She'll Be Coming 'Round The Mountain," accompanied by the sounds of much laughter.

CHAPTER 20

Leaden gray skies, filled with threats of snow, hung thick as Race steered the Chevy crate up Highway 71 toward Columbus. The distance from Cincinnati to Columbus was about a hundred miles, but they had to stop for a morning appointment on the way. "Located way out in the boonies," Stan explained.

As usual, Stan had the directions printed out, and went over them thoroughly before they left that morning. Stan had an organized notebook consisting of a page for every client, including directions to each location. The notebook, he proudly explained, had been thought up and compiled by Ellie.

For the first few miles, Stan dozed, his head lolling toward the window and his breathing coming short and even. Race enjoyed the sensation of the miles melting beneath the car. If only for a brief time, he felt free. Like being in the hideaway, he was alone with his thoughts.

Glancing over at Stan, he realized how easy it would be to ditch the old guy and run for his life. Not hurt him, but just leave him and run. How far could he get heading straight north? A person could be in Canada in a matter of a few hours. Slick and clean. He hadn't been thinking. He should have grabbed his cash stash from the back of his dresser drawer. Next time... Come to think of it, this whole setup really could buy him some time. Being a good boy and becoming *trustworthy* as Goforth had put it. By biding his time and planning carefully, he could escape from Toon, Savvy, creep school, probation, and the whole stinking mess.

Sometimes, late at night when trains rumbled over his hideaway, making the windows rattle, Race often considered catching a freight car and leaving Cincinnati. What would it take to make it in another town? On his own? He didn't need much—a job and a place to live. But in the very next thought, he knew he couldn't leave. He had to take care of Nealia. Vince would have expected it of him.

However, lately his mother had been doing better. The counseling seemed be working with her. She'd begun to take a more serious look at her life and her responsibilities. She wasn't drinking as much. Maybe now was his chance. Once he was sure she'd be okay without him, he'd make his move.

Stan roused just before time to turn off the highway onto the side road heading to their morning appointment. They were on blacktop for a while, but then a right turn took them onto a graded road full of potholes and loose gravel. Race tried his best to miss the holes, but the road was a mess.

"Bad road, eh?" Stan remarked.

"Bad car," Race said through clenched teeth. "The thing corners like a dump truck."

"I know. I've been thinking pretty seriously about getting a new one."

Race was studying the printed directions that he'd taped to the dash, when Stan said, "Want to help me?"

"Help you what?"

"Pick out the car."

The directions said the road was supposed to curve to the left, go down a hill into a small valley and then on the left-hand side of the next hill would be the farmhouse he was looking for. He waited till he actually spotted the house and barn, before he could answer. It also gave time for the words to sink in.

"Why me?" Race said as he pulled into the long, rutted driveway.

"You're my driver."

Race pulled the crate to a stop in front of the house. "Whatever," he said coolly as he got out. But inwardly he was bewildered. Surely the fat guy couldn't be serious. Probably like Goforth, just more conning and conniving.

By the time they reached Columbus, powdery snow was forming soft sweeping swirls across the highway. They grabbed a late lunch. Race was starving, even though the lady at the farmhouse had loaded them down with her homemade chocolate chip cookies.

At the concert hall, Race let Stan take the lead as usual. Pretty ironic to be led by a blind guy, but Stan always seemed to know where he was going. Race never failed to be amazed at how Stan sensed when some obstruction was in front of him, and then deftly moved to avoid it.

Now Race followed Stan through the shiny halls of the concert hall as though he'd done this thing all his life—while all the time trying not to stare. Tall windows along the outside walls spread soft light upon the muted pastel paintings in gilt frames that lined the inside walls. The marble floors were buffed to such a high sheen, Race could see their reflections as they walked along. The click of Stan's cane reverberated down the hall like the sound of a toy cap pistol.

The hallway led them to a carpeted foyer overhung with glittering chandeliers as big as a dinner table. They took the elevator down to the lower level where they met up with the center's director—dapper guy named Chad who habitually stroked his trim goatee.

Stan briefly introduced Race to Chad, but the man's mind was obviously on a million other things. After the director had expressed his relief that the piano tuner was indeed in the building and on the job, he took them backstage to where the shiny black concert grand piano sat waiting.

There was nothing to clean off the top of this instrument. In a few moments, Race had all the tools laid out and Stan went to work.

"I'll be down in one of those front seats if you need me," Race said. "Just give me a high sign."

Without looking up, Stan agreed. "Good idea," he muttered.

Race found his way from backstage to the door leading out into the theater area where he sank down into one of the plush cushioned front seats. He was pretty proud of himself that he'd had the foresight to bring his backpack containing his school stuff.

Using Stan's client notebook as a makeshift desk, Race attempted to muddle his way through a few algebra problems. Stan's notebook made him think about the girl named Ellie. It didn't surprise him when Stan said she'd thought of organizing his client information in a portable notebook. That just seemed to fit her. She looked like she had her life all in order. She was probably a straight A student. Probably never missed a day of school—ever. But then when you have a real home, and a real family, the rest is a snap.

But he still wondered about her. Wondered how he could find out more about her. Since she hadn't run away from him the first time she met him—and surely she knew where he came from—maybe there was a chance she didn't even care. Now that would be different.

The entire theater was a buzz of activity. On the stage, soundmen checked mikes and speakers, workers set up chairs and music stands, while the lighting technicians played with the spotlights. Other people trotted up and down the stairs doing things Race could only guess at. Very distracting. Finally, he folded his paper and stuck it into his algebra book, slid down in the seat, laid his head back and quickly fell asleep.

He was awakened by someone softly shaking his shoulder. He reacted like a tightly coiled spring suddenly released, nearly slamming the worker in the head.

"Hey, cool it, buddy," the guy said as he stumbled back a few steps, his eyes wide.

Race quickly realized where he was and felt his face grow hot. "Sorry." He bent down to pick up the book that had spilled to the floor, hoping to hide his face.

The guy jerked his thumb toward the stage. "The tuner-guy says to tell you he needs to talk to you."

"Okay. Thanks."

The man walked off, shaking his head.

"We've got a little problem," Stan said when Race had joined him on the stage.

"We?" Race didn't have any problem here except that he'd nearly flattened a guy.

"I've been working on this thing for over two hours and the pianist still isn't happy with the sluggishness in some of these middle-range keys. I've finally figured out that it must have to do with the humidity."

Stan popped open his watch and felt the hands. "It's getting late. There's no way we'll make it back home before your curfew."

Race shrugged. "So?"

"I'm going to keep at this. I feel sure it'll be resolved before curtain time. Chad's ordering in sandwiches, then he's keeping two seats open for us down front for the concert tonight."

Stan cocked his head like he did when he listened closely. "You okay with that?"

"Whatever."

"We'll just stay at the Holiday Inn down the street and go back to Cincinnati in the morning."

Stay the night? Now Race was kicking himself big time. Why hadn't he thought to grab his wad of cash. What a prime opportunity this would be to split the scene. Neither Vince nor Wynn would have ever been caught short like this—especially Vince. He would have been on top this thing from the get-go.

Maybe he should just split, anyway. The blind guy always had money with him. Race wouldn't have to hurt him, just tie him up good. He'd have the entire night to make tracks. Canada was starting to sound really good.

"Call Goforth and let him know what's up," Stan told him. "Chad's offered the use of the phone in his office. One of the workers will show you where it's located."

"Like Goforth's gonna believe me?" Race protested.

"Tell him I'll call him from the hotel tonight. But I can't stop right now."

But Goforth *did* believe him. Or if he didn't, it was a great act.

"Cool," was Goforth's reply to Race's explanation. "You get to experience a live symphony concert. What a great opportunity for you."

"Stan said he'd call you from the hotel tonight."

"Tell him I look forward to it. Later, Race."

And he was gone.

Race felt lightheaded. Didn't these doofuses know how wide they were opening the door for him to split?

Race felt oddly smug as he watched the members of the orchestra finding their places and begin tuning their instruments. Stan had finally solved the problem of the sluggish keys by drying out the soundboard with a hair dryer of all things. Pretty clever. But as he confided to Race later, some of the problem had to do with a nervous and temperamental pianist. "The tiniest details needle them when they're uptight," he said.

Race wasn't sure what he expected from the concert, but nothing could have prepared him for the cascade of sounds that came spilling over that stage and down into the place where he was sitting. Ready for total boredom, his plan was to again lean back in the soft seat and get some sleep as soon as the lights dimmed. The plan went awry.

Suddenly the entire auditorium erupted into an explosion of music. Dozens of musicians played instruments he'd never seen before, all working together to create unbelievable music, following a director who lifted them up and drew them after him with one small white baton.

Race knew what it was to have rap and be-bop pump into him for hours on end. It rocked his head, it made his body want to gyrate and dance. But this—this drove straight into his chest, deep into his gut.

Crescendos built up and exploded like clusters of fireworks spraying in a million different directions. Gentler tones hung softly on the violins and soothed the ache inside him. Happy melodies flew freely from the flutes. French horns gave forth thick dark melancholy notes.

Number after number played on with pauses only for thunderous applause. Race could barely catch his breath, as tangled confused powerful emotions erupted from his insides. He'd never known there could be such music. It wrapped around him and soaked into every pore. What he'd heard on the radio in his hideaway trifled in comparison to the *aliveness* of it being performed only a few feet away from where he sat.

Intermission came and Stan excused himself, saying he needed to check the piano one more time. Race stayed put. On the floor beside him, he picked up a program someone had dropped. Almost every word was foreign to him— names of the music, names of the composers. He knew none of it. Looking around the auditorium at all these people, at the stage filled with seasoned musicians, suddenly it struck him how little he really knew about anything.

Toward the close of the concert, a melody came forth that Race recognized as the one he'd heard Stan play at the Dotson's. As it had on that day, the beauty of it made his insides ache and his eyes burn hot. His head was screaming out at the stupidity of all of this, screaming at himself to cool it. Chill. Cut the garbage. But nothing worked. He'd lost his footing and had fallen into a rushing stream, and was being swept merrily along with the steady flow, at first fighting and flailing, then finally giving up to the power of the current, letting it carry him wherever it willed.

As the final notes died away the pianist, sweat-soaked after his powerful performance, took several bows. Before the lights came up, Race quickly wiped wetness from his cheeks.

Stan informed Race they'd been invited to a reception given for the orchestra members following the concert. "Plenty of food," Stan added, although Race wasn't sure if that fact was for his benefit or for Stan's. The man loved to eat.

Stan was right. The large reception area was replete with several long tables loaded with platters of crackers and cheese, chip and dips, tiny sandwiches (of which Race could have eaten a dozen), fruits, veggies, and a wide array of cookies and cakes.

At first Race held back, feeling very much out of place. But then Stan said he was going to need a little assistance.

"Buffet tables are always a challenge," he admitted. "Not like someone setting a plate in front of me." He smiled. "I usually send the cherry tomatoes rolling to the floor."

Such a thought hadn't occurred to Race before. For the most part, he'd succeeded in ignoring Stan's limitations. He couldn't very well ignore this. As they worked through the crowd, people spoke pleasantries to them. At one point the pianist came and fussed over Stan, thanking him again and again for solving the problem.

Race finally got Stan to a place where he could sit down. He then headed to the buffet and proceeded to stack two plates as high as he could with everything he could find, and they ate it all.

When it was time to leave, Race went back into the auditorium to get their coats, his backpack, and the tool case. Because they'd arrived so early, the Chevy was parked close to the entrance. Stan led the way, his cane making a muffled sound through the fluffy layer of fresh snow. He was almost at the car when Race saw him slip, lose his balance, and hit the ground.

In an instant, Race dropped the tool case, and when he did, it hit his big toe in a flash of white-hot pain. Ignoring it, he rushed to Stan's side. Kneeling down, he asked, "You okay?"

Stan chuckled. "I think so. I'll tell you more when I get up."

"You better stay still for a minute."

"Good idea, Race, but this snow's kind of cold on the backside—in spite of my ample cushioning." Again, he was chuckling. "You know, when you can't see, you get pretty good at learning to fall. There's an art to it. Remind me to teach you sometime."

By the time Race had his employer on his feet, a couple of the orchestra members had come by to help. They assisted Race in getting Stan up and into the car. One was a young guy who'd played the kettledrums. He didn't appear to be much older than Race.

After Stan was safely in and said he felt fine, the young guy turned to Race and asked about his toe. "I saw that tool case hit your foot."

"It's okay," Race insisted when, in fact, the toe was throbbing like a bad boy.

Later that night, Race was sprawled across the humungous bed in his hotel room—Stan had reserved adjoining rooms—with an ice pack easing the pain in his big toe.

He'd clicked through about a jillion channels on the television, but couldn't keep his mind on any of them. The music kept running through his head. There'd been nothing drab about that concert hall. Or about that music. Even the music seemed filled with color.

Using the remote, he turned down the sound on the TV.

"Well, big shot, isn't this the point where you were going to tie up the blind guy, take his money, and trip out on your merry way to Canada?"

After positioning the giant pillows just right, he pulled the thick, flowered comforter over him and heaved a deep sigh.

"And you were going to tie him up with what—his shoestrings? Yeah right."

CHAPTER 21

The music didn't even have a name—just a number. *Piano Concerto No. 2 in C Minor,* is how it was listed on the concert program that he'd saved. Race had no idea what a *con-serto* was, nor how to pronounce the composer's name. Something like *Rack-moni-off.* But that didn't matter, because he dug around and found it in a music store in the mall. Then he played it over and over at the hideaway trying to pick it apart and discover why it had given him such a gut-punch. He remained clueless.

The February nights weren't as cold as they'd been in January, so his nights at the hideaway were less stressful. However, he dreaded the time when the dark nights would grow increasingly shorter. The darkness had become his friend. His protection. He'd become very good at keeping hidden as he moved from point to point.

To think that they used to *rule the night*—the pack, that is. Brazenly they walked the OTR streets, daring anyone to cross them. And now he slunk around through the shadows.

"Sorry Vince, but I gotta do what works for me," he whispered as he approached OTR through back alleys after one particular night at the hideaway. "You just gotta understand."

Suddenly there was a sharp report of gunfire, followed by sirens and shouting and screaming. Race jumped closer to the back of an empty building and froze, unsure whether to move forward or backward.

The noise seemed to come from a few blocks away. Swallowing the fear, he waited a few minutes giving time for the attention of any nearby cops to be diverted to the emergency at hand, then he made a run for his apartment. As he swung himself up on the fire escape that led to his living room window, he could make out a small figure huddled there. Automatically he reached for his knife that wasn't there.

A head popped up from the curled-up ball. "Race? That you?"

"Pinky! What're you doing, man? You wanna get me..."

"Hey bro, just lemme in for a few minutes. We be sittin' ducks out there tonight. Every cop in OTR got a mad on. Shootin' first; askin' later."

Race moved past him. "It's open. Sometimes I leave it unlocked."

"Wish I'd known. My bones is half froze to death, man."

"Why'd you come here?" Race asked after they were inside.

"I just run. Hard to think when bullets is flying."

"I got a couple burritos in the kitchen. Want one?"

"Don't know as I can eat nothing—my stomach's like rocks be sitting in it."

Race got the burritos anyway, and Pinky managed to get his down and a Coke as well.

"You can't stay here long, Pinky." In spite of the fact that Race had been taking crazy chances breaking curfew several nights a week, he suddenly realized he really didn't want to have his setup messed over. And having Pinky in his apartment could mess it over really bad.

Pinky sat huddled in the corner of the couch. He was getting some height on him, but he was still skinny as a pencil. His dark eyes always had a darting-around, scared look to them—like he was expecting someone to punch him out any minute.

"You gotcha a good thing going down, man? Don't need us no more?" Pinky had wadded up the empty burrito wrapping and now he tore little bits of it off as he talked, not looking up.

Race didn't know any more—about anything. He thought about the note from Wynn. How bound was he to what Wynn wanted? Had Wynn ever done what Race wanted? "I got some choices now, Pinky."

"It's cause you's a whitey. They don't give Wynn no choices."

"It's because Wynn was packing, Pinky."

"They say you had a knife." Pinky tore more pieces off the wrapping. "You had a knife and you was busted doing a little two-bit shoplifting deal." He shook his head.

Race let the last remark go, but he was pretty sure he knew about Wynn and the choices. Race had had a gut feeling all along that Wynn wanted to be locked up. That he'd turned up his nose at any choices presented to him.

"It's got nothing to do with white or black, Pinky. The guy I work for doesn't even know my color. He can't see me."

"Can't see? You mean the dude's blind?"

Race nodded.

"What you do for a blind dude?"

"Drive him around."

"Sweet." It was quiet for a minute before Pinky said, "Savvy and Toon's done right by me. Hawk don't even want me around him no more. Got his own friends, he say." He looked up at Race for a moment. "Me and him used to be tight as you and Vince was."

Race disagreed on that. Nothing Hawk and Pinky had could ever compare with him and Vince. Hawk was nothing like Vince. Nothing. Hawk cared about nothing and no one but himself. He'd never treated Pinky as good as Vince had treated Race. But Race kept quiet.

"Toon say Hawk's gonna get cut down to size someday." He went back to pulling off bits of paper. "The whole mess be solved if you just listened."

"Listened to what?"

"To when you coulda got us all in the Dragons. Just one little fight—you coulda done it one-handed—and we'd all be wearing purple now. And be safe."

Race shook his head. Pinky really believed this crap. They'd gotten to him big time.

"Pinky, you get caught up in that gang stuff and it gets worse, not better. The moment you're in, you're marked. Challenged by any other gang wannabe. You heard about the Latino gangs coming together now? And what makes you think the police can't aim at a purple jacket? It stands out like a neon sign. And you'd be out of school for good."

"You so high falutin' now. You don't know nothing. The Dragons is where it's at, man. It's all cool. They tight—watching they backs." Pinky threw the wad of paper on the coffee table in front of him and stood up. "They all be steaming mad at you, Race—Toon, Savvy, the Dragons. Even Hawk."

"How about you? You steaming mad at me too?"

Pinky shook his head and studied the floor. "Things so mixed up in my head now. You, Vince and Wynn was my heroes. I don't know no more. It's all mixed up."

Race sure knew what he meant about being mixed up.

Pulling on his coat, Pinky added, "I do know one thing. I's done for good being picked on. I's getting me a gun."

"So you can go keep Wynn company?"

"No, man. So's I can protect myself. If they takes me out, I is taking dudes with me."

As he listened, Race knew he, too, was in danger. When he was with Stan, when he was at his hideaway petting Monty Mutt and listening to a *con-serto*, he allowed himself to forget. How stupid he'd been. He never did have that luxury—and didn't have it now.

"Pinky, I need a knife. Can you get me one?"

Pinky's face lit up with a flicker of hope. "You gonna come back and help us?"

"I don't know yet. I told you I have choices now."

"You dreamin', man. You got no more choices than nobody else in OTR."

"Hang on a minute and I'll get you some cash for the knife."

"I got money, man. More money than I done ever had. Pay me when I get the thing. I'll let you know when I gets it and where you be meeting up with me."

"It's a deal. Thanks, Pinky."

"Thanks for nothing. You still be a yellow traitor in my book."

He crawled through the window and disappeared into the night.

The used-car salesman grew more and more befuddled. His frowzy white mustache twitched as he looked first at the blind guy who couldn't look back at him, then at the kid beside him, whom the salesman obviously disdained. Race thought it was hilarious.

Several weeks had passed since Stan mentioned getting another car. Race thought the matter had been forgotten, but here they were.

Stan had come to this car lot on a recommendation from his nephew, Ryan, who as Race later learned, was Ellie's father. "If Ryan trusts them, that's good enough for me," he'd told Race as they pulled into the lot.

A glass partition surrounded the salesman's small office. On the walls beneath the glass, hung plaques that screamed out that *Roy Rentie* was the number one salesman in the place.

"Tell me exactly what you're looking for," Roy said as he leaned back in his big overstuffed office chair, "and I'll do my best to assist."

"What do you think, Race?" Stan asked.

Roy looked at Stan. "Excuse me, sir, but don't *you* have some idea of the kind of vehicle you're looking for."

As soon as he'd let the word *looking* slip from his lips, Roy's mustache twitched again.

"Well, what I mean is..."

Stan chuckled. "Tell you what, Roy. Ridiculous as this may sound to you, the state of Ohio frowns on issuing a driver's license to someone like me. A little narrow-minded, I know, but that's the way it is. And since it's been a few years since I've been behind the wheel, my man, Race, here is going to help me." Stan leaned toward Race and asked again, "What do you think?"

Race knew full well what he thought. But he hesitated. He'd never been asked his opinion before. It was hard to believe that Stan was serious. At any moment, someone would burst into the glassed-in office yelling, "Hold it right there! Cut! Just joking, Graham Kyle Paloma! Nobody, nowhere, really gives a flying rip what you think."

It didn't happen. There was only silence. Race glanced at the stuffy salesman sitting there in his starched shirt and tie.

Race cleared his throat and turned in his chair to face Stan. "You need a smaller car. One that's easier to handle," he began, "especially on some of those gravel roads."

Stan nodded. "Go on."

"Mid-sized, but with good gas mileage. Not too expensive, but nothing cheap, because your business depends on your transportation." Race thought a minute. "And lots of trunk space," he added. Because Stan kept a lot of stuff in that big Chevy trunk. "Probably something like an Accord, or a Camry."

Roy started to speak, but Race interrupted, "And no more than four or five years old."

"Sounds good to me, Race," Stan said. To Roy, he said, "Got anything on your lot fitting Race's requirements?"

"Come with me." Roy said, still not looking at Race.

Test driving was a rush. The fun of driving different cars without the fear of being fingered by the cops. Really wild.

Stan ran his hands over the dash of each one as Race explained the features and described the colors. They opened the trunks, and Stan reached his chubby arm in as far as he could, feeling around to check for roominess.

The entire afternoon seemed unreal, but Stan capped it off by actually picking out the car right then and there—fully relying on Race's input. And with no little price dickering on Stan's part.

He instructed Roy to make a couple of phone calls, one to nephew Ryan and another to Stan's bank, after which they drove out of the lot in a new-looking silver Honda Accord.

"Let's go show Ryan and Anita," Stan suggested. "See what they think."

Ryan and Anita Crosslin's two-story frame house was located near the university district.

"They need a big house," Stan explained, "because Ryan and his wife run their accounting business out of their home."

In the midst of giving directions, Stan explained that Ryan was the son of his brother, Calvin, who'd been many years older than Stan. "I was the baby of the family," Stan said, "but that doesn't mean I was babied. On that Nebraska farm, we all worked. Daddy had me out on that tractor before I was four."

Race tried to imagine a chubby little toddler driving a tractor down the long rows of a big field. But it was impossible. His mind couldn't make the connection. Mostly because he was thinking about Ellie—wondering if she'd be home when they arrived. After all, it was only Thursday, but it was close to time for school to be out.

Luck was with him. Ellie and her younger brother, Warren, were both there—it was teachers'-meeting week, Race was told. Amidst introductions and much fussing over the new car, Race had no time to think. The next thing he knew, he'd followed them into the house. As Anita took his coat she smiled at him. Race immediately saw where Ellie got her good looks.

"Stan enjoys having you as his driver," she told him. "He's had some real duds in the past. We're always thankful when he gets a good one."

Race felt his face flush. He managed to mutter a thank you, before he followed everyone into the spacious sunken living room and found a chair in the corner. One wall held a big-screen TV like he'd seen at Savvy's apartment. But this room was much warmer than Savvy's. Across the room, tall windows looked out over a sloping, tree-filled back yard.

Race listened as Stan and Ryan chatted back and forth about finalizing the paperwork on the car purchase, transferring insurance, finding titles and such; but Race's mind was mulling over Anita's remark. He'd never thought about Stan having other drivers. That's because he didn't think much about Stan at all. Of course, the man had had other drivers. Who were they? Why had they been duds? And what made Race any different?

Deep in thought, he failed to notice when Ellie approached him from the side. He jumped when she spoke his name.

She paused. "Sorry, Race. Didn't mean to startle you. What can we get you to drink? Tea, lemonade, Coke? Or we have hot spiced cider."

"Coke's fine," he told her, wishing somehow he could make himself more inconspicuous. While he desperately wanted a chance to talk to Ellie, he felt totally out of place in her big house. Any moment someone might turn to him and say, "And tell us, Race, where do *you* live?"

"Why, in the ghetto, of course, where the toilets plug up and the faucets leak. Short on heat and food, but long on exciting crime, drugs, and violence."

Then someone might ask, "Tell us, Race, what do you do for fun? Any hobbies?"

"Well, if you call being lightning fast at stealing really slick cars a hobby..."

Warren, who appeared to be about eleven or twelve, bounced around the living room with the pent-up energy of a large puppy. At first he was full of questions about his uncle Stan's car, but when that bored him, he sat on the floor by Stan's chair playing games on someone's cell phone.

Finally, his uncle asked, "So Warren, how's your lawn business? Is this snow making you any money?"

"Is it ever. The whole neighborhood wants their walks shoveled. It's a booming business. And," he added quickly while he had the floor, "I finally saved enough to buy me a new bike."

"That right?" Stan reached out to feel for Warren's shoulder and gave a friendly squeeze. "I'm proud of you. Really proud of you!"

"You'll have to come out later and have a look."

When Warren told his uncle to *have a look,* he didn't get all bent out of shape like the car salesman. Stan's blindness was no big deal to Warren.

Ellie brought Race his drink, but disappeared back into the kitchen.

When the conversation went back to the adults, Warren brought the cell phone over to Race. "You know how to play this game?"

Race shook his head. He'd never messed around much with a cell phone.

"You know any games?"

"Video games."

"You any good?" His dark eyes studied Race intently.

"Pretty good."

"Wanna come upstairs to the game room? I've got some great ones."

Race wasn't sure. He was scared to move.

Just then Ellie crossed the room and headed toward the stairs.

"Ellie," Warren said, "wanna join Race and me in some video games?"

She smiled. "Sure."

Race was instantly on his feet, following them up the stairs.

CHAPTER 22

The game room was exactly that—a big room full of games. A regulation-sized pool table sat in the middle of the room. Off to one side, a racecar setup with seemingly miles of tracks that looped and whirled around filled a full third of the room. Two computers sat upon two separate desks, their screensavers creating swirls of changing colors. Bookshelves lined one wall filled with books, photos, boxes of board games, puzzles, and all sorts of plaques and trophies. One of the shelves held a television set. They settled in front of the set and proceeded to play one video game after another, in all of which Race creamed them both—relentlessly. They didn't have any of the games that Race really liked, such as *Mortal Kombat,* the one he'd mastered while hanging out at Mad Malone's. This collection consisted of tamer stuff, which at any other time would have bored him to tears.

At first, he considered letting Ellie win, but found he didn't know how. He'd always played hard and played for keeps. He didn't know how to do it any other way. But it didn't matter, because they were good sports. And they both asked him to show his techniques.

"I want to know how to beat him," Ellie said with a laugh, jabbing a thumb at her younger brother.

"No way," Warren countered. "Teach me to beat the socks off her."

Race liked hearing Ellie laugh and he liked the sweet smell of her sitting there on the floor next to him.

"Well, then, let's let you two slug it out on the next one," Race suggested.

"Oh yeah," Warren said. "Look out, Sis. I'm lethal now."

"In your dreams."

As the two siblings went after it, Race's eyes trailed up to the bookshelves and there among a group of family photos, he noticed a framed photograph of a man and woman with a little boy on the woman's lap. It sort of looked like a younger, slimmer Stan.

He stood up to take a closer look. It sure did look like Stan. "Is that your uncle Stan in that picture?"

"Yeah," Ellie said, but didn't look up. "Whoa," she yelled as she worked the controls. "Gotcha that time. Thought you said you were lethal, dreamer boy."

"Who's this with him?" Race picked up the photo to study it.

"Marie and little Charlie." But Ellie's eyes still never left the screen. "Gotcha again!"

"So who's Marie and little Charlie?"

Now Ellie looked up at him. "My aunt and cousin. You know, the ones who got killed."

"Killed?" Race suddenly saw Vince's lifeless body sprawled on the ground and blood running down the sidewalk and into the gutter.

Now Warren looked up as well. "Didn't Uncle Stan tell you?"

Race shook his head.

"I'm surprised," Ellie added. "He talks about it pretty freely now. It happened a long time ago."

Of course Stan never told him. Race never wanted to talk to Stan, or listen to Stan.

"That's how he lost his eyesight," Ellie went on. "And that's why he limps. You've noticed that, I'm sure."

Race nodded dumbly. He'd followed behind Stan up dozens of sidewalks for weeks now, but he'd never noticed any limp. Because he'd never paid any attention.

"What happened?" he wanted to know.

Ellie was standing by his side now looking at the photo over his shoulder. Again, he could smell the cleanness of her. "Drunk kids in a stolen car," she said. "Hit them head on. Aunt Marie and little Charlie died at the scene. Uncle Stan spent months in the hospital. Had to learn to walk all over again, like a little baby. Severe head injuries caused him to lose his sight."

"Uncle Stan was a graphic artist," Warren put in, "before the accident. Dad says he was one of the best in the business."

"He's still the best in his business," Ellie put in as she returned to her place in front of the ongoing game. "Just a different business. Uncle Stan's the greatest!" She glanced back up at Race. "But I guess you've already found that out."

If Anita hadn't called them to come down for pizza at that very moment, Race wasn't sure what he might have done. Because his stomach was doing the old burn job again, with a little lurching thrown in for good measure. *Drunk kids in a stolen car.*

When he came back into the living room, Stan took him aside. "We can stay and eat pizza with them," he said in a low tone, "and that will make you late for curfew." He rubbed his top lip with his finger like he did when he was thinking. "So—we can leave now and still make your curfew, or..."

Race waited. "Or?"

"Or we can stay and you could spend the night at my place and take the bus in the morning. I have an extra bedroom. You're certainly welcome." He paused again. "I'll let you decide."

Race wasn't sure he even knew his own mind anymore. Stuff inside his head swirled and tumbled. He wasn't sure who he was or what any of this was all about. He wished he could get to the hideaway and think. Just think. About what he'd just learned about Stan Crosslin. About what the heck he was going to do about the threats coming at him on his own home turf.

He'd told Pinky the other night that he now had choices. It had surprised him when he said it. He guessed it was partly true. At least he had one choice. Here. Now. Tonight.

Race took a deep breath. "We can stay."

"Great. We'll call Goforth from my place."

Once they'd polished off the pizza and Stan and Race had their coats on to leave, Warren once more insisted they see his bike before they left. Their breath showed in frosty puffs as they went out the back door and onto a wide patio.

Stan made a great production of feeling all over the icy cold bike, asking about details of color and style, and commenting on how awesome it was and how proud he was of Warren for all his hard work and discipline. Race stamped his feet and tried to get warm.

"Go get the Honda warmed up, Race," Stan said. "I'll be there directly."

As Race got in the car, he heard Ryan yell out the back door at his son. "Warren, make sure you lock that bike up in the garage before you come in. You don't want some nut to come by and steal it."

Race's mind suddenly swept back to that sweltering September night in a yard not too far from here. He'd been the *nut* who'd stolen some kid's bike.

He started the car and cranked the heater up on high. "Vince, man," he whispered into the empty car. "You sorry so and so. These fat cats aren't like what you told me. Not *anything* like what you told me. How could you have been so wrong?"

He started the car and cranked the heater up on high.

"How did you feel when your brother was killed?"

Race hated when the counselor asked that question. He didn't really like their counselor much. A mousy-looking guy with hair the color of muddy water, pale skin, and scraggly growth on his chin that Race assumed was supposed to be a beard. Delvin Knowles was his name. To Race, he was Troll Knowles.

Race and Nealia were scheduled to meet with him every Monday night of the world. The Troll met with them separately for about 15 minutes each, then in a session together. When the Troll first asked Race the question, Race refused to answer. It was too stupid a question to deserve an answer. How're you *supposed* to feel when your brother's shot in the back? If you feel at all, you'll get a gun and kill somebody— anybody. Or sink a knife into somebody's belly. Or get some pot and lace it with a little embalming fluid. Or you slit your own wrists. Or you *don't feel* and just keep on trucking.

In later sessions, when the question came up, Race resorted to smart-aleck answers like: "Happiest moment of my life," or "Made me wanna do triple back flips." The Troll never batted an eyelash. Just kept on asking stupid questions.

Now as he tossed and turned in the bed in the back bedroom of Stan's neat little bungalow, he wondered how Stan felt when his wife and son were killed. When he had to lie there in the hospital for months, unable to see, wondering if he'd ever walk again. Did he ever want to slit his wrists? Did he want to shoot somebody? How did he *feel?* And what did he *do* with his feelings? Now the question didn't seem so stupid any more. And Race *really* wanted to know.

At creep school the next day, the halls were bustling with activity. The halls were always crowded, but this was different. There were kids in the hallways who were definitely off-the-wall straight—unlike the weirdo student body of creep school. Race stopped a kid from his computer class to ask what was going on.

"Aw, some do-gooder creampuffs from another school volunteered to paint our shoddy walls." He screwed up his face in disgust. "Are we supposed to kiss their feet or what?"

Race watched as the straight kids headed for the gymnasium. He craned his neck as he walked by the open doors to the gym where he saw them spreading out tarps and opening paint cans.

Nothing to concern him. He headed for the computer lab, his favorite class. He'd never had much opportunity to mess with a computer before, but he liked everything he was learning. Most of the guys stayed with *hunt and peck* on the keyboard, but Race wanted to learn the *qwerty* keys and really *type*. He sized it up early on and quickly realized that that was the only way to get up any speed. And he wanted to be fast. The instructor seemed willing to help him get it down pat.

In the lab, they were allowed to set up free email accounts and email one another. Most of what Race got from the other creeps in class were dirty messages or links to porn sites. He wished he could send a *genuine* email. He wondered what it'd take to get Ellie's email address. Would Stan tell him? Or maybe he'd get really brave and ask her himself the next time he saw her.

When the bell rang, Race stepped out into the hall to see it filled with kids on ladders happily painting away as if they had good sense. Dumb. Why didn't they wait till spring break or something when the place was empty? What if a bucket fell? Or worse yet, didn't they know some of these creeps would love nothing better than to knock over a ladder just to see someone hit the floor?

As he headed to his locker he looked up at a girl on one of the ladders. His heart thudded in his throat and his knees went soft and mushy. Ellie Crosslin! Of all the lousy luck! There went any chance he had to impress this chick—right down the toilet. Should he duck and run, or keep moving? Too late now. She was coming down the steps. She'd be at the bottom the very moment he passed her ladder. She wore a baggy sweatshirt and a faded pair of jeans, which fit her perfectly. An aqua bandana covered her hair. In her right hand, she wielded a paintbrush.

The entire scene moved into slow motion as Ellie's sneakers touched the floor and she turned around and saw him. The friendly smile had fled.

"Why hello, Race." The soft words came at him through a sort of gray fog. "I didn't know you went to school here."

Race instinctively moved into defense mode. A part of him marveled at how easily he slipped back into the no-expression, no-emotion glare he'd learned so well. "Well, now you do. Big whoop-de-do." He whirled his pointer finger in the air and kept right on walking.

CHAPTER 23

For a while after the incident with Ellie, Race beat himself up big time, telling himself how stupid he'd acted. Stupid, stupid, stupid, stupid. But then he convinced himself he didn't really give a flying rip. What did it matter what Miss *Eleanor* thought anyway? Did he ever really think he had a chance with her?

The real stupidity, he concluded, wasn't how he reacted to seeing her at creep school, but rather his thinking for a moment that she'd ever give him the time of day. The stiff shot of reality had sobered him up like a slap across the face. Just what he needed. After all, probation wouldn't last forever. Soon he'd be free again. They'd all go their separate ways, and the fat blind man would find another driver. Meanwhile, he'd force himself to remember who he was and where he belonged. Any day now, he'd have a knife again and it'd be business as usual in OTR.

Pinky's call came a couple weeks later, in mid-March. "Be in *your* alley off Race Street at two," he said so softly Race could barely hear him. "I gots you a present."

"Presents are free."

"This present be fifty."

His alley off Race Street. Why would Pinky choose that place? It was no secret how Race got his name scuffling in that alley—Vince had told the story so often he practically wore it out. "See ya, Pinky. Thanks."

The roll of bills stuffed in his drawer fluctuated in size from week to week. High-dollar deals were a thing of the past. Race's pay from Stan was split—half in his pocket, half to pay for the shoplifting spree. That didn't leave a whole lot, but it was steady. Strange, but he looked at the money he earned from Stan differently than money from stealing cars. Hard to explain, but the earned money seemed more real, more solid. He wasn't sure why.

Race knew he was doing Stan a good job, not only because of the comment Ellie's mother had made about his not being a *dud*, but because of things that Stan said.

Stan liked to tell people about Race running to pick him up off the pavement in the snowy parking lot. The first time Stan told the story, it made Race uncomfortable. After all, it hadn't been any big deal. Next time Stan told it, Race *liked* hearing it. And with each succeeding time, he enjoyed it more.

"This is my driver, Race," Stan'd say. "He drives my car, carries my tool case, and picks me up when I fall down." This was always followed by his soft chuckle, as he would then relate the details.

From the roll of bills, Race counted out two twenties and a ten. He paused a moment, then decided to stick in an extra five for Pinky's trouble.

In the kitchen, he fixed a cup of hot coffee, then went to the living room and cranked up the volume on the television in an effort to keep himself awake till two. As he sipped the scalding liquid, he hoped against hope that Goforth wouldn't call while he was out on the street.

Goforth's calls didn't panic Race anymore. For the most part, they were pretty predictable. Of all the times Race had violated curfew, he'd never been caught. About once a week, the PO dropped by creep school for a few minutes. Race figured he must have several naughty little charges at the school to check up on. Race would be called out of class to go to the administrative offices. Goforth would meet with him in a vacant office and ask a few questions, pull his glasses out of his pocket, put them on, look over the papers, put the glasses back in his pocket, nod a few times, and leave. During one of those visits, he had asked, "You making any friends here?"

Race snorted. "Here? You gotta be kidding."

"A man needs friends, Race."

"I got my own friends."

Goforth looked at him with a steady gaze that made Race squirm. "Do you, Race? I wonder. I really wonder."

What the heck was that supposed to mean? Race didn't have a clue. But later on the comment bugged him. In the back of his mind, he wondered how much Goforth really knew about him. Of course, he knew about Vince's murder, but did he also know about Race's connection to Wynn?

The night was breezy and biting cold as Race headed down the darkened streets toward Race Street. He kept thinking how good it'd feel to be armed once again. No more naked, helpless feeling. Pinky had really come through for him. Race would have to think of a way to thank him—short of throwing in his lot with the Deuce Dragons, that is.

A few noisy ladies were still working the streets. Didn't they ever get cold? Or tired?

No sirens tonight. Relatively quiet. His feet crunched over bits of broken glass. The wind caught a McDonald's cup and sent it scudding across the sidewalk in front of him. Bits of paper and an empty plastic bag whirled around in their own private eddy in the concave of a vacant doorway.

As he turned into the alley, his heart began pounding and his stomach churned and burned. *What's the deal with that? I'm just picking up a knife from my little buddy, Pinky.*

The streets were dark, but the alley darker. It took a moment for Race to make out Pinky's small form as he stood about halfway into the alley. Race picked up his pace. "Hey, man. What's up?" He pulled the cash from his pocket. He'd make this quick.

"It's a nice one, Race."

Race could see the shiny blade flickering in Pinky's hand. "Sweet." They were face to face now. Race handed the money over. "I stuck an extra five in there for you, buddy."

Race had seen Pinky scared before, but never like this. His eyes were wide and his breath short. "Didn't have to do that man." But he took it and shoved it into the pocket of his baggy jeans, making the chains jingle.

Race felt the knife in his hand. Pinky was right—it had a lovely feel, perfectly weighted.

"This is no place for chit chat," Race said. "Let's split. Catcha later."

"Later." Pinky turned to walk toward Vine.

Race shivered in the cold. As he turned to go the opposite direction, he'd only taken a couple steps when three figures came out of the shadows and closed off his exit. Of the three, he only recognized Piston, but all wore purple.

"Hey there, big man. Word has it you wanna be jumped in. You ready to be a big man again—be a Dragon. "

So Pinky had double-crossed him. Anger exploded through him like a grenade. If he lived through this, Race would rip the little twit apart.

Every muscle went taut as he balanced the knife lightly in his hand. No wonder he'd been nervous. He should've listened to his street smarts. Vince would have.

This was it. His first time to fight alone. He'd stay cool and let them play it out. Maybe they were bluffing. Stalling.

"You got it wrong." Race's voice echoed down the dark alley canyon. "Nobody jumps me in. Not now, not ever."

The crunch of footsteps from behind him let him know there was no bluffing tonight. They were done waiting. They had him trapped.

"We gives you a chance to come in nice and easy." Piston's gruff voice sliced through the darkness as he moved slowly forward. "Now all them little favors is over. You comin' in on Dragon terms."

A voice behind him added, "Tonight you be changin' your mind about Dragons."

Another voice. "And we doin' it in your own little alley, *Race Paloma.*"

The first blow was a kidney punch to his back, forcing out a groan of sudden, sharp pain. Race whirled and plunged with the knife, and heard a scream. He got someone. He had no time to relish the pleasure as his arms were grabbed from behind. Something hard came down on his right wrist and the knife clattered to the pavement. A fist in his stomach doubled him over, knocking the wind from him. As he struggled to straighten up, a fist hit his jaw in two hard slams, jarring his brains.

Race heard soft moaning off to his left. The guy he stabbed, maybe.

"Get that knife," Piston ordered. "We gonna test his new toy."

Race used the pause to suck air into his lungs and get his feet back under him.

"Can't find it," came the answer.

Piston's swearing filled the cold night air. "It's gotta be there. Keep lookin'. We gonna slit him wide open with his own shank."

Race knew if they found that knife, it'd take a year to get him sewn up—if he lived. And he *wanted* to live. He did. He really did. Vince never had that choice.

Race made a sudden move to violently rip his arms from his holder's grasp, kicking back as he did so. He was free. As hands groped to regain their hold, his fist connected with a soft midsection followed by a whoosh of expelled air. The half-second of freedom was short lived as hands and fists knocked him to the cold, hard, filthy pavement.

"You babies stand back." It was Piston's voice again. "He's had his chance."

Piston's big boot landed the first kick, hitting Race in the ribs. All he could do now was curl into a ball to ward off the worst, but the pain was like fire coursing through his body. The kicks came so fast that all sense of reality faded. In the distance he heard pitiful cries of pain, but could hardly register that the cries were his own.

Through the rain of kicks, Race heard a voice yell, "I gots it. I gots the knife."

"Lemme have it!"

At that moment, wild screams of sirens slashed the night air.

"It's the fuzz, man. Split!"

Race could feel vibrations from the pounding of running, retreating feet. Within seconds, red and white lights whipped in a frenzy around the dank alley walls. For the first time in his entire life, a police siren sounded beautiful.

Without opening his eyes, Race knew he was in a hospital. Strange smells. Strange sounds. As consciousness moved over his body, so did the awareness of pain. There wasn't a spot on him that didn't hurt. His jaw ached, sharp stabs of pain moved in his wrist. It hurt to breathe.

So, his little game was over. No more driving the silver Honda. No more listening to *Rack* whatever-his-name-was. No more Monty Mutt. No more Ellie. No more computer lab. It'd been nice while it lasted. But who'd have thought he'd ever be sad to see it go? And it wasn't just the thought of lockup. Before now, that's all it'd been—that he didn't want juvie. But now... It was no longer what he *didn't want,* it was what he *did want.*

Soft voices broke his chain of thought. He guessed he'd have to open his eyes. The task seemed monumental. Slowly Goforth's face came into his blurred view—his face calm, quiet. It was good to see him.

"Hello kid," he said softly.

Race tried to speak, but couldn't. His throat was dry and his chest hurt, so he gave a little nod and tried to smile. It hurt to smile.

"You're a stupid fool, Race. I was going to wait till you felt better to say that, but it needs to be said. You are one stupid fool."

Race made another little nod.

"You had it made, Race." He slowly shook his head. "What the hell were you doing in a dark alley at two in the morning? And whose blood was splattered all over the place?"

Race opened his mouth to speak and closed it again. Even if he could talk, he hadn't a clue what he'd say.

Goforth let out a deep sigh. "Okay. Now that I know you're awake and the doc says you'll be fine, I'm outta here. When I come back, we're gonna talk. So get ready. Hear me?"

Race nodded again. Later that night, it registered in Race's dull mind that Goforth hadn't been angry. In fact, he'd looked almost...what? Disappointed? Sorta spooky. Race wasn't sure how to handle that.

Nealia, however, was her old self, crying and sobbing and begging Race to straighten up and promise her that he would never, never break curfew again. Every time she tried to touch him, she made something hurt. The nurse finally instructed her not to touch Race at all till the soreness left. Trouble was, the only time she ever touched him was when she wanted to make a scene.

During the night, in the darkened hospital room, Race thought things through till he had it all figured out. No doubt he was on his way to juvie now. Hopefully, it wouldn't be for very long. And, also hopefully, since everything else had been going pretty smooth, maybe they wouldn't be too hard on him. He made up his mind he'd make the time count.

While inside the walls, he wouldn't let any deadhead pull him into any mindless gang wars. He'd keep his nose clean, study, get his GED, then do something with his life. Just what, he wasn't sure.

But what if he was sent to the same facility as Wynn? Then what? They'd be bound to each other. To watch each other's backs. To hang tight.

Throbs of pain in his chest made him catch his breath. Broken ribs, he'd been told.

Could he ever break from Wynn? From the pack? From his past? He had to. There had to be more to life than banging around OTR. There just had to be.

CHAPTER 24

"How would you like to go to Kentucky?"

Propped up in the hospital bed, Race attempted to feed himself breakfast left-handed, and chew with a painful jaw.

Goforth hadn't bothered to sit down when he came in. He just stood there by the side of the bed. It was tough enough for Race to eat in his predicament without someone gawking at him. And he was starved. Even cooked oatmeal looked good. Now a spoonful of the pasty stuff hung in mid-air.

"Kentucky?" His stiff jaw made him talk funny. Not broken, he'd been told, just stiff. Like the wrist. "What's in Kentucky?"

"Stan spends a few days in Kentucky every spring. Says he has several accounts there and he lines them all up and handles them in one fell swoop."

"Stan?" Race was dumbfounded. He'd been so sure the job was history. He'd broken curfew, for heaven's sake.

"Yeah. Stan Crosslin. Remember him? Or did you have a worse head blow than we thought?"

Race grinned and maneuvered the spoonful of gray oatmeal into his mouth. He hadn't eaten cooked oatmeal since he was very small. Uncle Dutch liked to cook oatmeal sometimes. Race remembered that now.

Goforth lifted the dome-shaped lid on one of the plates on Race's tray. Two slices of toast lay there cooling. He proceeded to butter the toast. "Jelly?"

Race nodded.

He pulled cellophane covers off tiny packets of jelly and spread purple on the buttered slices. "You need to know," he said, "the judge wasn't too crazy about the idea." He placed the slices of toast in a neat row on the plate. "About giving you a second chance, that is."

A second chance. Maybe his head injury *had* scrambled his brains. He was hearing things. Hallucinating.

"We talked him into it. Stan and I did. Stan more than me. He said you needed to get out of town for a few days. That, and Stan's willingness to take responsibility for you, seemed enough to persuade the judge."

Stan had gone to bat for him. Why? Nothing was making any sense.

"Well?"

Race laid down the spoon and looked up at Goforth. Funny, but he hadn't even thought about giving his hard-core, glare-stare. Where had that hardened stare gone? And when? He guessed you didn't think about such things after you'd had your head bounced around on the pavement and your guts kicked in. "Well what?"

"You *do* have a choice here, pal. Do you want to go to Kentucky with Stan Crosslin, or not?"

Race paused a minute. Out of Cincinnati—clean out of the entire state. No discussion. "Yes, sir. I do."

"Okay. It'll take a few days for him to get the appointments set up. He usually goes later in April. He's changing his plans to accommodate the situation."

Race nodded.

"You're being released from here this afternoon." Goforth lifted another domed lid and wrinkled his nose at the pile of scrambled eggs. "I expect you to go straight home. And between now and the time you leave with Stan, don't stick one toe outside your door after curfew. Got it?"

Race nodded again.

"You got a suitcase?" Goforth paused a minute, then shook his head. "No, of course you don't. Dumb question. No problem, I have an extra I can loan you."

The PO pulled his glasses from his pocket, held them a minute, then hooked them back again. "I hope I don't need to tell you, we've put our necks on the chopping block." He reached out to put his hand lightly on Race's shoulder. "Please, pal, don't drop the guillotine." He turned to go then. "Finish your breakfast. I'll catch you later."

Race nodded. His shoulder felt warm where the hand had lain.

Goforth paused at the door. "I expect you to tell me every last detail of what happened in that alley." He gave a funny little salute. "Whenever you're ready."

The suitcase was brought into his hospital room before he was dismissed. Race ran his hand over the hardness of the dark green case, then flipped open the clasps and opened it. Inside was a silky-feeling dark green divider that hooked and unhooked. He guessed you could put shirts and jeans on one side and socks and underwear on the other. He unhooked the divider and there lay a pair of very cool sunglasses with the tag still attached. There was writing on the tag: "You might need these. Goforth."

He hadn't been inside the apartment for ten minutes when the phone rang. It was Pinky.

As soon as Race heard his voice, the anger welled up and made every part of his body hurt all over again. "You dirty little traitor. If I ever get my hands on you, I'll pulverize you. You knew..."

"They say they just wanna talk. Honest Race. They just wanna talk to you."

"And you believed them? You're dumber than I thought."

"I gots you another knife, Race. Better'n that other one. You'll see. I brings it to you tonight."

"No Pinky. Stay away."

"Ain't gonna stay long. I just brings it to you window. You grab it, I runs."

"Why're they after me, Pinky?"

"You da kingpin, man. You know that."

The very sound of the word made Race laugh. "Kingpin? I'm no kingpin."

"They say when you comes in, all the little wanabes'll come tripping in easy."

That was the stupidest thing Race had ever heard.

"They wants you in really bad. Race? You sure you don't wanna change you mind? They all be really tight. It's cool as sliced ice. Know what I mean?"

"Pinky listen, I don't know why they think what they think about me, but I'm not gonna be no Dragon. And I don't want no knife. Don't come. You hear?" And he hung up.

Race paced about the apartment cont like a caged animal. Just knowing he couldn't go to the hideaway made him feel even more trapped. Stan had called the hospital and told Race they were leaving first thing Sunday morning, and it was now only Friday afternoon.

He rummaged through his school things and tried to work on homework. This was the first school he'd missed since starting creep school. How much had he missed? Should he call about make-up work? And if so, who? He had no idea. Maybe he'd ask Goforth when he called. But why wait for him to call? After all he had Goforth's number. Slumped down on the couch, he started a couple of times to punch in the phone numbers, then chickened out.

It wasn't really his problem. Let Goforth figure it out. He's the one who suggested Race get out of town.

There was no position where Race didn't hurt. He got up from the couch and headed to the kitchen. He put together several cracker and cheese sandwiches and opened a Coke. He wished they had a kitchen table. With chairs. Then he could at least sit up and do his homework. They had had a table once, but one of Nealia's muscle-bound *friends* splintered it in a fit of rage. They'd never gotten another one. They never sat down to eat together, anyway.

Race looked around the dingy kitchen and thought of Adelaide Dotson's yellow kitchen. How the sunlight had filtered in through yellow curtains and how the four yellow plates and tumblers sat one after the other in a neat row in the drain tray. "Not everything is brought to you by the color drab, Vince old boy," he said softly. "Not everything."

He drained the last of the Coke, crushed the can and tossed it into the overflowing trashcan.

"And I want to tell you something else, brother dear. I'm getting really fed up with sleeping on that lumpy old couch."

Walking down the hallway to the once-shared bedroom, Race stepped inside. Chaos. Pure chaos. It had always been chaos, but it had never bothered him until now. It was time.

There didn't need to be two beds anymore. That'd give him about twice as much room in here. The bed wasn't worth saving. He'd take it down the back way to the dumpster. Someone would have it picked up before daybreak. And all the old magazines and stuff that Vince loved to collect. What to do? He needed trash bags.

Back to the kitchen. He rummaged every cabinet. No trash bags. Marcus' mama would have trash bags.

He was in luck. Daneesha handed him a whole box, but he shook his head. "Just two or three," he told her.

"You cleaning?" she asked in a surprised voice.

He nodded. "Cleaning out Vince's stuff." He looked over at Marcus. "If I find any cool stuff, Marcus, you can have it."

Marcus grinned.

"You don't mind me saying it," Daneesha said softly, "it be high time."

"I don't mind. You're probably right."

It wasn't nearly as tough as Race had thought it would be. And it wasn't all Vince's stuff anyway. A lot was his. Much of it went into the trash bags. Outgrown t-shirts and fast food toys, and one really cool yo-yo, he placed in a pile for Marcus. After the bed was out in the dumpster, the extra space made work easier. He forgot about the pain in his ribs.

Perhaps when he returned from the Kentucky trip, he might even tear out the ratty carpet. Surely, he could find something to put on that disgusting floor. Maybe after he was finished, he'd actually have a decent room to live in.

He was so engrossed that the sound of Nealia coming in the door around four shocked him. But nothing could have shocked him more than her violent reaction to his evening's work.

From where he was sitting on the floor in the middle of his room, he saw her enter the hallway, weaving a little from side to side. It took a moment for her fuzzy brain to register what he'd done, then he saw the fiery anger explode in her eyes. She ran at him with one long, gut-wrenching scream. "Noooooooooo."

She was on him in a windmill of flailing fists on his head, his back, his tender broken ribs. "You can't do this. Can't take my Vince. You can't. Can't. Can't. Nooooooooooooo. My Vince. My baby."

"Mom, stop it. The ribs. You're hurting me." He struggled to ward off the blows, to grab wrists, to get her under control. Nothing was working. Her drunken mind was incoherent. In one desperate move, he reached out and grabbed at her legs, knocking her backward into the hallway with a heavy thump. As soon as she was down, he jumped over her and ran for the front door. He had to get out of there before he hurt her.

His first instinct was to head for the hideaway—his only safe place. He went flying out the front door and onto the street and was almost to Fourteenth Street when it hit him. Kentucky! His second chance. He was risking it all by being out here. How bad did he really want it? He felt as though he were being pulled in a million different directions. The pull to be with Monty Mutt in the safety of the hideaway was enormous. He just wanted to be left alone. By everyone. By the whole world.

His breath came short and ragged. He leaned over and put his arms around his midsection to ease the pain of breathing. "God," he whispered to the night, "how I wish everyone would just leave me alone." He turned back toward home.

Even in her drunken stupor, Nealia's mind had been clear enough to lock both the door and the window. Not sure what to do next, he slumped down in a heap in the hallway in front of their door. Sooner or later, she'd leave. He'd just have to wait. Cold and aching, he leaned his head back against the wall and tried to sleep.

CHAPTER 25

W hen Goforth offered to pick Race up and take him to Stan's house Sunday morning, Race was surprised, but he didn't refuse. Race's only stipulation was that he'd meet him at a bus stop on Vine. Goforth agreed. Race felt really stupid standing there carrying the green suitcase, with his backpack filled with textbooks on his back. No way would he want to be near his own hood. The fact that it was early Sunday morning and the streets were deserted saved the day.

"I've talked to the school," Goforth said as Race climbed into the beat-up little blue-and-rust Volvo. "They'll work with you on your assignments."

Race nodded. He figured he could probably study as good or better on a trip as he could at the apartment.

As they drove along in silence, Race thought about thanking the PO for what he'd done—the suitcase, the sunglasses, this ride, and all that stuff—but the words just wouldn't come.

The Volvo rolled to a stop in front of Stan's house. Race grabbed his stuff from the back seat.

"Okay, pal. Have a good trip."

Race nodded.

"And please—remember about the chopping block."

He nodded again. Over a stupid tightness in his throat that he couldn't explain, he squeaked out, "I'll remember." Then he watched for a minute as the rusty Volvo drove off.

The front door of Stan's house opened before he could reach for the knob and there stood Ellie. He'd not seen her since the chance meeting in the hall at creep school.

Her eyes widened at the sight of his bruised face. "Oh my gosh!" Then, collecting herself, she stepped back to let him in. "I heard you got hurt. It looks really bad."

"Bad enough."

"Just set your things down and have a seat. Uncle Stan's almost ready." She tucked a dark strand of hair behind her left ear. "I'm working back in his office this morning."

Race had turned to stone. He couldn't move. He needed to say ... to explain ... But how can you explain what you don't know?

She hesitated a moment, waiting, her gentle hazel eyes studying his face, making him feel warm. Then she turned to go.

"Ellie."

She stopped.

"I'm sorry about the other day. I was ..."

"Rude?" She smiled.

He nodded and smiled back. "Good word. Sorry I was rude."

She stepped back toward him, so close that her clean, sweet smell wafted over him softly like the touch of kitten fur. "Race, I *knew* you attended school there. Before I ever went that day, I knew."

"You did?" Now he felt stupider than ever. "But you said..."

"It was supposed to come off coy. I guess I'm not very good at that kind of stuff. Being coy, I mean. Never even learned how to bat my eyelashes."

Race's mind was having trouble keeping up, trying to remember just what was said that morning.

She looked up at him. "Heck, why do you think I volunteered for the project in the first place?"

"You...?"

"Hoped I'd see you? Uh huh. Well, now the secret's out. Catcha later." And she was out the door and gone.

Race steered the Honda south along Highway 75. It'd taken about fifty miles for him to finally relax. Maneuvering the interstates wasn't exactly a piece of cake, but he'd made it without getting totally turned around, and now he was on a straight course to Lexington. No sweat.

Stan had gone over the details of the trip before they left that morning, explaining where they'd be going, where they'd stay, and the appointments he had lined up. "I used to live in this area," Stan told him as they reviewed the maps. "Still have lots of friends there."

By afternoon, they left the interstates for the lesser state roads.

"You ever been to Kentucky?" Stan asked him.

"Nope." Race learned a long time ago that shrugs, head shakes and nods make no impact when you're talking to a blind man. He was forced to answer. "My great-grandfather came from Kentucky." Race remembered his aunt telling him that once.

"That right?"

Stan waited a moment like he always did to see if Race would say more. Then, "What part? Do you know?"

"Dunno. Nobody talked much about it."

Race was wearing the cool sunglasses Goforth had given him. They were the kind he'd have picked out himself. Or swiped for himself—whichever. Strange that Goforth should do that. Goforth was a tough dude to figure out. At first Race had been sure the PO was bent on softening him up just so he could use him. That's what he'd been told they do. He wasn't so sure any more.

As the sun warmed the car, Stan as usual, began to nod off. White clouds spread across the sky in wavy riffles, like they'd been combed through by the wind. Race had never noticed clouds much before he'd started driving for Stan. No reason to look up, he guessed. But he noticed them now. A lot. When he watched clouds move and change shapes and colors, somehow, some way, it made him feel free.

They were headed for a farming community, Stan had told him, and would be staying with a family there. As they traveled south and west, the land rose and fell in repeated waves of rounded hills.

Could this be how normal people feel? Race wondered. Driving along in the family car for a little weekend jaunt? If so, he could probably get used to this.

For today, for this moment, he'd try to forget he was a kid on probation within inches of being tossed in the slammer, with a soused mom who locked him out at night, and a gang who was intent on wiping him out. Right now, he was going to enjoy himself.

Driving along in an almost dreamlike trance, he approached a small rise, and there on the other side lay endless stretches of soft green pasture dotted with fat, black cattle. Tight clumps of shade trees standing here and there were all that broke the solid greenness of the landscape— that and one clear blue pond fed by a trickling ravine. Clear reflections of graceful willows replicated greenness across the smooth surface of water.

Never had he ever seen anything so beautiful. The starkness of the black against the green was so incredibly beautiful, it took his breath away. So much so that he actually, audibly, gasped in surprise.

The sound startled his dozing companion.

"What is it, Race?" Stan straightened up. "Everything okay?"

Race had slowed the car now. There was no traffic to speak of. "Just so beautiful," he mumbled.

"Oh yeah. The countryside, you mean. Forgot to tell you about that. Pull over and stop. Can you? Is there a shoulder?"

"Naw. That's okay."

Stan reached out and touched Race's arm. "You really need to. You need to soak it in. Take it from one who wishes he had done more of that."

So he did. Race stopped the car on the shoulder and just looked at the green grass, the black cows, the towering trees, the glassy pond, and wished he could get out and run and run and run and never stop running. He'd pull off his shoes and feel the grass on his bare feet, and reach up and grab a strand of the combed clouds. He was sure he could do that.

"My brother always told me we lived in a world that was *brought to you by the color drab*," Race said in a near-whisper.

"That the brother who was murdered?"

"Yeah. Vince. Wish he could have seen this."

"Probably seemed that way, Race. I mean, like Vince said about the color drab. The truth of the matter is, each man colors his *own* world." He paused a moment. "Even me."

"What's a con-sert-o?"

The sun hung low in front of them and apricot rays broke in and through banks of layered clouds and splayed out in fingers of light above.

Stan cocked his head. "A what?"

Race had for so long wanted to ask the question and now he'd finally worked up enough courage to get the words out and now he had to ask it again. "A *con-sert-o*. C-o-n-c-e-r-t-o."

"Oh. You mean a *con-cher-to*. That's how it's pronounced."

"How the heck was I supposed to know?"

"By asking questions. That's how you find out things, Race. Ask or look it up."

"Okay, so what's a *con-cher-to*?"

"It's a composition for an entire orchestra, but with one instrument performing the solo part. That could be a horn, or violin..."

"Or piano?"

"Right. Or piano. So, may I ask what brought about this interest in concertos?"

"You played it at the Dotson's house. Then I heard it at the concert in Columbus."

Stan turned a little toward him. His dead eyes, which used to bug the heck out of Race, didn't bother him anymore. He wasn't sure when that had changed. "You remember the piece I played at the Dotson's?" He didn't disguise his surprise. "That was a long time ago."

"But I remember."

"And you heard it again at the concert?"

"Yep."

"And recognized it."

"Yep."

"What piece was it? Do you know the composer?"

"The name on the program was *Rack-something-or-other.*"

Stan chuckled. "*Rock.* It's pronounced *Rock-mah-nuh-noff.*"

"Looks like *Rack.*"

"Sergei Rachmaninoff. And it must have been his Piano Concerto No. 2. You have fine taste in music, my friend. The man was a musical genius."

"I got the CD in my backpack."

Stan cleared his throat. "You learned the name of the piece and the composer and then found the CD?"

"Is that okay?" This was the most Race had ever shared about much of anything with anyone since Vince died. Maybe Stan was making fun of him.

"Okay? Well, I guess it's okay. Just hard to believe you'd be tormenting me by my knowing it's in your backpack and I'm not getting to listen." He rubbed his chubby hands together like a little kid. "Stop the car and let's pop that puppy in the player."

Wingate Hill Farm, owned by Albert and Laura Embry, sat at the end of a long, curving, rutted drive lined with tall cedars bending gracefully in the wind. The house itself, situated at the base of a steep hill, was almost completely screened from view by sprawling shade trees, which were just now showing fringes of spring green. Behind the house were barns, sheds, grain bins, and a long, low building which Race was certain had to be the stable. The late afternoon sun transformed the white structures to a pinkish hue.

Stan had talked a little about the Embrys, telling Race how big their operation had been in years past, and how they'd cut back since their four sons were all grown and gone from home.

"Albert will probably always have a few head of cattle and enough horses to keep him busy," Stan had said as they came within a few miles of the farm. "I can't imagine him ever retiring."

Race attempted to navigate the ruts in the drive and still watch the horses running wild and free in the pasture that bordered the drive. Then he saw the colts—two of them— bouncing alongside their mothers on little legs that looked much too thin, too spindly, to hold up anything. They were so tiny. So frisky. So beautiful.

"See any stock?" Stan asked.

"Yeah. A few horses and a couple of little colts."

"Foals."

"Foals?"

"Colts are males. Fillies are female, and if you don't know for sure, then they're foals."

Race couldn't take his eyes off them. "Foals then. Two running alongside their mothers."

"Car must have spooked them."

Presently, as they neared the house, the horses slowed, then stopped and bent their magnificent heads down to graze while one foal nuzzled beneath its mother to nurse.

Race hoped against hope he'd get to touch one before they left.

CHAPTER 26

Albert's leathery face, browned by years of sun and wind, spread in a wide grin as he approached their car. He pulled off a sweat-stained cap to show a thick shock of gray hair that blew every which way in the soft spring breeze. The man's long legs were as bow-legged as every cowboy Race had ever seen on television.

Chickens that had scattered when the car approached, moved warily back, scratching in the gravel and making soft clucking noises. A couple of overgrown hound dogs got up from their resting spot on the porch to come check them out.

By the time Race got out and came around the car, Stan was out and the two men were hugging and greeting one another like long-lost friends.

"And who's this young fellow?" Albert came at Race with his large hand extended. Race grasped a hand that felt as though it were lined with steel rods.

"My trusty driver, Race Paloma. Race, meet Albert Embry."

Race had the presence of mind to at least say, "Pleased to meet you," while extricating his still-tender right hand from the vice-grip.

"Welcome to Wingate." Albert studied Race with deep-set, laughing, dark eyes shelved over with bushy white brows. "What happened to your face?"

"Just a little run of bad luck," Race managed to say.

Albert nodded and thankfully changed the subject. "You came at a busy time," he said. "Foaling time. Got one right ready to drop. Maybe tonight."

Race wasn't sure how to reply to that, so he opened the trunk and started unloading their suitcases, but he kept thinking about a foal being born.

Laura's kitchen was almost as big as Race's whole apartment back in Cincinnati. And did it ever smell good. Chicken was frying in two large skillets, and a pan of hot rolls had just emerged from the oven. On another cabinet sat two cobblers in deep cake pans with juices bubbling over the sides. One peach, one cherry.

Laura looked like a little kid clad in a shirt and pair of blue jeans. Her gray hair hung in loose curls around her face, and only there—in her cheeks and around her eyes— did lines and wrinkles give away her age. After she and Race were introduced, she came over to him, stood on tiptoe and kissed his cheek and gave him a hug.

"Welcome to Wingate Hill Farm, Race." Her eyes held that same laughing quality as her husband's. "Race," she repeated. "What an apt name to have here in Kentucky. Racing is what we're all about. Horse racing, that is."

Albert showed them their rooms upstairs. Stan took the one closest to the stairway and the bathroom. Albert offered Race the corner room with windows on two sides. "From there you can see almost all that's going on at Wingate," Albert told him.

After they were settled in, they sat down to more food than Race usually ate in a month. Every time his plate was empty, they passed him something else and he took more. He'd always liked fried chicken, but he'd never tasted any in his whole life that was as good as this. The rolls melted in his mouth, the mashed potatoes were fluffy as cotton candy, and the cobblers were rich and sweet with a flaky crust that crumbled under his fork.

As they ate, Albert and Laura caught Stan up on all the goings on of children and grandchildren, who, as Albert said, had "scattered to the four winds."

"I guess that's what we get for having four sons," Laura added with a laugh.

When they had slowed down their eating pace, and Laura was pouring mugs of coffee, Stan said, "Now Race, I pay for my keep by tuning their piano. You pay for your keep by helping Laura clean up the kitchen. Is that a deal?"

Albert laughed a deep, full laugh. "Goodness, Stan. You shoulda told the boy that before he ate. Then he'd at least have had a choice."

"For a meal that good," Race replied, "I guess I'd do most anything. Just point me in the right direction."

Later, as Laura showed him how to put leftovers in refrigerator storage dishes, and how to scrape off the dishes and stack them for her to put in the dishwasher, he realized that he had just replied to her with a reasonable and coherent answer. Maybe he *could* converse normally after all.

"You're gonna get out your fiddle and play for us, aren't you, Albert?" Stan asked when the four of them were settled in the spacious den.

Albert laughed. "And bore that there youngster out of his mind? I'm betting he's a heavy metal fiend."

Race was sitting comfortably and sleepily on the leather couch. He grinned at Albert and nodded. He couldn't deny it.

But Stan said, "You got this guy all wrong, Albert. He's gotten hooked on Rachmaninoff."

Laura turned from where she was straightening ranching magazines on the coffee table. "Rachmaninoff? My stars."

"Well then, that settles it," Albert said, pulling a black violin case down from a shelf beside the piano. "Heavy metal, classical, and now Bluegrass! Gotta love it all."

As Albert tuned up his fiddle, Laura went to the piano to accompany him. Albert's hands of steel moved that bow over the strings so fast it was a blur, and his feet bounced around light as feathers.

Albert and Laura ran from one tune to the next in rapid succession, making Race wonder how many songs they really knew. They'd probably played together for a lifetime. Race could hardly remember a moment in his life when he had felt any more whole, or more satisfied.

It was nearly eleven, after plenty of music and cups of coffee, when Stan announced he was ready to call it a day. "Our first appointment is at eight-thirty, Race."

"Want me to wake you?" Laura asked Race as she started clearing away the coffee mugs.

"I might need that, Mrs. Embry. Thank you."

"We're just home folk, Race. You can call me Laura."

"Okay. Laura."

"Hey, Race," Albert said. "Grab your jacket and come with me to the stable. I better check on that mare once more before I turn in."

Race's heart sped into overdrive. "Would it be all right?"

"Gabby's pretty gentle, but we'll let her be the final judge."

The stable held aromas that Race had never smelled before, and yet he felt he'd been inhaling them all his life. The warmth, the closeness, the softness of it all—exactly how he expected it would be. A couple of horses looked over stall doors and nickered. How many days would he be here? Four? Race's mind ran out ahead trying to think how many hours he could spend right here in the stable.

Albert led him to a stall where a mare lay on her side. She was breathing heavily.

"Well, well. Looks like you might just see a foal born tonight Race." Albert stepped inside. "You squeamish?"

Race shrugged. "I dunno."

"Good time to find out." Albert stepped to the mare's black head and knelt down, talking to her softly while stroking her head and her side. Motioning to Race, he said, "Step over here quietly and kneel down with me. Let Gabby see and smell you."

Race did as he was told, terrified that he might do something wrong. Albert guided his hand to the mare's flared nostrils and Race felt a puff of warm breath on his hand. "Now gently touch her nose. Let her know you're a friend."

Hesitantly, Race touched the silky softness of the nose. "Hello, Gabby. I'm Race," he whispered. "I won't hurt you."

"Good job," Albert told him. "Now come around here where we can assist."

Race's heart pounded in his throat with such force, he was sure Albert could hear it. At the mare's backside, they again knelt down side by side. Gabby's tail had been wrapped in a blue binding, obviously to keep it out of the way. Her shiny black sides were swollen balloon-like.

Suddenly, like in the blink of an eye, a gush of water spewed out and a tiny hoof emerged.

"Ah, watch close. This is going to happen fast."

Race didn't want to miss a thing. Next, a miniature head coated with white filmy stuff appeared. For a few minutes, everything was still. Albert kept patting the mare's side, talking soft words of encouragement to her. Gently, he pulled the filmy stuff off the tiny face. "Another few minutes..." he said. Then, "Put your hands here, Race." He motioned below the foal. "Like this."

Race had to scoot closer and did exactly as he was told.

"Now the next time she heaves, give a tug—real easy-like."

And suddenly there it was. Almost in his lap. An entire complete perfect little foal lying there in the straw. Race stared at it. The whole thing was like a dream. Albert worked quickly to pull the filmy stuff off the tiny body. "Grab those old towels there by the door, Race. Race? Over there by the door."

Albert then showed him how to rub the body and dry it off.

"It's a filly," Albert announced

"A little girl," Race said using his new-found knowledge. Then felt stupid.

"You got it," Albert said with a laugh. "And look, she has her mama's blaze."

"Blaze?"

"The white place on her nose. We call it a blaze. And three white stockings. Great coloring."

Gently he moved the foal closer to the mare's head and she began to lick her baby. Within a few minutes, both mare and foal were up on their feet, with the foal nosing around in an attempt to nurse. If there was anything in the entire world more beautiful than this, Race couldn't imagine what it might be. He was barely aware of Albert patting him on the shoulder telling him what a good attendant he'd been.

Lying in the upstairs corner bedroom that night, Race dreamed of black cattle in lush green pastures, and frisky black foals leaping and kicking up delicate hooves under a blue umbrella sky dotted with hazy bluish clouds. And in the midst of the beauty, he and Vince walked along a gurgling stream lined with lacy green willows, talking and making plans.

It was so real that when he woke up with a start, it took several moments to figure out where he was. So different. The quiet of the room. The quiet of the house. The quiet of the outdoors. "Vince," he whispered into the stillness.

He rose then and moved to the window. The entire place was bathed in a milky moonlight—trees, flower gardens, the giant cedars along the drive, the buildings, the stable. He knew he'd never get back to sleep. On the dresser lay Vince's lighter. He picked it up now and ran his thumb over the embossed lettering.

Deftly, he pulled on his jeans, shirt, and, carrying his shoes, tiptoed down the stairs and out the front door. He didn't even think about his jacket. He headed toward the stable, not bothering to pull on his shoes until the rocks along the path hurt his tender feet, forcing him to stop.

Opening the stable door, he inhaled that wonderful aroma of horses and hay and leather. He expected to have to feel his way around in the dark, but a few lights left burning lent a soft glow and he could see perfectly.

"Hello, Gabby. It's me again. Race."

The mare put her elegant head over the stall door and Race petted her nose and the side of her face.

"You are beautiful," he whispered. "The most beautiful thing I've ever seen."

He opened the stall door and there was the foal lying curled up in the corner. "Can I see your baby again? I'll be really gentle with her. I promise."

Closing the stall door behind him, Race moved slowly, cautiously, over to the filly and sat down in the soft straw beside her with his back against the wall, talking evenly to Gabby as he did so. He touched the tiny head, then a soft, soft ear. So exquisitely perfect. He leaned over and pressed his face against the furry warmth.

When the first sob sounded from deep inside him, Race didn't even know what it was. A sound so foreign, he didn't recognize it. That sob was followed by another and another and another. Presently, he was lying in the straw against the filly as the sobs wrenched and shook him to his very core.

He heard beautiful music, saw a conductor in white tie and tails leading a well-trained, highly disciplined orchestra. He saw Stan and Adelaide playing *She'll Be Coming 'Round the Mountain* and heard their silly laughter while he sat on the floor holding an orange cat. Yellow plates and yellow tumblers sat in a drain tray in a yellow kitchen. Warm cherry cobbler placed before him on a flowered plate. And there was Vince lying in a pool of red blood, the brown basketball rolling slowly away from the body. And the tidal wave of sobs kept coming till he felt his guts were being ripped out from inside him. He called out to Vince. Calling him back. And it hurt so bad. Worse than it had ever hurt before in all these months. All these long, dry, empty months. Nothing *nothing* could hurt this bad. "Vince, Vince. Why'd you have to go and die? Why'd you leave me behind? Why?"

After a time, Gabby came over and lowered her head and nuzzled her baby and then nuzzled the boy who lay beside her. Both slept.

CHAPTER 27

"Race? You in here, son?"

The voice sounded distant and far away. For a long moment, Race couldn't think where he was. He lifted his head to see the foal noisily nursing at Gabby's side. Then he saw Albert looking over the stall door.

"Never met a boy yet that didn't want to sleep with a new foal," he said smiling. "Matter of fact, I'd kinda like that myself. Except these old bones would make a heap of protest."

Race was sitting up now, brushing straw from his hair and clothes. He remembered the awful crying and hoped it didn't show on his face. When Nealia spent the night crying, her face always looked puffy.

"I didn't really mean to spend the night," Race answered. It hadn't occurred to him when he came in here in the wee hours of the morning that he might have been doing something wrong. Thankfully his host didn't appear upset.

Albert opened the stall door, stepped inside and petted Gabby's nose, then came around to check out the filly.

"Want to help me feed? If so, you'd better get inside and get cleaned up for breakfast."

Race nodded. "Just show me what to do."

"By the way, did I tell you what we've decided to name the little filly?

"Nope."

"Gabrielle's Race. Or Gabby's Race for short."

Race smiled. "You really mean it?" He knew he sounded like a little kid, but he didn't even care.

"I really mean it."

Stan's appointments took them into three surrounding counties—into homes, schools, churches, even one retirement center. Now that was a hoot. Race found himself talking easily to the residents who stood around to watch the piano tuner at work.

Each drive took them through magnificent scenes of rolling hills and sweeping valleys, of forests filled with lacy pink and white dogwood coming into bloom, cut through by clear bubbling streams. Race found he wanted to describe each scene to Stan. And he did. In fact, he could hardly stop talking—kind of like when he'd had too many beers. Vince always said that was the only time Race ever talked. It was that same light-headed, floaty feeling, but without the booze. He couldn't have explained it if he tried. He only knew it felt good. Really good. Almost like someone had taken a scrub brush to his insides. Every time he stepped out of the car, he wanted to take a deep breath of the clean fresh air—and he did, even though his tender ribs still complained.

They worked hard together, putting in as many appointments as the day would allow. The evenings meant laughter around the Embrys' dinner table. Albert could tell tall tales one after the other without taking a breath, until finally

Laura would tap his arm gently and say, "Now, now, Albert. That's enough. You're boring our company to tears." But she was wrong. Race never tired of hearing Albert talk. Especially when he talked about horses.

Goforth called only once while they were away. He asked how things were going and Race said, "Cool, man. Everything here is really cool."

Goforth asked a couple questions about his schoolwork, and Race assured him he was keeping up. Then he said, "Goforth?"

"Yeah."

"I helped deliver a foal."

"You what?"

"A foal. You know. A baby horse. I helped deliver it."

"Well, Race Paloma. I guess that's about the best news I've heard in a long time. A very long time."

Race wasn't exactly sure what that comment meant, but it sounded good.

Each morning brought them closer to the end of the visit—something Race didn't want to think about. On the afternoon of the last day, Stan tuned Laura's piano. Since Race wasn't needed, he spent the afternoon in the stable. Albert showed him how to groom the horses, hang up the hay nets, and muck out the stalls. Who'd have thought that it could be fun to shovel horse poop?

At one point, Race stumbled into a question he'd been wanting to ask. "Albert, did you know Stan before he..." But he got flustered and couldn't finish.

"Before the accident?" Albert completed the thought easily. "No I didn't." He spread fresh straw on the floor of one of the stalls while Race watched. "Wish I had. And you're probably wondering how he happened to know all of us here in Kentucky."

Race nodded. It was exactly what he was wondering.

"It was Laura actually. She felt our community needed a local piano tuner—which was true—so she wrote to the *Emil Fries School of Piano Technology* in Vancouver, asking for applicants and Stan answered our petition. We were exactly what he needed during those early years of his healing.

"It's tough enough to lose your sight," Albert went on, "let alone being crippled and losing your family all in one fell swoop. But that's what happened to Stan. You can't hardly tell about the legs. His limp's almost gone now."

Albert leaned heavily against the stall railing, pulled off his cap, smoothed back the unruly mop of hair and replaced the cap. "Course he blessed the socks off all of us as well. He was active in about every community event we ever had, the schools included. The guy is nuts about kids. But I guess you know that."

Race hadn't really thought about it. But he thought about it now. "Why'd he ever leave here?"

Albert laughed. "He sorta outgrew us. Plus his nephew, Ryan, wanted him living near them, especially after Stan's older brother—Ryan's dad—passed away. The family thing, you know."

Race thought about Ellie and Warren and understood. They needed their uncle close by.

"When he moved away, he promised he'd come back every year and take care of us. He's been true to his word." Albert grabbed a nearby pitchfork. "We got one more stall. Let's get to it." With a shake of his head, he added, "It's been good to have a little help around here. I surely do appreciate it. Just want you to know."

Race smiled and nodded.

Race had the car loaded before breakfast the next morning. When it was time to leave, Laura hugged him and again planted a kiss on his cheek. Albert gave him one of those steel-rod handshakes that only he could give, then looked at him with his dark penetrating eyes. "Now son, know that you're welcome in our home any time. Understand?"

Race nodded. How do you tell someone *thank you* when words sound so trite? Those two little words could never in a million years say what he was feeling. He blinked against the stinging in his eyes, quickly grabbed for his sunglasses and got into the car.

Nights alone in the upstairs bedroom of Wingate Hill Farm had given Race space to think. Back home, he always had *time* to think, but no space. The closeness of it all suffocated good thoughts and good dreams. During his thinking times at Wingate, he determined he would get up the courage to ask Stan the question he'd wanted to ask for weeks now. But they were more than halfway home and still he hadn't asked.

As the fence posts, and the farms, and the pasturelands whipped by them, the knots in Race's neck and shoulders returned, and the burning in his stomach awakened just like before. *Same ole same ole.* If only he never had to go back.

Stan was again talking about his boyhood home in Nebraska, and especially about his father, how strict, yet good and kind he was. One story led to another and was beginning to wear on Race's fraying nerves. "You make the guy sound so perfect." His voice sounded sharp. "Nobody's *that* good."

"Oh now there's where you're wrong, Race," Stan replied. "There are many, many good people in this old world. You just haven't had a chance to meet them all yet."

"Oh yeah right. Lotsa good old dudes—like the drunk kid who took out your wife and kid."

A heavy silence filled the car.

Race figured if he was in this deep, he just as well ask his question. "So how did you feel when you lost your family? And your sight? Huh? Tell me how it felt." He hated the way the words dripped with sarcasm. This wasn't the way he'd planned to ask. But the anger overpowered and won.

"Oh, *and* my business," Stan put in. "Don't forget that one. Because I lost it all, Race. I lost everything that ever made my life worth living."

"So? How did you feel?"

Stan's voice went soft. "Mad as hell, Race. Madder than that even. More angry than any person could ever be in one lifetime. I let it eat me alive."

Funny, but that wasn't the answer Race expected. Too naked. Too bare. Too open. But he nodded. *More angry than any person could ever be in one lifetime.* Now that made perfect sense.

Race plunged on. "You don't act mad now. What happened?"

"I told you the other day. Remember?"

"You told me? What?"

"Every man colors his own world. I finally decided I didn't like the color of hate and anger." He gave a deep, raspy sigh unlike anything Race had ever heard from the man. "I guess you could say Race, that I didn't want my life to *be brought to you by the color drab.* There are just too many other colors to choose from."

Fortunately, Race needed to stop for gas and the subject was closed.

Nealia, true to her ditzy self, never remembered a thing about the night she screamed at him, hit him, and then locked him out. In fact, when he arrived home, she thanked him for taking care of Vince's things, saying she could never have done it alone. Race could only shake his head. The never-ending, merry-go-round of crazy-making. He was sick to death of all of it.

He tried to recapture that wonderful clean scrubbed feeling he had at Wingate, but he couldn't. It was gone. Gone as though it'd never even happened. If only he could get to the hideaway and have at least a tiny bit of the peace and freedom he'd experienced at Wingate. But the risk was too great. So much more was at stake now.

Later Race would wonder how he ever heard the noise at the living room window since he was asleep back in his own bedroom. All he knew was that something had awakened him and it hadn't been a dream. A glance at the clock told him it was only two. Too early to be his mother coming in. He lay there a minute listening. Maybe the sound had come through the thin walls to where Marcus was sleeping next door. Then he heard it again. A click. A tap. Maybe a mouse in the kitchen?

Jumping up he hurried out to the living room. He stood there a moment shivering in his under shorts and t-shirt, listening. When an object hit the living room window, he jumped.

Slowly he moved toward the window. There was nothing on the fire escape. He pressed his face against the window and looked down. There in a heap lay Pinky getting ready to throw another piece of glass or rock or anything he could grab. His face was horribly bruised and swollen, his shirt and jeans were torn and bloody.

Race unlocked the window and threw it open. "Pinky."

"Can't make it up there, Race. You gots to help me."

In a matter of seconds Race had pulled on his clothes and was on the ground. "Good God, Pinky. What happened? Who did this?"

Pinky gave a lopsided grin through bloodied lips. From his pocket, he pulled out a purple bandana and waved it limply. "I is in, man. I's a Dragon. I's the leader now."

"Dumb stupid fool. I oughta leave you out here to rot."

"Aw Race. You can't do that, bro. What you tell Wynn?"

"You got any broken bones?"

"I dunno." The low moan that escaped his lips sounded like a wounded animal. "Ain't nothin' in me that don't hurt, Race. Nothin'."

Race knew that feeling well. "I gotta get you inside. If I lift you, think you can grab the fire escape railing and pull yourself up?"

They gave it a try, but Pinky was too weak and in too much pain to even reach up, and Race was afraid he'd hurt him worse. Race had seen lots of kids who'd been jumped in, but he'd never seen anyone beaten this badly. Waves of hot anger rolled and boiled inside him. The worst part was, he didn't know who to be mad at—empty-headed Pinky for allowing this to happen, or the merciless Dragons who beat up a skinny, defenseless, out-numbered kid that was half their size.

"I'm gonna try to pull down the bottom ladder so we can get you up. Haven't done that for years." He reached up for it and pulled hard. "Rusted." He pulled again and it gave a little. "Don't want to take you up the front stairs if we can help it."

On the third try, the aged rusted hinges broke free. Now came the work of getting his injured friend up the ladder. Race put Pinky in front and let him rest his body back against Race's chest, and thus they crept slowly up, resting every few minutes.

Pinky stumbled through the living room window, crawled on all fours to the couch and there he collapsed.

Race brought a wet cloth and antiseptic from the bathroom.

"So why're you here, big man? Why're you not celebrating with your new brothers? Shouldn't there be some big wild celebration? They finally got what they wanted."

Pinky sucked in his breath hard as Race touched his swollen face with the cool cloth. Both eyes were nearly swollen shut and turning dark purple. No telling how long he'd lain behind the building. Or how long it took to drag himself there from wherever the beating took place. "I thought so too. But they say to get outta there." He had to rest between words. "I 'posed to meet 'em in the morning. Tomorrow I gets my jacket, Race. My purple jacket."

"I'll kill 'em. I swear I'll take that Piston apart and spread the pieces all over OTR."

"I done it myself, Race. I done it all myself. Got sick of hearing Hawk and his homies dissin' me all the time. Toon say to me, 'You sick of his dissin'? Show that boy. You let them Dragons jump you in. Then you be over Hawk when he come in. And 'sides all that, them Dragons be watching you back bigtime.' Toon kept saying that."

Pinky winced and groaned as Race doctored the cuts and scrapes best he could. God only knew if he was bleeding internally. "Toon has rocks in his head. Why'd you listen to that moron?"

"Sound good to me, Race. Real good. Savvy even agree. 'Do it boy,' he say. 'Show 'em all up.' Then he say, 'Show 'em you's a man.'"

The swelling anger made Race's throat go tight. "Why are they so all-fired hot on you being a Dragon anyway? What do they care?"

"Can't figure it out, Man, but they something there."

"Something there, what? What do you mean? Talk straight."

Pinky drew in a painful breath—probably broken ribs. "I seen 'em be with Piston sometimes."

"Toon and Savvy?"

Pinky nodded, then he made like he was going to get up off the couch. Race gently pushed him back down. "Idiot! What do you think you're doing?"

"Gotta get outta here 'fore your mama get home. And I gotta go tell Hawk. He ain't never gonna believe this. Can't wait to see his stupid face."

"You're not leaving here tonight. You'll have plenty opportunity to show off your war wounds. I'll bed you down in my bed and I'll take the floor. We'll close the door and Mom'll never know." Then he added, "She'll probably be soused, anyway."

To Race's great relief, Pinky gave no more argument. And Race was right. He had Pinky up and out the door before Nealia awakened the next morning. But not before a phone call had come for Race. A call he never expected. It was Sharkey.

Thankfully, Pinky was in the bathroom admiring his bruises when the phone rang in the kitchen. Race wasn't sure how he would have handled it had Pinky been standing there listening.

Sharkey wasn't one to mince words. "Kid," he said, coming right to the point, "you been hanging out in one of my junked travel trailers?"

The question hit him square in the gut. He was too stunned to even think up a good lie. "Yeah," came the soft reply.

"Sorta thought it was you. Don't know why. By the look of the stuff, I knew it had to be a kid."

His private place. Someone else had seen his secret hideaway. He felt betrayed. Violated. Never mind that it *was* Sharkey's property to begin with.

"I suppose you don't think I ever go back there, but I try to walk the place every few months or so, just to check it out."

Race still hadn't said anything. His one last shimmering soap bubble of hope...

"Hate to do this kid, but I can't let you keep your stuff out there. Too big a liability. Understand?"

Race must have mumbled something because Sharkey went on. "You know, somebody might be chasing after you and want to get to you bad enough to put a bullet into Monty. You don't want that do you?"

Race's brain twirled and tumbled. He'd never thought of that. Somebody shooting good old Monty Mutt. His buddy.

"Plus with all them candles and stuff you could start a fire out there, and I can't afford that." Another long pause. "I saw the doggie treats, so I knew you figured out Monty's a pussycat in disguise." Race almost had to smile at that remark.

"So just come on out to the shop. You can load your stuff in my pickup. I'll help you take it home."

What could he do? Just like all the other messes in his life, the decision had been taken completely out of his hands.

"And Race. Just so's you'll know, I'm having all that fallen razor wire repaired. Shoulda done that a long time ago. No hard feelings I hope?" Not waiting for an answer, he said, "It's for your safety and mine. Now when'll you be out to get that stuff?"

"In a few days, I guess."

"Call first."

"Okay."

Poof. Just like that, his private little sanctuary was gone. Just like when Uncle Dutch was taken away and never returned. Just like the moment Vince was gunned down. Just like the hundred dollars Sharkey had given him last fall. Just like his freedom when the cell door slammed shut. Poof. Poof. Poof. His entire life equaled a gazillion *poofs*.

CHAPTER 28

Pinky emerged from the bathroom limping, moving like an old man, but raring to go—the purple bandana tied in a valiant do-rag around his head. His face looked like he'd run it through a meat grinder.

"Let's split, bro," he said. "I gots people to see. You coming, right?" He squinted up at Race through puffy eyes. "Hey man, what's up? You whiter than a whitey."

"Nothing that concerns you."

Out on the street, Race said, "You go find your playmates, Pinky. Get your precious jacket. You don't need me there. I need to find Toon. Where's he been hanging lately?"

"Playground, park, market, a empty alley. Toon, he be all over OTR. Just walk, you find him."

"I thought he hung tight with Savvy."

"Sometimes. Sometimes not."

At Fifteenth Street, they split. The Dragon's pad was somewhere over on Liberty. Race watched Pinky limp away. If they hurt him again, Race knew he'd have to get a knife and take them on. Whatever it took.

He found Toon stretched out on a picnic table in the park nearest the Music Hall. Probably sleeping off a high.

Race took a paper cup he'd picked up while coming through the market and filled it at the water fountain. Standing up on the seat of the picnic table, towering over Toon, he poured the water straight into his ugly face. Toon sat up sputtering, shaking his head, his dreadlocks flying in all directions.

"Race? You punk. What you do that for?"

"Toon, you're a royal scumbag."

"What I do, man? I ain't even laid eyes on you for weeks. I got no beef with you."

"You sent a skinny little kid into a lion's den, that's what you did. I suppose you think that's funny. Why don't you let 'em jump *your* ugly ass in? Why you gotta pick on Pinky?"

As the words tumbled out, they served to fuel his pressure-cooker of rage. He reached down, grabbed a handful of Toon's shirt front and yanked hard, snapping Toon's neck back. "How about if I give you a little taste of what Pinky got last night?"

At that moment, a voice sounded behind him. "Race Paloma. You leave poor old Toon alone."

Race shoved Toon backward, nearly knocking him off the table. He turned to see Savvy sauntering toward them. He stopped a few feet away, his feet apart and his beefy hands on his hips. "Now what's got you all hot and bothered today?"

"As if you didn't know."

"You all concerned for your pink little homie? Why's that got you all upset? He got exactly what he wanted. He's happy. You should be happy, too."

Savvy's reference of Pinky's lighter skin made Race even more angry. He jumped off the table and faced Savvy. "Why'd you have to egg him on? You knew he'd do exactly what you said."

Savvy laughed. "Right on. That baby aims to please. Just the kind we like."

"We? Who's we?"

Savvy dropped his hands and took a couple steps forward. "Race, you need to come up to my place for a while. I got someone you'll want to talk to."

"You don't have anyone I want to talk to."

"You're wrong there. But I'll let you decide." He turned to go. Then added, "You know Toon's not worth your time."

"Hey, bro," Toon said in a bewildered whine. "What you mean by that?"

Savvy ignored him. To Race he said, "You coming or not?"

There was something about Savvy that Race despised, but maybe if he went along, he could find out more. More what, he wasn't sure.

Race hadn't been in Savvy's apartment since his shoplifting snafu. It hadn't changed, except for the fact that four or five guys Race had never seen before were lounging around the place. With a wave of his muscle-bound arm, Savvy sent them off into a back bedroom.

As Race sat in the bright, open living room, he remembered their first visit and how Wynn just sat there, silently letting the pack be run over by this low-life outsider. But immediately following that thought, Race felt the aching pang of missing his close friend. Was it because Wynn was so closely linked to Vince?

Race refused the beer Savvy offered. "You said you had someone for me to talk to. I don't need your beer to do that."

"You know, Race," he said with a half-smile, "I've missed you. Your probation about over? I understand you been free-wheeling all over the place, driving around some old blind guy."

The reference to Stan made Race bristle. But isn't that what he himself had called his employer only a few weeks ago?

Just then, the phone rang making Race jump. Savvy picked up a cordless off the table beside his chair. "Yeah? Okay. Uh huh. He's right here." Handing the phone to Race, he said, "It's for you."

Race hesitated. "What the heck...?"

"Take it." Savvy waggled the phone at him.

"Hello?"

"Race, that you?" It was Wynn.

For a moment Race couldn't speak. He glanced over at Savvy who wore a disgusting smirk.

"Hey bro," Race said softly wishing he could take the phone outside. "What's up?"

"This call be so far off their rule book—if I gets caught I gets slammed bigtime. So I gotta talk fast. I knows all about Pinky, bro. It don't matter now, what gone on before. Don't matter. Understand?"

Race didn't understand anything. The room seemed to be slowly spinning, making his stomach roll.

Wynn hurried on. "What Pinky done was plain dumb. You and me both know that. But he done it and it's over. You gotta get in there now and take care of him."

"In there?"

"Race. Think. *Think.* I ain't there. Somebody gotta watch him. You the onliest one, man. It be all up to you."

Race couldn't believe what he was hearing. Everything inside him wanted to scream. To slam the phone on the floor. It wasn't Race's fault Wynn landed in the slammer. He did it to himself—just like Pinky did this thing with the Dragons all by himself. Why'd they want to dump it all on Race's head?

The silence hung heavy between them. Then Wynn said, "It ain't all so bad. They's some okay dudes in that Dragon bunch."

"But Vince said..."

"But Vince *nothing*." Wynn's voice went so loud it hurt Race's ear. "Don't give me no Vince stuff, man. Vince ain't here. Ain't here. Remember?"

The words cut Race like a clean knife. "I know that."

"Then live like it. We is here. We is now. Things is changing in OTR. Need you to give me your word, bro. They be easy on you. I knows that for sure."

Race wanted to know how Wynn knew all this, but he was in no position to ask. He wanted to say, "If you'd seen Pinky, you'd be killing, not joining," but he couldn't say that either with Savvy sitting there. Why did Savvy set this up? And how?

"You hearing me?" Wynn said. "Talk to me man. Give me your word. You want to do something for Vince? Then do this for his homie. And for Pinky. Tell me I got your word."

Race released a heavy sigh. Suddenly, he felt old, tired, and beaten. What was the use? Wynn was right. OTR *was* changing. How long did he think he could escape the pressure? The Dragons were growing stronger every day. Why fight it? "You got it," Race said with a total lack of conviction.

"You won't regret it, bro. I gotta go now." And the line went dead.

Savvy reached over for the phone. "Wise decision, my good man." His eyes narrowed. "Somebody'll be in touch to set up the time."

Race stood to his feet. "I'm not doing this for you, dude. This is my decision. *I'll* decide the time *and* the place."

Before slamming out the door, he heard Savvy yell, "Better not wait too long!"

Well there you go. More *poofs*. No more job. No more Stan. No more Honda. No more out-of-town trips. No more school with its neat computer lab. And, he realized with more sadness that he thought possible, *no more Ellie.*

For several hours, he wandered aimlessly around OTR not knowing where to go, what to do. Would he tell Stan good-bye? Or just drop out of sight? And how long would it take Goforth to catch up with him? *Move over, Wynn.*

Late in the afternoon, his wandering took him closer to his apartment. He just as well go home. Shut out the world and sleep. If he stayed on the streets, he might just strangle somebody.

At the top of the stairs, he could hear laughter. Nealia's laughter. Strange. His mother seldom laughed these days.

He opened the door to see an overgrown Neanderthal he'd never laid eyes on before. The man had planted his wide backside in their overstuffed chair. Nealia was perched on his lap and his hand was up her blouse. The place reeked of cheap whiskey. Nealia's laughter trailed off as she looked around at Race.

"Hey little darlin'," she said, her voice unnaturally high and giddy. "Come on in here and meet my new friend, Carlisle. I met him while you were away." She pulled Carlisle's hand out of its resting place. Neanderthal man looked at Race with dull, glazed eyes.

"Got awful lonely without you here, little darlin'. You know? Awful lonely. I didn't know how much I'd miss you, but I really did miss you. But Carlisle here came into Malone's and we got to be friends. Hit it off fast, didn't we Carlisle."

Neanderthal grunted.

As she blathered on, Race walked slowly in their direction.

"I'm very happy to meet Carlisle," Race said through clenched teeth. "Looks like he was just leaving." He took hold of his mother's arm in an attempt to pull her up but she pulled back hard. Her strength surprised him, but she always was stronger when she'd had a few drinks.

"Now Kyle darlin', you cut that out," she whined.

Neanderthal didn't change expression. "I don't remember you being the one what invited me in."

"Get out of here."

"Race, don't be that way now. This is my company."

The rage that had been building inside Race ever since last night hit its boiling point. This time he grabbed his mother by both her arms. Taking her by surprise, he turned and threw her onto the couch. Neanderthal did nothing to hold her, but in a flash he was on his feet—his very large feet.

Race's anger shut out any thought of reason as he plowed into the giant, which was akin to attacking an elephant. He got in a few slams that jarred his arms all the way to his teeth. Before he knew what had hit him he was in a half-nelson that made him wonder if he would ever catch another breath of air. Nealia screamed for Carlisle to please not hurt her *darlin'*.

"Now then, Sonny," Neanderthal said in his deep, gravelly voice, "why don't you be a good little boy and go outside and play till I make up my mind to leave. You catch my drift?"

Race gave as much a nod as the clinch would allow. As soon as he did, he was free, gasping for breath as he stumbled toward the door. He went out slamming it as hard as he could. If he'd only had his knife...

By nightfall, Race had made up his mind. He was out of here. He still had a little cash. A freight train would probably work best. He could be a long way from this place in a few short hours.

He spent the rest of the day moving from one darkened video arcade along Vine to another, staying off the streets as much as possible since it was past his curfew. He had no way of knowing when Neanderthal would be gone. If Vince had been there, his brother would have splattered the guy. Vince knew the moves to put on big guys and bring them to their knees. Race never bothered to learn. Now he wished he had. Too late now, but he still wished he had.

A strange air of restlessness hung in the streets. There was always a sense of restlessness in OTR, but more so tonight. Knots of loud, agitated blacks moved along here and there. In one of the arcades Race overheard sketchy details of what had enflamed the anger: some black kid had gotten himself shot and killed by police in some dark alley off Republic Street by trying to resist arrest.

Nothing new there. Every dude he knew in OTR ran when the cops pursued, no matter their color, no matter their age, no matter what they were doing. Race had learned it from little up—it was better to take your chances and get the heck out of the way.

CHAPTER 29

Around three in the morning, when Race climbed in their apartment window, the place was empty. He shut himself in his bedroom, securing the door with a chair shoved under the knob just in case Neanderthal returned. Nealia might have given her new friend a key. It'd be just like a brainless thing she'd do.

For a long time, he tossed and turned, unable to sleep. He felt like a rat caught in an ever-shrinking maze. The plan to jump a freight—which a few hours ago had sounded like the perfect answer—now seemed a stupid move. After all, he was now a kid with a record. It'd only be a matter of time before he was tracked down, no matter where he ran. How long could he hide? And where?

When he did fall asleep, he dreamed of blazing guns and flying bullets while he was trapped, alone and terrified, in a dark alley.

He awakened to the jangling of the phone out in the kitchen. It took him a minute to get the chair out of the way, the door opened, and make his way down the hall. Grabbing the phone, he mumbled hello in a sleepy voice.

He heard Stan's voice greeting him from the other end. That was a surprise since his employer seldom if ever called. It'd been only two days since he'd last seen Stan and yet it seemed more like a million years. The sound of Stan's voice had a strange, calming effect on Race.

"Hey there, Race. I called to tell you my good news. I've been asked to tune at the Music Hall. Remember how I told you I'd love to get that chance? Well, it's finally come my way."

"When?"

"Tomorrow. Tuesday. Around three or so, they said."

"Cool."

"I knew you'd be happy for me. Their regular guy is sick and a concert is coming up."

Race let himself imagine for a moment what it'd be like to have something to look forward to. Something to get excited about. Even straining at it, his mind just couldn't get there.

"We only have two appointments," Stan said. "The first is out west of town. That'll give us plenty of time to eat lunch and get to the Music Hall." He was quiet a moment. "I'll see you in the morning then."

"See you."

As Race hung up, he realized what time it was. He'd never been late for creep school and he didn't want to start now—on his last day. While he was still in Kentucky, he'd been anxious to find out how well he'd kept up. Now it didn't really matter. He made up his mind he'd have this last day of school. After that, he'd have his last day with Stan on Tuesday—finally getting to see the inside of the Music Hall. After that he'd either be jumped into the Dragons, in jail on his way to juvie, or on a freight headed out of town. And he wasn't really sure which would be worse.

All through the day, Race felt as though he were swimming underwater with everything and everyone moving in fuzzy, wavery shapes around him. His head throbbed and pounded with pressure. Later he couldn't remember talking to a single person at creep school, although he knew people had spoken to him. The pride he thought he'd feel at having kept up while in Kentucky turned hollow. A joke. What was the use of any of it? His mother had been right all along—nothing good could ever last in OTR.

That night he sat on the couch till long after midnight, mindlessly staring first at the television, then at the pink and green lights doing strange things to the room. Sirens were a natural part of living in OTR, but tonight one was screeching almost every fifteen minutes. Race shut it all out. It didn't concern him. What'd he care if they were all out there killing one another?

He knew he should be sorting things out. Planning. If he did leave town, he should be deciding when to go and what to take. Instead, everything inside him had shut down. Like someone had flipped the *off* switch. He didn't even care if Neanderthal came back. Part of him almost wished he would.

He must have dozed a couple of time because he didn't remember hearing Nealia come in. But he was awake and moving early. He'd at least have one last day with Stan.

Their morning appointment was a new client, a piano teacher who lived in a nice house in the burbs. After clearing off the instrument, opening it up and laying out Stan's tools, Race stood close by to watch. Usually he found a comfortable chair and got out of the way, but not today. Today he felt a strange drawing to stay close by and watch as Stan worked: his sensitive fingers moving expertly from string to string, his mouth moving as he counted. He always cocked his head a little to the right to listen as the tuning hammer tightened or loosened pegs.

Starting in the middle, Stan brought one string to perfect pitch—using the tuning fork as his guide. From there he moved all the way up, then all the way down the sounding board, adjusting every key to the pitch of the first. At intervals, he tapped the tuning fork on the edge of the piano, then held it to his ear to listen for the pitch. Stan worked in slow, methodical movements with no wasted motion.

"Every string is tuned to the first key I tune," Stan once told him. "If that one key is off pitch, then every single key in the entire eighty-eight will be off pitch."

Race remembered the day Stan had said that. They were driving through one of those beautiful valleys in Kentucky on a sun-splashed day.

"It's rather like life itself," Stan went on. "If I base my life on values and principles that are off pitch, or out of tune, then every facet of my life will also be out of tune." Then he said, "No one *has* to be out of tune, Race. Tune your life to the principles that are right, fair, and honorable."

But the words made little sense. Because it didn't seem to Race that it mattered much what *he* did—ever. He could only take what life handed him—which was pretty dismal stuff. But later, during times when he was all alone, he mulled over what Stan had said, trying to make sense of it.

When you grow up on the streets, as Race had, you develop a gut feeling when something's about to come down. He'd felt it the evening before when there were so many sirens screaming, but he ignored it. He should have turned on the news, but he didn't. Wallowing in his own problems had drowned out his inner gut feeling. Had he listened, it would have warned him, as it had so many times before.

They were on their way to the Music Hall deep in Over-the-Rhine. By the time Race reached Fourteenth and Vine, the telltale signs were everywhere. The riot had already swelled into mob violence in broad daylight. Large crowds of angry disgruntled blacks moved in undulating waves along the streets, some with bandanas tied around their faces like he'd seen once in a low-grade western movie. Hastily scrawled signs shouted out their anger: "No justice; no peace," "No more black blood," "Cincinnati cops: stop killing black people!" But the voices shouted even louder—a virtual chorus of fiery rage.

Now Race noticed the lazy plumes of pale gray smoke billowing up from several different areas. Ahead he watched as random individuals stepped in and out of stores through the broken-out front windows, staggering beneath the weight of armloads of free loot. High-style shoplifting the easy way. Not a cop in sight.

Now Stan sensed it. "What is it, Race? What's happening?"

"I shouldn't have come down here. It's outta control."

Race was frozen, staring in unbelief at the bizarre scenes unfolding before him. To his right, in a recessed doorway stood Savvy, his arms folded across his broad chest, his legs apart like a soldier at parade rest. He was flanked by two men, one white, one black, both dressed in expensive three-piece suits.

Cars lined ahead of them down Vine Street, also caught unawares in the melee, were slowing and stopping. Suddenly, the crowd—as if of one mind—turned their attention from roaming and looting to converging on the slowed cars.

Jerking from his trance, Race wrenched the wheel to turn and gas it and make good their escape. But he was two seconds too late.

The windshield exploded on the passenger side as the first rock found its mark. Stan's head flung backward from the blow. He groaned, and grabbed his head as blood streamed between his fingers. Screams of "Get whitey, get whitey, get whitey" sounded like a wild, eerie, inhuman chant as the crowd closed in on the car, bashing windows with ball bats and table legs. Now the doors were open and Race saw Stan being dragged out by dozens of angry hands.

Race fought like a mad man against blows from sticks and fists, screaming Stan's name over and over. He had to stay on his feet. He had to get to Stan. He had to.

It seemed he struggled relentlessly for hours, staving off the blows, but actually it was only a few short minutes. Suddenly someone was pushing and shoving toward him, yelling his name. *Two* someones. Hawk and Pinky. Reaching his side, they made a wall of defense, shouting at the mob to leave him alone. "He's a friend," Pinky yelled. "He lives here!" While Pinky yelled and waved his arms, Hawk tried to pull Race away to safety behind the car.

"C'mon man. Let's get you outta here. No place for a whitey, no matter who he be."

But Race yanked his arm free. "Let me go! Stop it. I've gotta help Stan."

"You see that crowd? They wipe you out like a ant, bro. What you care about no rich, blind man nohow."

"Yeah, man, what do it matter?" Pinky was now standing behind his cousin, his purple do-rag tied around his neck.

Heading back toward Stan and the mob, Race yelled back, "Pinky, call an ambulance. Remember, you owe me."

He pushed his way back through the angry crowd, now beginning to thin out. Their interest in a limp, white man on the asphalt was waning. Seeing Stan lying there motionless exploded Race's anger as he flattened a couple of stragglers, discouraging the rest. They left him alone in search of easier prey.

Even before he knelt down, he knew his friend was in bad shape. *His friend.* Suddenly he knew. This man *was* his friend. Perhaps the truest friend he'd ever had.

Leaning down close, he said, "Stan. It's me, Race. Can you hear me?"

Race couldn't tell if the low groan was an answer, or an expression of pain. They'd beaten Stan to a pulp. Pulling off his own shirt, Race used it to gently dab at the worst of the bleeding.

"Hang on, Stan. Help's coming. You're gonna be all right. You've been through worse than this, man. It's gonna be okay." Blinking back burning tears, he said, "Don't leave me, Stan. Please don't leave me."

CHAPTER 30

The television in the ICU waiting area blared out the gory play-by-play of the riot, which was concentrated right in the middle of Race's own neighborhood. The streets he'd known nearly all his life—now in total disarray. He sat staring at the scenes as they unfolded, shivering in the cold until Anita finally noticed and asked a nurse to bring him a blanket.

When Ryan, Anita, Ellie, and Warren first joined him at the hospital, they tried to force him to see a doctor, but he refused. "I'm okay," he insisted. When they brought it up again, he just shook his head. They also insisted that he eat something. He refused that too.

Outside, it grew dark. Only one family member could be in Stan's room at a time and Warren refused to go in. The three others took turns throughout late afternoon and early evening. At around seven-thirty, Ellie came out of Stan's room, walked over to Race and sat down on the couch beside him.

"Uncle Stan's asking for you."

Race looked at her. "For me?"

She laid her hand on his arm. "For you."

Part of him wanted to run to Stan's side. The other part was terrified. He stood up on shaky legs.

"You can't stay long," Ellie said softly.

He nodded.

The room was dim and reeked of acrid hospital smells. Stan was hooked up to every weird machine imaginable, his skin looked pale, washed out.

"That you Race?"

Race swallowed hard. "It's me." He moved to Stan's side.

"Ryan's told me... It's pretty bad in your neighborhood." His voice was weak, his breathing labored.

"It's bad."

"Your mother... She okay?"

"I called her earlier. She's staying inside."

Stan gave a slight nod.

It was quiet a moment. There was so much Race wanted to say. All the words were spinning around inside his head.

"Want to thank you, Race. Loved having you as my driver—and good friend."

"Stan?" He reached down for the man's hand, the one with no needles in it. "Stan, do you want to see me now? What I mean is, I *want* you to see me now."

Stan mouth formed a slight smile. "Race, my boy. I already *know* what you look like—inside and out." He took a long slow breath. "But lean down here."

Race leaned closer to allow the sensitive, gentle fingers to travel over his forehead, eyes, cheeks, ears, hair, chin, then back to the wet cheeks.

"Don't cry, Race. Everything's going to be all right."

"It's never gonna be all right," he choked out the words, "if you're not all right."

"Not true. Not true." He paused a moment to get his breath. "You're so close to finding that perfect pitch, Race. So close."

"But I need you to help me. Help me find it."

Stan shook his head ever so slightly. "Your heart knows. You have a gentle heart. I knew that from the start. Trust it, Race. Trust it." Their hands were still clasped. Stan squeezed his hand ever so softly.

Just then a nurse stepped in. "Time to leave now," she said just over a whisper.

"I have to go now," Race said. But Stan didn't release his hand.

"Your brother, Vince, told you *drab. Brought to you by the color drab,* you said." Another slow raspy breath. "You're not him. Remember. That's what *he* saw... That's not what *you* see."

Race lay his cheek against Stan's forehead. "Thank you, Stan. For everything."

"Good-bye, Race."

"Bye, Stan."

Stan died just past midnight. Ryan, Anita, Ellie, and Warren drew Race into the room with them and they all cried together, openly.

They wouldn't hear of Race going back into OTR that night.

"Stan said he wanted you to spend the night at his house," Ryan said, "or if you don't want to be alone, you can bed down in our spare room."

Race thought a moment. "I'd like to stay at Stan's house— if that's okay with you."

Ryan smiled. "It's fine with us."

Goforth leaned back in his chair, making it squeak in protest. The glasses were out and on his face, about to be pulled off and returned to his pocket. He held up a legal pad, studying the notes he'd scribbled there.

Race had just finished spilling his guts, telling everything he knew about the Deuce Dragons, giving Piston's name, Savvy's name, and Toon's, and explaining in detail how the car theft ring operated. About the gang growth in OTR which Savvy seemed to promote. Then he added the part about seeing Savvy in the midst of the riot.

"You know, you'll be giving this to the police as well."

Race nodded. He'd become more and more convinced that Savvy had been brought into Cincinnati to ratchet up the Dragons—and to weaken their pack. The night Wynn was caught, and Race barely escaped—it had all been a setup. Another ploy by Savvy to apply more pressure.

"And you know," Goforth went on, "your life won't be worth a plug nickel when the bad boys find out you snitched."

He nodded again, then followed it with a shrug.

"You're all right with that?"

Race looked at Goforth. "If I wasn't, I'd be wearing purple right now."

Goforth shook his head. "Sorry, Race. But you're just not very good gang material." Then he smiled.

"You're probably right."

"Best thing will be to get you out of the city altogether." Reaching over to a corner of his littered desk, he pulled out a letter. "We seem to have the solution right here. You know of a family by the name of Embry? From Kentucky?"

"Albert and Laura. Stan's friends. We stayed with them."

Goforth nodded. "They heard about Stan's death. Seems they think they'd like to have you come stay with them for a while."

Race studied Goforth's face to see if he was kidding.

"Can't imagine why they'd want a problem kid like you. Must be a little crazy. But then they do say something here about *work*. Probably slave labor. What do you think?"

In Race's mind, he saw those green hills, the rows of thick cedars, the big two-story house, and the horses, and the foal. *His* foal, Gabby's Race.

"Well, what do you think? Want to go shovel horse manure for a while? At least till things cool off here?"

Race nodded.

"You know, Pal, now that you're gonna get out in the world, you might want to learn how to talk."

Race grinned. "I'd like that, Goforth. I'd like that a *whole* lot."

In May, Race finished his year of creep school with passing grades. Laura had supplied him with a laptop so he was able to keep up with all his classes, including computer lab. And now he had Ellie's email. They kept cyberspace heated up with their exchanges.

Troll Knowles somehow succeeded in convincing Nealia to check into a rehab center to dry out. Perhaps it would take, perhaps it wouldn't. Race realized now that that was her problem, not his.

At the Cincinnati bus station before Race had boarded to leave, Goforth stood by his side. "Race," he said, "there'll be days when you'll feel like a dried up little turd that the cat buried in the sand. Some days you'll still be boiling over with anger. Other days you'll feel like you can conquer the world. That just means that you're human, right? But if you're made of what Stan thought you were made of, you won't let anything stop you."

Race had plenty of time to think about those words—and about the things Stan had taught him—as he shoveled out stalls, groomed horses, helped Albert in training Gabby's Race, and when he saddled up one of the mares and rode out across the pastures with the wind blowing past his ears.

It was near noon on a hot day in July. Sweat dripped off Race's nose and chin as he spread another pitchfork full of clean bedding straw on the floor of a stall. He never tired of the sound and smells of the stable, and he loved putting his muscles to the task.

With the pitchfork in mid-air, he heard Albert calling his name. Sticking his head out the stable door, he called back, "Yeah? Whatcha need?"

"Somebody here to see you."

Race shaded his eyes and looked up toward the front drive. Through the veil of trees he saw two cars: the Crosslin's big SUV, and behind it, the little silver Honda. Race studied the scene for a moment, then smiled. Leaning the pitchfork against the door, he walked toward the house.

As he approached, his heart jumped as he saw Ellie standing by the Honda dressed in a breezy blue blouse, denim cutoffs and blue sandals, her hair blowing free in the wind. She smiled as she saw him and held up the keys, jangling them in the air.

He tried to insist that he was hot, sweaty, and stinky, but that didn't stop the hugs as the whole family converged on him.

"We know Uncle Stan would want you to have the car—after all, you picked it out," Anita told him. "So we decided to bring it and surprise you."

Race walked around the car. He tried not to think of the rock flying through the windshield, the crashing of the windows and the cruel hands pulling a defenseless blind man out that door. He touched the warm hood. "It looks great."

"Just broken windows," Ryan said. "And a few dings. Not much. The insurance covered it."

"The title's in the glove box," Warren said. "Cool, huh?"

"Cool," Race agreed.

"Want to take it for a drive?" Anita said.

Again, Ellie jangled the keys. She tossed them to Race. He reached up and caught them midair.

Race glanced over at Albert. "Well, I don't know. I've got a lot of work..."

"Aw Race. Get on outta here. The work'll be here when you get back."

He looked at Ellie. "Come with me?"

She nodded.

Laura reached for his arm. "How about taking a quick shower first? It wouldn't be a smart move to *totally* gross the lady out."

Race grinned. He headed to the house on a dead run, scattering dogs and chickens as he went. He flew up the porch stairs, slammed into the house, and took the stairs to his room three at a time.

Time was precious. He didn't want to waste a single second.

NORMA JEAN LUTZ BIO

Norma Jean Lutz's writing career began professionally in 1977 when she enrolled in a writing correspondence course. Since then, she has had over 250 short stories and articles published in both secular and Christian publications. The full-time writer is also the author of over 50 published books under her own name and many ghostwritten books. Her books have been favorably reviewed in *Affair de Coeur, Coffee Time Romance, Romance Reader at Heart, and The Romance Studio* magazines, and her short fiction has garnered a number of first prizes in local writing contests.

Norma Jean is the founder of the Professionalism In Writing School, which was held annually in Tulsa for fourteen years. This writers' conference, which closed its doors in 1996, gave many writers their start in the publishing world.

A gifted teacher, Norma Jean has taught a variety of writing courses at local colleges and community schools, and is a frequent speaker at writers' seminars around the country. For eight years, she taught on staff for the Institute of Children's Literature. She has served as artist-in-residence at grade schools, and for two years taught a staff development workshop for language arts teachers in schools in Northeastern Oklahoma.

As co-host for the Tulsa KNYD Road Show, she shared the microphone with Kim Spence to present the Road Show Book Club, a feature presented by the station for more than a year. She has also appeared in numerous interviews on KDOR-TV.

As a writer who loves writing for teens, and hanging out with teens, Norma Jean has launched the **Clean Teen Reads** website and blog. Lots of fun stuff for teens! Check it out here:

www.CleanTeenReads.net
The Site for Teens Who Love Books and Stories

If you're a newbie author and need help. Look no further. Helpful information can be found on the Be A Novelist blog site:

www.beanovelist.com/be-a-novelist-blog

Why struggle out there all alone when you can benefit from Norma Jean's many decades of experience in the writing/publishing industry? Contact Norma Jean: **normajean@beanovelist.com**

OTHER TITLES BY NORMA JEAN LUTZ

Norma Jean Lutz Classic Collection

Sweet teen romance novels previously published in the 80s and 90s and re-released under *NUWSLink, Inc. Publishing.* All six are available in both print and digital on Amazon.

Flower in the Hills
Tiger Beetle at Kendallwood
Rockin' into Romance
Oklahoma Exile
Forever is Over
Lingering Dreams

The Tulsa Series

Christian Historical romance, set against the backdrop of the infamous 1921 Tulsa Race Riot. All four titles are available in the Kindle Store.

Tulsa Tempest
Tulsa Turning
Tulsa Trespass
Return to Tulsa

www.ingramcontent.com/pod-product-compliance
Lightning Source LLC
Chambersburg PA
CBHW061017120726
47910CB00006B/1994